PRAISE FOR
R. FRANKLIN JAMES

STICKS AND STONES

4 Stars: "A fast paced mystery with lots going on…. I really liked the human touches…. Hollis finds a box of letters written to the dead woman in her probate case and I learned a lot about Hollis from the way in which she reacted to the letters. She goes way beyond what was required for her job to see that the outcome of the case is what it should be. Hollis also comes in contact with a young man named Vince, 'a revering addict on the other side of withdrawals.' Hollis buys him lunch several times and when he asks her why she is being so nice, she answers, 'Because I could.' Readers are sure to be captured by this plot-twisting, exciting mystery. It is a real page turner and I certainly am going to keep reading this series."
—Cyclamen, Long and Short Reviews

"Who knew a simple nursery rhyme could be so dangerous? Someone knows. Someone has all the answers Hollis seeks. You'll want to keep turning the pages to see if Hollis survives long enough to uncover the truth."
—I Love a Mystery Reviews

"*Sticks & Stones* is a great read, a fun legal mystery about a great researcher who really knows her stuff. Holly is in fact more than a researcher, she's really quite the detective too …. I enjoyed reading the book, the plot moved at a fast pace, and Hollis was a great character that is easy to like. There was even a light romance, which did not overpower the plot."
—Mystery Sequels

"Twists and turns keep this debut novel exciting to the surprising end."
—Michele Drier, author of *Edited for Death* and *The Kandesky Vampire Chronicles*

"Hollis is a character you sorta warm up to, you have to get past her cool exterior and suddenly you realize you REALLY like her and care what happens to her. "
—Bless Their Hearts Mom Blog

"R. Franklin James' new book has everything a reader could ask for in a good mystery: intriguing plot, fascinating characters, and a few shockers thrown in along the way."
—Shirley Kennedy, romance novelist

5 Stars: "This mystery kept my attention from beginning to end. Although I had my suspicions of one character, the solution to the mystery surprised me. And that, my friends, is the mark of a good mystery."
—Self-Taught Cook Blog

"A fast paced plot with many twists coupled with a smart and determined protagonist make this a most enjoyable read."
—Kathleen Delaney, author of the Ellen McKenzie real estate mysteries

"A smooth running story where slowly pieces of the puzzle are revealed. Being a book lover I liked the setting she created with the book club .... The author manages to reel the reader in with her delightful storytelling and likable characters. It's a great first book that lovers of the old-fashioned detective genre surely will appreciate!"
—Fenny, Hotchpotch Blog

"A satisfying, clean mystery with several twists that kept me guessing, and also left me anxious for the next book in the Hollis Morgan Mystery series."
—W.V. Stitcher

"A fast paced mystery that keeps the reader wanting more. I love a good mystery and this is one of the better ones I have read in awhile. A fun story for sure!!!"
—Kathleen Kelly, Celtic Lady's Reviews

"The story line was interesting, as were the characters. The book flows steady without any dull gaps. I really liked the author's way of writing…. If you love a good murder mystery, you should get a copy of this book."
—Vicki, I'd Rather Be at the Beach Blog

"This book allows the reader to take part in the investigation; I felt my suspicions sift as each new clue was revealed. This is a remarkable, well-rounded mystery and I HIGHLY recommend this to anyone who enjoys crime fiction."
—Heather Coulter, Books, Books, and More Books

"This first book written by Ms. James is a winner for anyone who enjoys a clean mystery which will keep you guessing until the end about 'whodunit.'"
—My Home of Books Blog

"This book is full of murder, mystery and of course mayhem. Thoroughly entertaining and a fast read, I can't wait for the next book in the series. Excellent debut novel, Ms. James!"
—Tammy & Michelle, Nook Users' Book Club

"This is R. Franklin James' debut novel, a fact which I find hard to believe. She has created a character I love in Hollis Morgan, and a great plot …. I'm going to follow the series and

R. Franklin James. I've found a winner."
—Views from the Countryside Blog

"Highly inventive... a wonderful thriller. The tension mounts as Hollis becomes the target of the killer putting her life in great peril. *The Fallen Angels Book Club* is loaded with twists and turns and red herrings that will leave you guessing all the while you are flipping pages to find out what happens next. When you finish this book you will heave a hugely satisfying sigh because you have enjoyed yourself immensely. Ms. Franklin James has provided us with a great new character in Hollis Morgan. I am already looking forward to the next book in this series from this very talented author."
—Vic's Media Room

"The author ... does a excellent job of creating a story line that's both realistic and suspenseful. There was never a dull moment. I really look forward to reading more from this author."
—Heather, Saving for 6 Blogspot

"A delightful read. It certainly contained mystery, murder and mayhem.... Like any good mystery, there was a mystery within a mystery and I found [Hollis'] exchanges with the older folks at the center refreshing and decidedly touching.... The reader could feel Hollis's fear with each event and her determination to clear her name. Very well written and very well thought out! Well done, Ms. James, well done!"
—Beth, Art From the Heart Blog

"*The Fallen Angels Book Club* by author R. Franklin James is an enjoyable first book in the new series featuring Hollis Morgan. Hollis is a good heroine as she is smart, determined and resourceful."
—Barbara Cothern, *Portland Book Review*

The Return of
the Fallen Angels
Book Club

The Return of the Fallen Angels Book Club

A HOLLIS MORGAN MYSTERY

———

R. FRANKLIN JAMES

Seattle, WA

CAMEL PRESS

Camel Press
PO Box 70515
Seattle, WA 98127

For more information go to: www.Camelpress.com
www.rfranklinjames.com

Cover design by Sabrina Sun

The Return of the Fallen Angels Book Club
Copyright © 2014 by R. Franklin James

ISBN: 978-1-60381-921-3 (Trade Paper)
ISBN: 978-1-60381-922-0 (eBook)

Library of Congress Control Number: 2015930785

Printed in the United States of America

For Sean and Stefan

Acknowledgments

⎯⎯⎯✦⎯⎯⎯

To Laura Meehan, Michele Drier, and Linda Townsdin, who helped me make this story a book.

To Kathleen Asay, Patricia Foulk, Terri Judd and Cindy Sample, who comprise the best critique group a writer can have.

To my real life angels who support and cheer me on: Joyce Pope, Geri Nibbs, Vanessa Aquino, and Barbara Lawrence.

To my amazing publishers and editors, Catherine Treadgold and Jennifer McCord, whose attentive reading and editing made this book so much better.

To Dawn Dawdle, thank you for believing in me.

To Leonard, the wind beneath my wings.

CHAPTER 1

HOLLIS STARED OUT THE RESTAURANT window at pedestrians huddled under umbrellas against the chilly Bay Area spring rain. Ordinarily she'd be irritated that Rena was late, but Rena was always late.

Actually she was grateful for the opportunity to go through her snail mail, particularly the envelope holding the invitation to the one-year reunion of her Hastings Law College class. It had taken her twice as long as most students to graduate, but then most students didn't have a break in attendance to serve time in prison. She gazed at the notice with satisfaction.

She'd done it. At thirty-three, she'd gotten the pardon, finished law school, and passed the bar. She was back on track.

She glanced at her cellphone. No messages.

John must still be in his interview. He hadn't been able to hide his excitement when he told her that if the final interview went well, he'd be offered a job. Then he'd leave his detective position with the San Lucian Police Department and become a special agent with Homeland Security. John didn't dwell on it, but she knew he was concerned that his years on the police force might be seen as a negative—too many habits and procedures to unlearn.

Thinking of Police Detective John Faber and their times together brought a smile to her face that was about more than self-gratification over achieving personal goals. A flurry of movement at the entrance caught her eye and she looked up to see Rena rushing toward her.

"Sorry, sorry." Rena placed her wet umbrella on the floor and reached over to give Hollis a lopsided hug before draping her tan trench coat across the back of her chair.

Rena had let her hair grow into a wavy mass of shoulder length dark curls that set off her oval-shaped face and *café au lait* skin. Her cheeks were rosy and her hazel eyes were wide and lively. In fact, she practically glowed.

"Not to worry," Hollis said, returning the envelope to her briefcase. "It gave me a moment to catch up with myself." She ran her fingers self-consciously through her unruly auburn locks. "Take a minute and get settled. I'm not in a hurry."

"Well, I am, but my meeting is right down the street." Rena brushed invisible lint from her tan cashmere top and smoothed black slacks tucked into black knee-high boots. As usual, she looked like a high-fashion model. They met when Rena joined the Fallen Angels Book Club. She'd been referred by their former parole officer, Jeffrey Wallace. Hollis resisted new members, but Rena won her over with her knack for predicting a character's true nature. She could also spot a motive a chapter ahead. Besides, Hollis owed Jeffrey. They all owed Jeffrey.

Hollis smiled to herself. The Fallen Angels Book Club had been Jeffrey's idea. Its then seven members had all been convicted of white-collar crimes. The book club had been her lifeline since her first year out of prison. Then, two years ago, one crisis after another forced them to turn from discussing books to being suspects in a murder, with Hollis leading the list. It had been a torturous few months; however, they'd come through it, their pasts exposed but otherwise no worse off.

Still, they hadn't met since. She missed the group, even though she and Rena had stayed in touch.

She briefly glanced down at her own conservative navy suit and simple pale-yellow-linen blouse. She was still finding her personal style after years of wearing a school uniform. But it was the almost two years in prison blue that did her fashion sense in. She motioned to the waitress, who came immediately and took their order.

"I thought you said this could be a long lunch." Hollis took a sip of her herbal tea. "I told my paralegal I wouldn't be back until two."

Rena moved her shoulders up and down. "Well, la-di–da! You told your paralegal. My, my, I remember when *you* were the paralegal. Things have changed. I hope now that you're an attorney you're not too good for the rest of us."

"Yeah, right. I'm the lowest associate attorney on the Triple D totem pole," Hollis said, then grinned. She'd rather be on the bottom at the law firm of Dodson, Dodson & Doyle than toiling in a pressure cooker law firm anywhere else. Triple D had been good to her, supporting her while she cleared her name and received the pardon that had made her dream of being an attorney possible. "But since your time is limited, let's get to the point. Why'd you want to meet today, anyway?"

"Did Mark tell you about my cousin?"

Mark Haddon was Hollis' friend and Rena's live-in boyfriend. It still surprised her that she had introduced the two of them. Mark had been employed as a Triple D junior lawyer, and Hollis took him under her paralegal wing. He was the first person Hollis let back into her life when she was trying to start over again after prison. In fact, he'd literally saved her life.

"No, he and I haven't spoken for about a month, not since he's taken on this corporate fraud case," Hollis said.

"I know. He's been obsessed with that case for weeks. We haven't had much time together either." Rena mouthed a thank you to the waitress, who set a large Cobb salad in front of her.

"He probably didn't want to pre-empt my telling of the story."

Hollis perked up, her curiosity piqued. "Okay, so tell me. What about your cousin?"

"Her name is Shelby Patterson. She's actually my second … no wait, third cousin. We share family on her mother's side. She's several years younger than I am. Her father died in a car crash when she was three and her mom remarried when she was five. Darol Patterson is a jerk, but he did adopt Shelby and give her his name. No one in the family likes him much, but he was Aunt Susan's—that's Shelby's mother—choice. They didn't have much money. No one in our family did, and yet, everybody got along okay."

Rena paused and Hollis knew from her strained expression that whatever was coming next must be sensitive.

"Then Darol's mother came into money. She owned some commercial buildings on land that the county wanted, and got about three million after taxes. We all celebrated. But no one celebrated more than Darol. Anyway, he quit his job and pressured his mother into buying him and Aunt Susan a home, and to put in a couple of widescreen TVs. Aunt Susan was embarrassed but she couldn't stop Darol from constantly begging his mother for support."

Rena stopped speaking for a moment to take a bite of her salad.

Hollis chewed a mouthful of her own lunch thoughtfully, and waited for her friend to continue.

Rena took a deep breath. "Anyway, we didn't know it at the time, but theirs was not a smooth marriage. From the outside it looked average, but no one has a marriage without problems. My own parents got divorced when I was fifteen, so it was just Mom and me until I married Christopher's father." She stopped speaking again to take another bite.

Hollis knew that Christopher's father was an archetype for the "bad boy." He had taken most of Rena's money, which led to her writing bad checks, which led to her going to prison, which led to her sharing a parole officer with Hollis when she got out.

Hollis grimaced. Who was she to judge? Her own stint in prison was a result of putting her trust in others above her own instincts.

"When Shelby turned twelve, her mom—my aunt Susan—died of a heart attack. I was twenty-two and in prison at the time. What no one knew, except maybe Aunt Susan, was that Darol had an adult son and daughter from a previous marriage. They all came to live in that house—"

"What house? Who owned it?" Hollis interrupted.

"Remember, I told you. Darol had nagged his mother into buying them a house. She knew her son, however, and that's why she put the house in Aunt Susan's name. Old Mrs. Patterson liked Aunt Susan, and other than questioning her judgment in marrying her son, they got along well. She didn't want Darol to have anything in his name that he could sell after she found out that Darol had a drug habit. His kids, too."

Rena paused and looked inward, as if returning mentally to that time period, then resumed.

"That's what I meant when I said from the outside everything seemed okay. Aunt Susan never said anything, but she was worried that Shelby would figure out about the drugs, so when Aunt Susan began to have health problems, she sent Shelby to live with relatives in LA. Everybody knew what was going on by that time. Didn't matter. After Aunt Susan died, Darol got his hands on the house because they were still married at the time of her death, and thanks to California's community property laws, it took only a year for him to overload it with liens and eventually lose it to loan sharks." Rena tapped the top of her head. "Oh, did I tell you he lost his job right after Aunt Susan died? Back then his drug habit was too obvious for any employer to ignore. Then Darol and his kids went to live with his mother in her house in San Lucian hills. "

The waitress came by to collect their plates and to refill their cups.

Hollis reached into her tote. "I think I need to take notes."

Rena nodded. "Anyway, to make a very long story short, Darol and his kids—to their credit—kicked their habits, but not soon enough. Darol's mother died several months ago. She had a wonderful spirit. In her will, she left family members and close friends small bequests. She even left me a few dollars and Christopher a small savings account toward college. But the kicker was she left Shelby her house—the one Darol and his kids lived in—with the understanding that Shelby would sell it and use the money to cover her living expenses and her tuition for college."

"Hold up a sec, Rena. How did Darol take that?"

"Well, Mrs. Patterson had basically disinherited her son and grandchildren. Darol was furious because he didn't get a thing from his own mother and now his stepdaughter was going to make him homeless."

Hollis listened and said nothing.

"Unbelievably, even with her stepfather's fury, Shelby still remained close to Darol. I guess she was desperate for family. He was the only dad she could remember. For her, I suppose, a lousy dad was better than no dad at all." Rena took a sip of water. "Despite his pleading to Shelby, Darol's family kept watch and made sure she wouldn't give in and allow him to get his hands on the house. Even so, since he still wasn't working, he started selling things out of the house. Gone were the antique furniture, silverware, and his mother's jewelry."

Both women turned silent when the waitress returned to remove their plates. Rena checked her watch.

"Anyway, once the good stuff was sold, he was onto Shelby to add his name to hers on the deed. He told her he wanted to get a small loan against his mother's house, to start his own computer repair business. Thank goodness we were able to talk her into refusing. He got his family to loan him money; I don't know what he's done with it. A few days ago Shelby got accepted into UCLA. We're all so proud of her."

Hollis stopped writing and looked up. "But ...."

"But now she needs money for her tuition, books, and college expenses. She's going to have to sell the house. It's still in her name alone. The market isn't that great, but if she's lucky she'll be covered for all four years. Needless to say, Darol and his kids have already put the word out that they'll refuse to leave. He's threatened to contest the will, saying that his mother wasn't of sound mind. He talked with somebody who told him he still had rights."

Hollis thought she knew where this was headed. But as she opened her mouth to comment, her cellphone rang with a jazz piano ringtone. It was John.

Rena waved her a go-ahead.

"Hey," she told John, "I'm with Rena."

"Well, tell her hi from me and tell her I think I got the job."

Hollis beamed. "Oh, John, I'm so happy for you. When can we celebrate?"

"I have one last meeting; they want me to have breakfast with one of my future colleagues. I'm taking a four o'clock flight to Oakland on Wednesday morning. How about dinner after I get back?"

"If that's happening, you must have gotten the job. Dinner sounds perfect. Love you, and congratulations."

She didn't try to suppress her delight as she slipped the phone back into her purse.

Rena gave a laugh. "Well, let me guess. He got the job."

"You know he's been on edge for weeks. This was his third interview. I'm so proud of him." Hollis grinned until she saw Rena's furrowed brow. "I'm sorry. I interrupted your story."

"No, no, I've talked too long already. You get the idea. What do we need to do?"

"I need to meet with Shelby and take a look at her

grandmother's will. Did she have a trust? Or, did Mrs. Patterson's family go through probate?"

"There was a trust. Everything has been finalized. And Shelby's eighteen—she's legally an adult."

Hollis sighed. "Well, that's good news. The process takes time."

"I'll get her to fly up in a few days. We're having a family get-together this weekend. She can stay with me."

"Sounds good. When can you get me the paperwork?"

"I'll talk to her Aunt Denise. She's Darol sister and a lot like their mother, old Mrs. Patterson. I'll let you know as soon as I hear." Rena looked down at her phone to check the time. "I've got to go."

"Me, too. I want to do a little research. Do you realize that Shelby will be my first client?"

New associates had to build their own clientele. It was common in a law firm for associates during the first year or two to work under the wing of a supervising attorney. Gradually, they would prepare specific assignments for simpler cases and then handle new matters by themselves.

Rena smiled. "Great, and she can pay you, too. Well, she can once you win her case."

Hollis grinned. If necessary, she would've probably worked pro bono for a first client. "Well, there's an incentive. Call me when you have something."

They hugged.

Hollis watched Rena walk swiftly up the street to a nearby high-rise. Her first client: even the sound of it had promise. Now all she had to do was win.

Chapter 2

~~~

It was quiet now. Jeffrey could hear the slow thump of his heart. He must have been unconscious. He knew he'd been shot in the stomach.

Agony.

He tried to sit up, but the pain pierced through his body like a red hot lance. He moaned. Even so, the hole in his stomach was nothing compared to the sorrow in his heart. He lay back.

Searing, unrelenting pain.

He clutched his stomach. Why was it so dark? The lights in his office should still be on. Wait, were his eyes closed? He was too weak to open them. Would someone find him before it was all over?

He was so cold. The cold started in his feet and was gradually climbing up his legs.

He wiggled the fingers on his free hand; they still worked. That could be a good sign. He rubbed them together and felt sticky ooze.

Blood. Through the creeping cold, the warm blood was soaking his shirt and jacket.

His blood.

It was oozing out like the slow and steady flow from an upended bottle of syrup. He thought about his life and how he failed. He tried to turn his head, but his brain was shutting down. His neck stiffened.

The cold reached his chest, and there was no more pain.

He prayed for mercy.

CHAPTER 3

⁓

THE PHONE ON HOLLIS' DESK rang—a number she didn't recognize. Rena had confirmed the meeting with Shelby for the end of the week. But maybe the young Miss Patterson had changed her mind about flying up to meet with an inexperienced attorney. Hollis had reviewed the Patterson trust with diligence to ensure the validity of the claim and the most expedient approach to liquidate the house. She braced herself for disappointment.

"Hollis, this is Gene."

She caught her breath. The voice from her not so distant past hit her like a rock.

She stumbled a little. "Gene, wow, how are you? It's been … gee, Gene … it's been almost a year. What's been going on?"

Gene Donovan was indeed a voice from her past. He was one of the founding members of the Fallen Angels Book Club. She smiled, remembering Gene's blond good looks and his love of manicures. A columnist for a local paper, he was gay, and at thirty-seven, the second oldest member in the club. Thanks to his brother, the owner of a local newspaper, Gene hadn't had to worry about checking the felony conviction box on an employment application. Like her, he hated small talk.

"I've got some bad news."

Hollis' heart skipped a beat. Typical of Gene: no niceties, just cut to the chase.

"What's wrong?"

"Jeffrey Wallace is dead."

Hollis leaned back in her chair. It was as if she was seeing herself from above and looking down. The shock was like a hole in her chest that didn't show.

Gene gave her a moment to absorb his words then continued, his voice subdued.

"He was murdered, Hollis, in his office. Somebody shot him."

"No, it can't be." Hollis shook her head. "He was one of the good guys. He was …." She choked back tears.

Gene murmured, "I know. He might have been my parole officer, but he was also a friend."

"When did it happen?"

"Last night. It came across the police log this morning, but I didn't notice his name until a little while ago. I knew you would want to know and I still had your number."

"Did he suffer?" Hollis' voice faltered.

"I don't have any details. I'll call you back after … after I see what else I can find out." Gene's voice became firmer. "They don't have any suspects. You know what I'm thinking?"

"That no one knew Jeffrey better than we did. We owe him." Hollis said in a steady low pitched voice, "We need to get the Fallen Angels back together."

AFTER WORK THAT DAY, HOLLIS and Rena stood on the balcony of Rena's condo overlooking the backyard and watching her six-year-old son Christopher play with Mark. Hollis could only imagine what it must be like to be a parent. She was relieved her own maternal instincts hadn't surfaced.

"I can't believe someone would kill Jeffrey," Rena said. She dabbed at her eyes with a tissue.

Hollis agreed. "Without his help, I wouldn't have a pardon. I wouldn't be an attorney." She wasn't the weepy type, but there was still an ache in her chest that wouldn't go away.

Jeffrey Wallace had been more than her parole officer, he'd been her mentor, and in some instances her guardian angel. If it weren't for his strong letter of recommendation to the court, the judge wouldn't have given her the second chance she needed.

Rena nodded. "Without Jeffrey, I wouldn't have met you in the book club and you wouldn't have introduced me to Mark." Her voice turned solemn, "And without Mark, I'd be lost."

"Speaking of the book club, I talked with Gene. I think we should call the group together again."

"Why?" Rena turned to face her. "We're a book club. What could we do?"

"If nothing else, say goodbye as a group." Hollis looked away. "And maybe we could use our skills and resources to repay in part what we owe Jeffrey. He gave us our lives back. The least we can do is help find out who took his."

"I don't know, Hollis." Rena frowned. "As much as I adored Jeffrey, I don't know if I should get involved."

"Should?" Hollis pressed.

"I mean, I've moved on since my parole finished. I didn't need to get a pardon like you. I didn't need a state license to do my job." She swallowed. "And I've got Christopher to think about. He takes up a lot of my time. And now I'm up for a promotion and—"

"And who gave you the contacts so you could get your job at Barneys? I don't remember Jeffrey ever telling us he couldn't spare the time to get involved."

"That's mean, Hollis," Rena muttered, looking down at her feet. "I can't ... no, I'll be honest. I don't *want* to play detective when it's clearly police business and could be dangerous. Jeffrey would be the first to agree with me, and you know it."

Hollis grimaced. Rena was right, but Hollis would have

pushed the point with Jeffrey, too. She sighed. "Okay, I understand why you don't want to participate."

They turned back to view the game of toddler touch football.

After a few more minutes, Rena took a step back. "I hate it when you agree with me. Oh, what the hell! I can't sit on the sidelines. I wouldn't be able to look at myself in the mirror."

Hollis broke into a big smile. "Are you sure?"

"I never did everything Jeffrey wanted me to do anyway." Rena rubbed the back of her neck. "What's a little risk of exposure? Besides, it will be good to have the Fallen Angels back together."

Hollis nodded. She didn't realize how much she had counted on Rena's participation until there was a chance she wouldn't have it.

"Thanks, Rena." She patted her on the arm.

"Yeah, sure. So when's the meeting?"

"Gene is going to contact Miller and I've got to locate Richard."

Rena waved to Christopher, who was riding on Mark's back like a cowboy.

"Richard, good luck with his paranoia. You're going to have to do some heavy guilt-tripping to get him to come back. But first, how are you going to find him?"

"When we were going through the murder trial, Richard admitted that he didn't work far from me. Except for the fact I caught him in a couple of understandable lies about his home life, I think he just wanted off the suspect screen." Hollis tapped her chin thoughtfully. "I'll stake out his office building—as soon as I find it."

The murder trial that had ended the year before had caused an upheaval in the lives of the Fallen Angels, whose past felony convictions were laid bare in the light of the six o'clock news.

"Do you have that kind of time? I mean, will you still be able to help Shelby?"

"Won't be a problem." Hollis waved her hands for her not to

worry. "I have a young friend who can help me locate Richard."

Hollis smiled to herself. This would be the perfect assignment for Vince Colton. Hollis was convinced her friendship with him was one of life's left turns. She met the teenager during the weeks she was waiting for her scores from taking the bar. He was sitting in the lobby at the police station battling the aftereffects of detox, while waiting for his mother to be released from jail on drug charges. She still couldn't explain why she reached out to help him, except that she had come to believe that everyone deserved at least one second chance. Since then they had become friends.

Now clean, Vince worked where he could, but he didn't earn enough for him and his mother to live on. He'd been begging her to let him run errands and fix things that needed fixing, but she'd been holding back. First, at nineteen, he needed to finish high school; he still didn't have his GED. Second, she couldn't afford to pay him. And third, she couldn't afford to pay him. She was accelerating her law school loan payments as much as possible, but it would be years before she would have any appreciable discretionary income.

But she did owe him. He had come to her aid when both their lives were in jeopardy. He risked his life for hers. After he came out of the hospital, his gruff street manner disguised the vulnerability of a young man who desperately needed a friend. She took on the role and never looked back.

Yes, Vince would work out just fine.

CHAPTER 4

"So, Hollis, what do you want me to do once I spot this guy?" Vince seemed to inhale his hamburger and fries.

She'd caught up to him the next day at his janitorial job in a furniture store, and as usual he was happy to be treated to lunch. He was wearing his standard uniform of a gray hoodie, worn jeans, and a drab, once-white tee shirt. She stared as he chased lunch down with a single gulp of a sixteen-ounce soft drink. He could be the poster boy for fast food eateries everywhere.

"Maybe you should slow down," she said. "Doesn't eating fast like that upset your stomach?"

"Not as upset as being hungry." He looked up from his plate. "I mean I eat all the time. I just have a big appetite."

He wiped his mouth with the side of his hand.

"If you say so." Hollis took in his tall, rail-thin frame. She dug into her purse. "Here's his picture." She handed him a newspaper clipping. "Anyway, if you spot Richard, just let me know. Don't approach him. Once I know where he works, I can find out the rest."

"Cool."

Hollis' fingers made water circles on the table. "Vince, you ever think about getting that GED? Things have started to settle down for you; maybe this is a good time to go after it."

He frowned. "Ah, why did you have to bring that up again? I keep tellin' you, I get along fine without it. Besides …."

"Besides what?"

"Forget it." Vince balled up his napkin, stood, and pulled his hood over his head.

"Wait, don't go." Hollis reached out across the table. "Besides what? Please tell me."

He slumped back in his seat and stared down at the top of the table.

"Vince, talk to me. You said we were friends. Friends talk to each other."

He looked up. A flush crept across his cheeks, but he was still unable to look her in the eyes.

Hollis sensed she should just sit and wait.

After a few moments he said in a trembling voice, "I don't have the money. You gotta have money for everything … for books and, and … for clothes. I'm not a kid anymore. My mom needs medicine, and, and … the shelter won't let us stay more than thirty days, and …." He stopped. Despite his rapid blinking, a slim line of a tear made a slippery path down his cheek.

Hollis ran her fingers through her hair. Not a kid anymore. She doubted he was ever a kid. She reached over and put her hand over his. He jerked it back as if he had received an electric shock.

She put her hand in her lap and pretended not to notice. "Hear me out. I'll make you a deal. I don't have a lot of money either, but I may be able to get you a job at the law firm in our mailroom. It's kind of a gloomy place and it doesn't pay a lot, but you'd have a regular paycheck and maybe benefits. In exchange, you have to promise me that tomorrow you'll look into what it takes to get a GED. Then, after you get your first check, you'll enroll in a class and keep going until you get that GED. Like I said, the job in the mailroom doesn't pay a lot but—"

Vince let out a loud "whoop" that got the attention of nearby tables.

The transformation of his face caught Hollis off guard for the second time that day.

"I can do it. I liked school. I can work for your law firm during the day and keep my cleaning job at night." He beamed. "Then I can pay for my mom. Maybe we can get out of the shelter and get an apartment."

His grin was so engaging, Hollis found herself smiling too. "Okay, then. Let's get busy. I'll check with my boss about a job. You keep an eye out for Richard and don't forget, tomorrow I want you to find out what it takes to get a GED."

"LET ME UNDERSTAND." GEORGE LOOKED at her over the rims of his eyeglasses. "You want the firm to hire an ex-addict to be responsible for distributing our confidential client mail?"

George Ravel was in his fifties and looked every year. He was average in height and weight, and his hair was thinning. Still his clothes fit him well, and despite his warm personality, he was formidable in court.

Hollis smiled sheepishly. "Well, when you put it that way, it doesn't sound so good. But I can give you my personal assurance that Vince is reformed. He's eager to work. He saved my life, remember?"

"I thought it was you who saved his life?"

"Whatever." She waved a hand in the air. "He put himself in danger to help me. He has integrity. Please give it some thought, George. If you can ask the management committee to approve the hire, I know Vince will fit in and do a great job."

"Tell me about Shelby Patterson." He pointed to the paper in his hand. "You want to open a client matter, but you left the space blank regarding retainer. Your first case isn't pro bono, is it?" George glanced over the office form.

"No, it's just that I haven't met with her yet. She's flying up from LA day after tomorrow. I'll meet her in the afternoon."

"You want me to sit in?"

Hollis sat up a little straighter. "No, I've met with first-time clients before."

"That was as a paralegal. Now you're an attorney."

"I didn't lose any skills. I know the routine."

He chuckled. "Okay, counselor, you're up at bat." He handed back the pages. "File this with the billing section. Let me know your case code."

Hollis gathered her notepad and files. "George, what about—"

"All right, I'll talk with Ed Simmons about your friend, but no promises. He'll probably point out we don't have the budget." He sighed. "I'll do what I can. But I better get all my mail."

VINCE WAS TRUE TO HIS word. A little after five o'clock that day he called Hollis at work from one of the few remaining phone booths in downtown Oakland.

"Where did you find a phone booth?" She suddenly realized that he might have had difficulty reaching her.

"They put them near shelters 'cause they know some people don't have cellphones." He raised his voice to be heard over the sound of traffic. "Anyway, I saw your dude. He works in that building where you thought he did all right. I picked him out easy from the picture. I followed him, but he takes BART and I didn't have the money to ride."

"Good work," Hollis said. "But Vince, you know I didn't want you to follow him." She sighed. "Never mind, thank you. I can take it from here."

He was silent.

"What?" She prodded.

"Ah … did you hear anything about the mailroom?"

"No, not yet. I did ask, though, and I'll let you know as soon as I do hear anything. I only mentioned it this afternoon. It could take a few days for me to hear back."

"Yeah, sure, I know."

She could hear the longing and hope in his few words. She said, "Things will work out, don't worry. I'll reach you through the shelter or the car wash as soon as I know."

AFTER TALKING TO VINCE, HOLLIS rushed to pack up her things and head for home. John would be at her condo around seven to take her out to dinner. She was glad he had a ride from the airport. She wanted the chance to get home, go for a quick run, and freshen up. She wanted to be at her best, and it wouldn't do if she was too preoccupied to summon the proper enthusiasm over his new job.

Over the past months, with ongoing guidance from her girlfriends Stephanie and Rena, her wardrobe had vastly improved. They might say she was still a work in progress, but her ability to choose what brought out her best features was much improved. She was letting her hair grow, and her auburn waves flowed softly around her face and shoulders. She put on a belted, off-shoulder dove-gray dress, matching drape topper, and black, knee-high boots, which brought her height close to five foot six. As a finishing touch, she carried her favorite red clutch bag.

John's appreciative look was all the reassurance she needed. Closing the door, he stopped in the foyer and held her at arm's length.

He swallowed. "You look beautiful."

She smiled a little self-consciously. "Why thank you, kind sir. You look pretty good yourself."

John bent his lanky six-foot frame in a mock bow. With thick brown hair as dark as his eyes, olive skin, and a smile full of gleaming-white teeth that lit up his whole face, he was one of those people whose strength of character showed on the outside.

"You know we don't have to go out. I can just sit here and feast on you ... along with some takeout." He took her hand. "There's something I want to ask you anyway."

Hollis' heart went into a rapid staccato.

"Really? Really, something you want to ask me? Now that sounds mysterious. I, I think we should get some food first ... yes, food," she stammered. "And I want to hear about the interview."

She took her hand back and tried to breathe normally.

"We can talk here, too, you know."

"John, come on. I got all dressed up so we could celebrate." She picked up her keys from the entry table. "Let's go eat and then come back and talk."

He smiled and sighed. "All right, lady, but you're going to hear me out."

"I will." She flashed him a smile.

PERRIO'S RESTAURANT IN SAUSALITO WAS "their" place. Away from the town center where the restaurants clustered on the water, it was tucked into a narrow alley and surrounded by several small jewelry stores. It backed into the hillside with a surprise direct view of the sparkling bay. Sailboats dipped rhythmically to the natural movement of the waves. The smell of the sea was pervasive and the slight chill of the evening air along with the soulful notes of a street musician's saxophone added to the ambiance. The community not only drew tourists, but kept natives in awe of how lucky they were to live there.

"Welcome back, you two." The maître d' and owner, Jason, smiled and pointed them to "their" table next to the window. "Good thing you made reservations. We're going to be full tonight."

John held Hollis' chair and then took his own seat. "It was only a matter of time before word of mouth would make your restaurant too popular to walk into without reservations."

Hollis accepted the paper with that night's specials. "I'm glad the restaurant has really started to take off. It won't be our hidden spot anymore."

"You two will always have a place here." Jason looked back over his shoulder. "I have to get back to the door. Enjoy your dinner."

The next minutes involved looking over menus that they knew by heart and debating the chef's recommendations for the day. Finally, their orders were placed and wine was in hand.

Hollis leaned in. "Okay, now tell me what happened."

"Well, I had just about given up on their making me an offer." He took a swallow from his glass of Malbec. "I'd had four interviews that day. I felt like a machine. But I now know that those guys were my future team members. Everybody was given the opportunity to vet me because we were going to be working together for long stretches of time."

"Wow, so how did they finally make the offer?"

He grinned. "You'll like this. They bring me into this room that looks like something out of *Star Wars*. It has this huge, almost floor-to-ceiling screen. I mean football field huge. And it has desks with terminals that stretch down rows forever. My boss, Phillip—he insists I call him Phil—Phil pulls me aside, hands me a file, and says: 'We're going to need your assessment by next Friday. Orientation is at seven a.m. on Monday.'"

Hollis' eyes widened. "Wow, that was the offer? That was it?"

"That was it. After six months of security background checking, physical tests, psych tests, and intelligence tests. Yep, that was it." John looked around the room, trying to locate the waiter. "I'm starving. I guess the chef is running a little behind."

"I'm not that hungry." Hollis twisted the stem of her wine glass.

He stopped her glass. "What's the matter?"

She sighed. "I'm sorry. I am so happy for you, but I found out two days ago that Jeffrey Wallace was murdered."

"What? Who did it?"

"They don't know yet. I heard it from Gene Donovan. I don't know if you remember him—"

"I remember him. The newspaper guy, right?"

Hollis nodded. "Right. Gene was supposed to call me back today with the details, but I haven't heard from him."

"I should be able to find out something once I get back to headquarters."

She smiled. "That would be the best. We need to have the details."

He frowned. "We?"

"Ah … I thought the Fallen Angels Book Club should get back together."

John shook his head. "I don't believe it. Didn't you learn anything the last time?"

He paused. The waiter appeared with their plates of food.

"The rib-eye for you sir, and our chef's special tonight for the lady—seared bass." The young man positioned the plates with a flourish.

After he left a thick wall of silence still stood between them. Finally Hollis said coolly, "What exactly was I supposed to learn?"

John closed his eyes and shook his head. "Look, I don't want to get into an argument. I'm really sorry about Wallace. He seemed like a standup guy. I'd come to respect his work, he was dedicated and—"

"Enough, I get it. You don't have to patronize me."

"I wasn't trying to patronize you. We're just talking. But it seems like I can't say anything right tonight." He shoved a forkful of food in his mouth.

Hollis said nothing and for the next few moments they ate in silence. The waiter came over.

"How's everything?"

"The food is delicious." Hollis smiled up at him and he left with a pleased smile on his face. She reached across to cover

John's hand with hers. "I'm sorry. I've been in a lousy mood. Will you forgive me?"

He raised one eyebrow and then shrugged. "Sure, why not? I've gotten used to having you around."

Hollis took the lead in turning the conversation to non-controversial topics and the results of his interviews. She knew she was successful when she recounted a funny anecdote that earned her a loud laugh.

"I am so proud of you." She picked up her glass in a toast and smiled. "It wasn't easy getting inside the politics of Homeland Security. I'm sure they don't often recruit local cops for management positions."

"It's no different than what you've accomplished."

"Fine, then let's drink to the both of us."

They clinked glasses.

He took a deep sip and paused. "Okay, okay, let's come to an agreement. I'll find out about Wallace's death and pass on what I can. But you and your club members can't play sleuth. Stay out of the detective business. Deal?"

With a little effort, Hollis lifted her lips into a smile. It was better than starting another argument. "Deal."

They tapped glasses again.

John moved for the check. "Let's go back to your condo."

"I'd like that." Hollis started to gather up her things and then stopped. "John, what were you going to ask me?"

He pursed his lips tight.

"I already got my answer."

She tried to keep her face expressionless, but slowly exhaled a breath of relief. She was pretty sure she knew his question, but it was one she couldn't answer.

THE NEXT MORNING, HOLLIS SAT in Starbucks, drinking tea and peering out the window as well-tailored men and women hurried past every few seconds. She couldn't stop the silly grin spreading across her face when her thoughts drifted to John and their night together. He was applying gentle pressure and her list of relationship concerns was breaking down.

It was amazing how many semi-bald men resembling Richard Kleh worked in the Talbot Building. But she was only looking for one particular man, and in less than a minute Richard emerged from the BART escalators. She would recognize his purposeful gait anywhere.

She grabbed her purse, dashed out the door, and dodged a car as she ran across the street.

"Richard," she called out about a half block behind him.

He kept walking.

"Richard," she called out again. She stepped up her pace to a slow run and caught up to him just as he entered the automatic doors to his building. She had to tap his jacket sleeve to get his attention. He frowned and looked down at her, as if trying to register where he had seen her before. After a few seconds, recognition entered his eyes.

"Hollis?" He held the door open for her. "Wow, this is a surprise. Why are you here?"

She smiled. "Hi, Richard, or are you using an alias?"

He still looked the same, perhaps a bit heavier; his tall frame hid his weight well. His cheeks turned red.

"You can call me Richard. I've gotten used to it." He looked over her head and around the lobby. "After the press had a field day with our prison records during the trial, there was no further need for the dual identity."

There was a momentary awkward silence.

Hollis asked, "Is there someplace we can talk for a few minutes? I won't take up much of your time."

He pointed to a small coffee cart surrounded by a scattering of café tables toward the back of the lobby.

"I've got a few minutes before my first meeting. What's up?"

He gave his order to the young barista. Hollis asked for water.

"Let's sit first." Hollis took possession of a table and sat across from her. "Richard, I've got bad news. Jeffrey Wallace is dead."

He put the cup of coffee down without drinking. His brow creased.

"When? How?"

"He was murdered. I don't have any details yet. Gene contacted me. He still works for the paper." Hollis leaned in. "Richard I tracked you down to let you know about Jeffrey, and that the Fallen Angels are thinking of going to the funeral service together to pay our respects."

Richard gave her a skeptical look. "Unless you've changed since I last saw you, you've never cared about things like paying respects."

"Unless *you've* changed since I last saw you, you're still a cynic." She shrugged. "Like I said, we owe Jeffrey. Maybe we can all attend the funeral and talk about getting together in the future to rekindle the book club." She took a sip of tea and paused, knowing her next statement had to be carefully crafted. "We might even be able to help the police. Each of us has a different perspective. We could search—"

"Whoa, wait a minute. Why *us*? Let the police do their job. We are not investigators." Richard looked down at his watch. "Look, it was good seeing you again, but I've got to get to my office. Here's my card. Let me know about the funeral. I'll go. Regarding the other, if you can pull us all together—just to talk, only to talk—okay, I'm in. I at least owe Jeffrey that."

"Thanks for the water." She put the card in her purse. "You'll be hearing from me."

BACK IN HER OFFICE, HOLLIS spent the rest of the day researching the Shelby Patterson matter. From what she found in public records and from her grandmother's trust, Shelby had a no-brainer case. It shouldn't take long to get the court, if she was forced to go that route, to take action against her father.

She hurried to prepare a status report for George. Shelby might be her first paying client, but her priority was to clear her thoughts and focus on finding Jeffrey's killer.

CHAPTER 5

T HE NEXT MORNING, HOLLIS DRESSED carefully, caught her reflection in the office window, and smiled. She wanted to remember the day she met her first client. Not that she was superstitious, but she had worked so hard for this day. True, she was years behind in her original life plan, but recently she'd adopted the attitude of better late than never.

"Hollis."

She turned and realized that Tiffany had left her post at the reception desk to stand in her doorway. She must have said Hollis' name a couple of times before she was heard.

"I'm sorry. I guess I was day-dreaming," Hollis said sheepishly.

Tiffany gave her a wink. "Ms. Patterson is here. I put her in the blue conference room."

Hollis nodded. "I'll be right there."

"MISS PATTERSON, CAN I CALL you Shelby?" Hollis entered the room with her hand outstretched. "Did you have a good flight?" Hollis knew her first job was to make her client feel relaxed and comfortable. Shelby Patterson answered her with a shy nod and smile. A small woman, slight in stature and matching Hollis' own five foot three, she barely looked her eighteen years. Her wavy black hair was pulled back into a tight ponytail that fell to the top of her blouse collar. She shared her cousin Rena's *café au lait* skin color and striking good looks. In contrast to Rena's large hazel eyes, Shelby's were deep-set and light brown.

"Would you like some water?"

Shelby shook her head.

Hollis smiled encouragingly. "Why don't you tell me how I can help you?"

After a long moment of hesitation, Shelby cleared her throat and spoke in a crisp business voice. "Rena told me she gave you the lurid details, but I would wrap it all up with this. My stepfather's mother died and left me her house so that I could pay for my college tuition. My stepfather, Darol Patterson, didn't get along with his mother because he used to be an addict and who knows why else; anyway, he always felt she didn't care for him. When he found out she left me her house he was, and is, pissed off. He wants to ignore her last wishes and stop me from selling her house." She licked her lips. "Could I have that water now?"

"Of course." Hollis went to the small refrigerator tucked into the credenza and disguised to look like just another piece of furniture. She took out two bottles and handed one to Shelby.

"Thank you." She took a long sip and cleared her throat. "Dad moved into the house about six months ago and refuses to leave. He's also brought his kids from his first marriage to move in, Sonny and Joy."

Hollis raised her eyebrows but said nothing.

Shelby continued, "He doesn't have the money to hire a lawyer. I don't either; his family will be paying your fees. But I start college soon and I need to sell the house." Her eyes started to tear up and she murmured, "And now there are these phone calls and other things."

Hollis leaned forward so that she could hear. "His family will pay your fees to fight him. That must be ... awkward."

Shelby kept her eyes downcast. "Yeah, well, they respect my step-grandmother's wishes, and they don't like my stepdad much."

Hollis made a note.

"Tell me about the phone calls and other things."

"Before you think it's my dad, it's not. He would never hurt me. I think he just doesn't want to let go of Grandmother's house. It's the only thing he has left of her. That, and he probably doesn't have another place to stay."

"Shelby, explain to me about the rest of it ... the phone calls. What's happening?"

Shelby frowned, looked at Hollis and took a gulp of water. "The calls are hang-ups, over and over again. They stop for a couple of days, and then they start over. There are other strange things as well. Last week I went to the driveway and found my car door open. The battery was worn down because of the interior lights. Then, day before yesterday, all four tires were flat; the air had been let out."

Hollis frowned. "Did you tell the police?"

"I live in LA. They said they can't chase down pranksters."

"But you don't think it's a prankster?"

Shelby started to tear up again. She whispered, "I honestly don't know, but this all started after my grandmother's trust was read. I think it's Sonny and Joy ... more likely Joy."

"But don't they live here with your stepdad in the East Bay?"

"Yeah, but they used to live in LA. They probably have friends who would do it for them." Her voice gained strength and she took another gulp of water. "Anyway, neither of them is wired right."

Hollis listened, resting her chin on her fist.

"How can I represent you?"

"Can you take care of selling my grandmother's house?"

"What about your family that's living there?"

"Evict them," Shelby said.

Hollis looked at her in surprise, but kept her thoughts to herself.

"I told Rena I would help you," Hollis said, scribbling a note. "Let me do a little research about the proper action before I take any steps to secure the house for sale. I don't want to waste anybody's money. Typically our firm doesn't handle landlord/tenant disputes, or maybe in this case, trespassing. There may be other firms that could serve you better."

Shelby got up and walked to the window. Her voice returned to its earlier meekness yet held an undercurrent of persistence. "I know how this must look—like I don't care about my stepfather—but I really do. But I feel trapped and … used, and … and anyway, Rena said you handle wills and trusts. If you could just help me get Dad out of the house … because he says he'll take me to court. He'll probably try to be his own lawyer to save money and maybe get some sympathy."

Hollis felt Shelby was moving onto safer ground. "Well, I can definitely help you with that. If he files a protest, I can prepare your response. From what I've read in the trust, you should have no problem retaining control."

Shelby turned to face Hollis. "Good. I'm in the Bay Area through the weekend; then I'm going back to LA." Her tone reverted to its former curtness and she picked up her purse. "If I hear from Dad, I'll let you know, and you'll let me know about the eviction. Do you need me to sign something?"

Hollis felt herself blush. She had forgotten to give Shelby the attorney retention letter. "Yes, yes. My fees are reasonable, but I'll also try to give your family a break on billing. I'm a new attorney with the firm, so I'm not sure … but I'll see what I can do." She pulled the form out of her folder and handed it over. "I'll call you tomorrow on your cell."

"All right." An expression of resolve settled on Shelby's face. "Whatever you can do will be appreciated." She quickly signed the paper and passed it back.

Moments later at the elevators they waved goodbye.

Hollis returned to her office, her thoughts racing over the details of her meeting with Shelby. The young lady had been riding a roller coaster of emotions: veering back and forth from anger over the squabbles with her family and excitement over the surprise inheritance and her plans for college.

Ugh, teenagers.

Hollis' family life in her teenage years mostly involved staying out of the line of sight. She'd also learned that feelings and emotions were not shared and best kept buried. The Morgans were grateful for their undemanding children, who seemed to understand that expressions of love and caring were not available to them.

The many faces of Shelby made Hollis wonder what kind of client she would be for her first case. She was tempted to call Rena, but immediately knew that with the signing of that retention form, she was constrained by attorney-client privilege. She would reserve her second guessing for later.

George finished his call and turned his attention to Hollis.

"Well, how did it go?" He smiled, steepling his fingers. "I remember when I signed my first client."

Hollis smiled back. "Yeah, it's a great feeling. I didn't realize how nervous I was until I almost forgot to get her signature, but here you go." She pushed the paper toward him.

He glanced down, signed as her supervisor and returned it to her. "Okay, so what magic are you supposed to work?"

"Why do you say it like that?"

"Because anyone who wants an attorney with no experience is either looking for a fee deal or it's a case that's a hard sell."

Hollis laughed. "It's probably both. But I know one of her relatives … and I have to start somewhere."

George chuckled along with her and then sat quietly as he listened to her lay out the details of the case.

"It's clear she loves her stepfather, so she's afraid to confront him. The trust is not in dispute. He doesn't have a leg to stand on. The house is hers." Hollis checked her notes. "Should I try to get an injunction against the siblings to stop harassing her?"

"You wouldn't be able to get one without some kind of proof." He frowned. "If she has a land line, she can check with the phone company, or if it's a cellphone, her service provider. They might be able to report missed calls. Also, this isn't a landlord/tenant issue. There never was a lease or other residency agreement. This is a trespassing matter, and that makes it a lot easier to deal with."

Hollis scribbled a note. "Okay, I'll talk to her about that. Next, I'll see about getting the house listed. I'm hoping when her stepfather sees the sign go up in the yard and realizes she has an attorney, he'll back off."

"Maybe." George peered at her over his glasses. "Keep me informed. Oh, and tell your friend he has a job in the mailroom."

A smile leapt to Hollis' face. "Oh, thank you, George."

George held up his hand. "He'll be on probation to start with. He has to prove himself."

Hollis nodded and quickly backed out of his office so he couldn't change his mind.

CHAPTER 6

"HELLO, FELLOW FALLEN ANGELS, WELCOME back."
Hollis came from around the large conference table
to give each member a hug. "I can't believe how glad I am to
see you guys."

Gene and Hollis had confirmed the attendance of each
Fallen Angel for a meeting at the club's old location in the San
Lucian Library.

"I can't get over it." Miller Thornton glanced around the
room. Pulling out a chair from the table, he added, "It's been
over a year and nothing has changed. The library still looks
the same." Miller's hair was a little grayer and his hairline a
little higher; other than that, at forty-five he still had the same
youthful face.

Gene Donovan walked slowly around the room, examining
the photos of historical Northern California that lined the wall.
"Miller, what are you talking about? None of this was here. Not
one of these pictures. And the furniture is all new. Remember
how we had to set up our own table and chairs?"

Miller frowned. "Really? Hmm …. Still, some of this stuff
looks familiar."

Richard sucked on his teeth—an annoying habit she remembered well—and rocked back in his chair. "Probably because you're a librarian. All libraries must look the same to you." He rose to his feet to give Gene and Miller pats on the back. "It's good to see you two."

"How did you know I worked in a library? Oh, yeah. I guess we don't have to hide our identities anymore." Miller pulled out a small sheet of turquoise colored origami paper from his shirt pocket and started folding it into a tiny crane.

Gene turned to Hollis with a pleased look.

"You look good, Ms. Morgan," he said, swirling an index finger about her hair. "New haircut, new style, even a new briefcase. Being an attorney must agree with you."

She performed a fake curtsy. "Why, thank you, Mr. Donovan. You look pretty good yourself. In fact everybody seems to have weathered the last year well."

"Everybody except Jeffrey." Richard stopped doodling and raised the cap off his bald head.

There was a momentary silence.

Miller stopped folding. "Is Rena coming?"

The door burst open.

"Hi, everyone, it's so good to see you all again." Rena entered the room and flopped into the closest chair. She wore an ankle-length camel coat and a maroon cashmere scarf that was doubled into a large knot around her shoulders. She held up her hand. "I know, Gene, I'm late."

As she unwound the scarf, Hollis caught a whiff of a tuberose fragrance.

Gene sat next to Rena. "Doesn't matter. It's good to see you." He leaned over and gave her a kiss on the forehead.

"Hi, Rena." Miller took her outstretched hand in his own and squeezed it warmly. "It's good to see you … all of you. What's everybody been up to?"

Gene looked boyish as ever with his blond hair gelled into spikes. He mockingly raised a manicured hand. "I'm still with the newspaper. About a year ago, I got promoted to editorial page chief, but I still love a good book."

"Until the trial, I never knew you worked for a paper. Had I known back then, instead of me coming out of pocket for our books, you could've gotten them for free." Miller shook his finger. "I manage a regional library system."

Gene shrugged. "Sorry, how was I to know? You told us you got the books at no cost."

"Yeah Miller, you should have said something," Rena said. "Isn't it interesting to find out as we go around the room how we moved on. I knew about you, Gene, because I saw your name in the paper." She sat a little straighter in her chair. "After the trial I officially changed my name to Rena Gabriel. I had gotten used to it. Now I work for a retail store—"

"Barneys," Gene interjected, then, "Sorry, go on."

Hollis wagged her finger. Gene was fashion conscious as ever.

Rena laughed. "Yes, Barneys." She swiveled her chair. "And yes, Gene, before you ask, I do get a discount."

He slapped his leg. "I knew it."

"Anyway, I still love to read too," Rena said. "What about you, Richard? You didn't end up testifying."

"No. My wife has a sensitive job in government, and I didn't want my name out there. Fortunately the DA gave me a break. I didn't have to testify at the trial unless they absolutely needed me." He looked around at each of them. "But you know, I'm glad I don't have to hide anymore. I was starting to confuse myself."

They all laughed with more than a little self-consciousness.

Gene pulled out a mint and popped it into his mouth. "I never changed my name."

Hollis crossed her arms. "Well, you guys all know my background. The trial spared nothing in revealing the details of my life." She leaned into the table. "Miller, what exactly do you manage for the library?"

"I'm able to request information from any library in the world. We obtained a new—"

"No offense, Miller, hate to cut you off, but I can't be here all evening." Richard pointed to his watch. "Gene, what did you learn about Wallace's death?"

Gene slipped on a pair of reading glasses—not the dime-store kind—and pulled a piece of lined paper from a folder in his backpack.

"He was shot in the stomach with a .38 caliber. He could have survived, but he bled out before anyone found him."

Rena hugged herself, her hands gripping her upper arms. "When did it happen?"

"Monday night in his office between eight and nine p.m. He was working late. His body was discovered by the janitor early the next morning."

Richard frowned. "There was no one else working late? No security walking around?"

Gene shook his head. "Due to state budget cuts, security is limited to the lobby. So they would have called him to tell him he had a visitor. He'd have to let whoever killed him into his office."

Hollis was silent.

"What do you think, Hollis? You're awfully quiet," Miller said.

She looked up from where she was taking notes. "It sounds like whoever killed Jeffrey knew he was working late and knew the cleaning schedule or was just lucky." She scribbled on a piece of paper as she finished her thought. "Was there anything else, Gene?"

"Yeah, the police don't have anyone in custody. They brought his son in for questioning, but they let him go."

Rena raised her eyebrows. "Jeffrey had a family? I mean it's not impossible but I just never saw him with a family. He didn't have any pictures in his office."

Miller wrinkled his forehead. "I never saw any either. I guess he wanted to keep his personal life private. He only had that stupid cat poster. It had a pocket in the back where he stuffed all his career acknowledgments and certificates. He didn't want those in view either." He shook his head. "I've known him longer than any of you, and he never mentioned a family."

"Would you want former residents of the prison population to know about your family?" Richard said. "I can understand his reasoning."

Hollis looked up at the ceiling, remembering the extent to which Richard had gone to hide his own background.

"The police always check out the relatives first." Gene, done reading, took off his glasses. "They look for a family dispute. His family would have known about his schedule."

"Geesh, I'm still getting used to the fact that he had a family," Miller murmured.

"When's the funeral?" Rena asked.

"No funeral. It's a memorial, set for this coming Wednesday." Gene took out another few pages of paper and passed them around the table. "Here's the article in the *Herald*."

Richard tossed the paper onto the table. "Well that's it then. There's nothing for us to do except attend the memorial. Can I get a ride with somebody?"

"Sure, Richard, you can ride with me." Miller folded the paper into a series of squares. "I'll pick you up in front of the main library."

"Hollis, do you and Rena want to ride with me?" Gene packed up his backpack.

Rena raised her hand.

"Sure, sure." Hollis folded her hands together. "By then the police might have caught the killer. I've asked a friend who used to work for the police to see what he could find out about the status of the case, so we'll see what comes up." She paused. "Er … hey you guys, what about our book club? What about starting it up again?"

Richard took a deep breath and let it out slowly, and Miller's right leg bounced restlessly up and down.

Miller spoke first. "Yeah, I'd be willing to try it out. But I'm not willing to get the books. Gene, your paper gets books. Couldn't you tap that resource?"

Gene nodded. "The advance reader copies go to the review section, but we also purchase published books at a discount. I know the paper has a few copies to give away. I can buy any extra books we need. So, to answer your question, yes, I can supply the books."

"I'd be willing to start up again," Rena said. "I haven't read nearly as much as when we were together. I guess I need the pressure of knowing we're going to have a discussion about it."

Hollis looked over at Richard. "Well?"

"Sure, why not? But no Saturdays. I can only do Wednesday or Thursday nights."

Gene moved toward the door. "Let's meet on Thursday, the week after the memorial."

After agreeing on the time, everyone walked out into the lobby.

Rena waited in the hall for Hollis to turn off the lights.

"You think Jeffrey would be happy to see us together again?"

Hollis gave her a sad smile. "Knowing Jeffrey, he'd be happier to see us staying out of prison."

CHAPTER 7

THE WIND CARRIED CHILLING FOG across the Bay, making insidious snake-like pathways between the gravestones. Mourners wrapped in overcoats and scarves lined up on either side of the mound of dirt. Some dabbed at their eyes with tissues, others looked as if they wished they could be anywhere else but there. Everyone looked somber.

Hollis and Rena stood closest to the casket at the far end of the gatherers. Richard, Miller, and Gene stood behind them.

"Is there anyone who would like to speak before we proceed?" The minister kept shifting from foot to foot. It looked as if it was all he could do to keep his teeth from chattering. His cassock waved gently with the wind.

Hollis looked around. There were about thirty of them gathered. Women outnumbered men, but not by much. She looked over at the family. Jeffrey Wallace's wife, brother, and son stood apart from the others at the head of the gravesite. Their faces were stoic, unexpressive, as if they were still in shock.

"Very well then we—"

"Wait, I want to say something." A large burly black man

wearing a beige trench coat over a suit without a tie came forward. He looked to be in his forties, with a shaved head and heavy mustache. He wore thick glasses and carried what appeared to be the Bible.

"Yes, please, go ahead." The Minister backed away to let him come forward.

"Er … my name is Warren, and Jeffrey was my parole officer for five years. I hate to say it, I gave him a real hard time at first, but he stayed with me. He didn't let me get away with anything, but he didn't let me dangle either. We weren't close friends, but I respected the dude. He was okay."

Warren stepped back and the crowd closed the aisle behind him

"Anyone—"

"I'd like to speak."

This time a young woman came forward, shouldering her way briskly through the group, saying "excuse me" repeatedly as she made her way to the front. Hollis had noticed her at the beginning of the service. She was extremely tall with pale blue eyes and thin blond hair that she wore in a bright red clip on top of her head. Despite the cold, she only wore a brown sweater and a thin beige sheath. Her nose had turned bright red. She wasn't pretty in the classic sense, but attractive in a quirky way.

"Jeffrey Wallace was a good man. He wasn't perfect. He sent me back to prison even after I told him I couldn't pass the surprise urine test because I'd made one little slip the night before. But I didn't blame him; he had to do his job. The thing is, he didn't give up on me either. When I got out again he found me work, and now I really am clean. That's it. Goodbye, Jeffrey." She took a tissue out of her sleeve and dabbed at her nose.

The minister, not wanting to preempt any further speakers, stood quietly. Hollis could sense more than see Richard shifting restlessly behind her. Rena had also started to rummage about in her purse for tissues.

When no one else came forward, the minister checked his watch and looked to the widow for a sign. She gave a curt nod.

"We should all bow our heads," he intoned.

A few minutes later the service was over, and a winding group of mourners passed by the casket. They trudged steadily to the family's receiving line formed at the end of the path to introduce themselves and give condolences.

Hollis tried to think of some inconspicuous way of getting out of the line without having to interact socially with a family she knew she would never see again. But she was gently herded forward by the people around her. She wondered if her expression looked as grim as those of the other Fallen Angels.

A few steps behind Gene, she approached the mourning family. She couldn't resist peering at the woman Jeffrey had married. According to the obituary, Jeffrey had been married to Frances for eight years. Even more of a surprise was that this was his second marriage. His first ended when his wife died in childbirth. Their son, Brian, had survived. She did a quick calculation; Brian must be in his mid-twenties.

The line moved at a steady pace, putting her one person away from an older man standing next to Frances. It was a safe guess that he was Jeffrey's brother. People were murmuring their sympathies, and the family of three stood with their backs together as if poised to ward off the furies.

Hollis was now next in line. The man was short like Jeffrey, but the resemblance ended there. Jeffrey always reminded her of a friendly puffin. His brother looked like a hawk.

"I'm Jeffrey's brother, Calvin, thank you for coming." He reached out his hand for a gentle shake.

"I'm Hollis Morgan, I'm a former … client. I'm sorry for your loss."

At the sound of a raised voice, Hollis looked ahead to see a young man grabbing Gene's arm.

"You're Gene Donovan? I need to speak with you." Brian, Jeffrey's son, put an arm around Gene's shoulder and pulled him aside.

Brian was his father's double—short, with brown hair and a solemn face. Hollis stopped behind Gene, who turned and gave her a questioning look.

"Ah, ah sure ... wh-when?" Gene stuttered uncharacteristically. Usually full of confidence, he must have been caught off guard.

Hollis left Calvin and stood in front of Frances. She could see that Brian Wallace had not loosened his grip on Gene's shoulder. But it was clear from her clenched jaw that Frances' plan was to ignore the interchange.

"I'm Frances, Jeffrey's wife, thank you for coming." Either she had repeated the phrase one too many times, or she was simply bored. She sounded like a robot.

Hollis sympathized and wasn't thrown off by her tone. "I'm Hollis Morgan. I was a client of your husband's. He was a very good—"

"You're Hollis? I was hoping you'd come," Brian said. Letting go of Gene's shoulder, he reached across his stepmother with his hand outstretched for Hollis to shake. "Are all of you in the book club?" He pointed to the five of them now bunched together and halting the receiving line.

Gene was going through his jacket pockets, searching for a card.

Hollis looked past Frances to Rena, who was stopped in front of Calvin. Frances, who could no longer ignore her stepson's conversation, was looking more irritated by the second.

"Yes, but maybe we should talk after you've met the rest of the visitors?" Hollis said in a low voice. "We're holding up the line."

"Brian, please." Frances' raised voice was strained.

"Sorry." He spoke urgently to Hollis and Gene. "Call me and

let's talk. My father told me about you and I think I could use your help." He gave his number.

Gene pulled a business card from his pocket and scribbled a number on the back. He handed it to Brian. "What kind of help do—"

"Yes, of course we'll call and set something up," Hollis interjected, not wanting to be any more obvious than they already were.

Gene let her lead him away from the line, and they headed down the grassy pathway, back to their cars.

Gene got behind the wheel. Hollis sat in the back.

"What was that about?" she asked.

"You tell me. I guess there's a dysfunctional family out there for everyone." Gene shook his head.

Rena slid quickly into the car, followed just as hurriedly by Richard and Miller.

"Now that was strange," Richard said, taking a knit cap out of his jacket pocket and pulling it down to cover his bald head.

"No, that was bizarre," Rena said, briskly rubbing her arms against the cold. "What could he want with us?"

"I don't know, and I get the feeling Frances may not know what he has in mind either," Hollis said, watching the mourners return to their cars.

When Brian reached his car, he looked back at them. Frances must have pulled on his arm, for he immediately climbed into the limo waiting to take them away.

Gene followed her gaze. "Yeah, I think you're right."

HOLLIS WAS FOCUSED ON WRITING a brief for George when the phone rang.

"Check your email," John said. "I just scanned information that was used this morning for a press conference. It's about six pages. Let me know if you have questions."

"John," she said, "thank you."

"Yeah, sure. I said I would do what I could."

"I appreciate it. I'll let you know if I have any questions."

She let a silence rest between them.

Finally she said, "Well, I'll call you later."

He grunted goodbye.

Over the next few minutes she retrieved the report and printed out the pages of photos, text, and charts. She quickly read the summary conclusions and picked up the phone.

John answered on the first ring.

"What do you want to know?" he asked without preliminaries.

"The length of time before Jeffrey was discovered was long enough for him to completely bleed out. Do they know how long that could be?" It pained her even to say it. "Does it mean he suffered?"

Faber was silent for a moment. "This is a preliminary report. The ME wants to see the toxic analysis before he finalizes it. Only then can that question be answered."

It was Hollis' turn to be silent as she struggled with what it all meant. The tox report wouldn't wipe out the finality of a bullet.

"If he was shot and just left to die, wouldn't that mean not only malice but possible premeditation?"

"Yes, Counselor, it probably would," he said.

Hollis made a thumbs up gesture. "Well, this counselor has got to get back to work." Her eyes wandered back to the half-finished brief on top of her desk.

Associate attorneys were used by their senior attorneys to do grunt work. It was a complicated probate matter and likely to be research intensive. No wonder George was glad to see her pass the bar.

John gave a small cough. "What about getting together tonight?"

"Do you mind if I take a pass? With the funeral and everything, I wouldn't be very good company."

"Sure, I understand. Why don't you call me when you're feeling better?"

She heard papers shuffling. "I better get back to cleaning out my files," he said. "Talk to you soon." He was gone.

Hollis sighed. She couldn't explain to herself what the matter was. The other night she'd been terrified John was going to ask her to marry him. Then she felt less terrified but more worried he was going to ask her to live with him. As it turned out, he knew her well enough not to ask anything of her.

She picked up the new case file and spent the rest of the day outlining the issues. When it was time to leave for home, she made five copies of Jeffrey's medical examiner report to take with her.

HOLLIS DID SOME CHORES AND took a long shower before picking up the copy of the ME report. Pouring herself a glass of wine, she carried it and the pages onto her townhome patio. She wasn't sure what role Brian Wallace thought the Fallen Angels could play in finding Jeffrey's killer, but she wanted to be familiar with the facts of his death.

She started with the photos.

Blood was everywhere. The color photos were as gruesome as she feared. She could see that Jeffrey had lost weight since she'd last seen him and had started to gray around the temples. He'd died in a pool of his own blood.

She shuddered.

She looked in the report for his age—fifty-four. The bullet had gone through his stomach sometime between five thirty and eight thirty on Monday evening. The time was set largely by the cleaning people and office personnel who said goodnight on their way out and less by the ME's determination of his physical condition. He evidently had eaten a late lunch. From the angle of the bullet, his killer wasn't much taller than Jeffrey. And from the trajectory of the bullet, he—or she—was right handed. There wasn't much more to go on.

Hollis frowned and picked up her cellphone.

"Gene, I know we said we would meet next Thursday, but

can you call the Fallen Angels together for a meeting tomorrow after work, say six o'clock?"

Gene agreed. "Yeah, that encounter with the son was a little strange. I can probably switch some things around to make a meeting." He paused, as if checking his calendar. "Sure, I'll call the others. Where do you want to meet?"

"It's too late to get the library." Hollis sighed. "We can meet in my firm's conference room. I'll make arrangements."

"You got it. By the way, what's the rush?"

"I've made copies of the medical examiner's report for everyone. I was going through it. It seems that Jeffrey was deliberately left to die."

She heard a harsh intake of breath.

"I'll start calling now."

CHAPTER 8

T HE NEXT MORNING HOLLIS WAS the first one in the office. It was her favorite time of day. She stopped to look out Triple D's almost floor-to-ceiling windows overlooking the Bay. The new Bay Bridge, which joined San Francisco with the East Bay, provided a picturesque backdrop. The sun had begun its rise over the Oakland-Berkeley hills and cast a warm yellow glow on the water as it chased the fading blue of the night sky away. But today she could hardly enjoy the sight.

She hadn't slept well.

In the middle of the night, the cold realization that Jeffrey Wallace had been murdered had finally hit her. She felt obligated to honor his life and the good he had done. Looking at his family, she'd realized there was a side to him she hadn't known; however, from what she did know, he hadn't deserved to die the way he did. She labeled her own file for Jeffrey's murder and placed the ME report and her notes inside.

The firm was coming to life. She heard the early morning banter and smelled the aroma of fresh coffee. In her inbox was the file George had returned. He'd written comments on one of her legal research memos, and she had to grudgingly admit his suggestions were right on.

She spent the next hour doing paperwork and making client contacts until her phone buzzed.

"Hollis, you have a call from a Mr. Brian Wallace. I'll transfer," Tiffany announced. Performance bonuses were being discussed this week. Hollis noticed Tiffany was executing her receptionist's role with renewed commitment.

"Brian, how can I help you?"

"I need to discuss something with you as soon as possible," Brian said, not even bothering with a hello. "I can take off work for an early lunch. Are you free at eleven?"

She agreed, curious about his urgency.

Hollis told Tiffany she would need one of the conference rooms for a morning appointment. Tiffany nodded and immediately entered the room assignment into the computer. That was one definite advantage of being an attorney over a paralegal; your requests were rarely questioned.

Hollis was finishing up George's morning assignment when Brian arrived.

She'd asked for the small conference room without the panoramic view. It limited distractions and kept conversations from wandering off point. Tiffany had put out glasses and a pitcher of water.

Dressed for the office, Brian wore a conservative light gray suit, white shirt, with gray tie. His light brown hair was slicked back and his blue eyes darted around the room. He sat down and began to fidget with the stapler on the table.

"Hollis, I need your help, and maybe Gene's too … maybe all of the Fallen Angels." Brian stood and paced the room.

She noticed the assumed familiarity with his use of first names.

"I understand you need our help, but it would help to know why."

"You already met Frances, my stepmother. She and Dad were

married about eight years. It seemed like an okay marriage to me—I wasn't living at home—and Dad seemed happy, until about six months ago. They'd gone on a vacation to Hawaii and when they got back, Dad told me that he and Frances were going to set up a revocable trust. If anything happened to him, he wanted me to be executor, but Frances would have access to all their holdings for her life—except ten percent, which would go to the Public Library Foundation. I am to have his separate property now and after she dies. I'm the sole beneficiary of their trust. If there are still assets after my death, then the Public Library Foundation receives the remainder of the trust."

Hollis busily took notes.

"Was the trust funded and finalized?"

"Yeah, five months ago."

"All right, what you describe is not uncommon. That's standard language for a revocable trust."

"I realize that, but about three months ago, Frances filed for divorce. Dad was surprised and I think, hurt. He didn't see it coming. None of us did."

Hollis wrote, then circled the word divorce on her note pad. Now she knew why he needed her help.

She put down her pen. "The trust takes precedent. The divorce wasn't final. I know you may not want to hear this, but unless there is language in the trust specifying otherwise, your stepmother—subtracting your father's separate property and the amount to the Public Library Foundation—will still have full access to his estate."

"I knew it." Brian rubbed the nape of his neck. "She already spends like there's no tomorrow." He stopped and held out his hand out as if to stop whatever Hollis must be thinking. "Look, I admit I would like the money, but I'm not desperate for it. I have a good job as a supply manager, but … but …."

Hollis offered, "But you don't think your father would want a woman who was getting ready to divorce him to have his hard-earned money after his death."

"Exactly."

"What do you think Gene or I can do?"

"Dad told me about the Fallen Angels. He was very proud of all of you, especially after the trial." He sat down again. "Gene can run a background check on Frances. He can use his newspaper connections. For some reason, she's very secretive about her past. My mom died when I was five. I think Dad must have been really lonely when he met Frances and didn't bother to learn much about her." He leaned across the conference table. "Hollis, Dad once told me you had the sharpest deductive mind he knew of. I want you to find out what's she's up to."

She felt her brows knit together. "Have you heard anything about your father's killer? Do the police have any leads?"

"What?" Brian looked startled. "Oh no, there's nothing so far. They talk or come by to see me every day. Er … I do know they're following up on the angle of possible disgruntled parolees."

She shifted in her seat. "I'm sure there's always that possibility, but after office hours it's not likely he would have let a—"

"Look, I'm not a cop. I think a parolee is a real strong possibility for a suspect, and so do the police." Brian took a swallow from the glass of water. He was starting to sweat profusely. "Do you think you can help me with the trust or not?"

"You have to understand that even with a straightforward court filing, it takes thirty days from the date we file to get a hearing."

"Okay, no problem. We can use the time to flush Frances out."

"During that interval I can run a public records check on her while Gene covers her friends and family background." Hollis looked down at her notepad. "But this can cost a lot of money. I'm not a private detective, nor do I want to get in the way of the police investigation."

"I don't have a lot of money." He played with his pen. "I was hoping the Fallen Angels and not your law firm could help with digging up the truth. And maybe you could help me with processing the trust as co-executor; then you wouldn't have to charge your full rate. You'd get paid out of the trust."

Hollis grimaced. George was right about clients looking for a fee break from new attorneys.

"Brian, did you tell the police what you just told me, I mean about the trust and divorce? Money is a great motivator."

"Yes, I told them. They asked me if I thought Frances killed my father and honestly, I don't think she did. Frances has her issues, but I don't think she's a murderer. Besides, she was conducting an evening seminar when Dad was shot."

Hollis glanced down at the time on her cellphone. "Okay, let me get things moving. Today is Thursday; I'll file a request for hearing on Monday. Then I'll talk with Gene and we'll get back to you."

Brian dabbed at his damp forehead as the two of them walked to the elevators. He held out his hand and she shook it. It was clammy. She hoped he didn't notice her wiping her hand against her pants afterwards.

"Thanks Hollis, I'll look forward to hearing from you."

HOLLIS WAS IN HER OFFICE munching on a lunch of flavored crackers when she called Gene.

"It didn't take him long to get over his grief," he said.

"That was my thought. It sounds like he wants us to play private detectives."

Hollis took some satisfaction from having Brian request their assistance. He would be her second client. She ignored the nagging concern that she would have to deal with John's warnings about police interference. "I'm not sure Brian knows what it is we'd be looking for."

"I think you're right," Gene said. "But we can put it out there with the Fallen Angels. As a group we might be able to come up with a few avenues to pursue. Although to tell you the truth, I'm sure Jeffrey would be skeptical that we would be able to avoid crossing over into police territory."

"Yes." Hollis was glad Gene wasn't sitting in her office to see her look of resolve. "But I think he would want us to help his son. We'll meet and decide then how to handle things."

"That'll work. Maybe while we're helping one Wallace, we can find out who killed the other."

AFTER THE CALL WITH GENE, Hollis got down to tackling Shelby Patterson's case. She'd finished checking out real estate agency references and had narrowed it down to two. The firm she finally chose offered to place more advertising and oversee getting the house and yard in shape. She looked up to see Tiffany standing in her doorway.

"What?"

"There's this guy waiting to see you in the lobby. You didn't tell me you had an appointment other than Mr. Wallace."

Hollis frowned. "I don't have any other appointments today. Why didn't you just call me and announce him over the phone?"

"He seems upset." Tiffany smiled weakly, turning to look over her shoulder. "We used to be able to talk about this kind of stuff when you were a paralegal, but you're one of my bosses now and I feel funny."

Hollis' curiosity clicked in. "First, I'm still me and I hope you're still you. So, for me, we're on the same team. But tell me the name of this mysterious gentleman and I'll come and talk to you after he's gone."

"It's Shelby Patterson's father, Mr. Darol Patterson."

Entering the lobby, Hollis could immediately see why Darol Patterson had caused Tiffany to lose her usual professional cool. He was strikingly handsome, brown-skinned, tall and with a presence—a man who oozed charm. For Hollis, the greater surprise was his well-tailored attire—navy sports coat, open collar white shirt, and gray slacks. He looked nothing like the drug-addicted loser Shelby had described, except for his piercing dark eyes, which projected agitation and frustration.

She took him to the same conference room she'd shared with Brian Wallace that morning.

"Mr. Patterson, what can I do for you?"

"I understand you're representing my daughter in a lawsuit." His voice was low, clear, and articulate. "I want to know what my rights are, and I'd like you to hear my side of the story."

Hollis shook her head slowly. "Mr. Patterson, you need to get your own legal representation. I can't advise you regarding your rights. As you said, your daughter is my client. I can't discuss or share any—"

"Okay, okay, I get it. If it gets to that point, I'll be representing myself." Leaning across the table, he let his eyes bore into Hollis', and his voice rose with just a little irritation. "Besides, I think you'd be better able to serve her if you knew my side. Wouldn't you agree?"

She gave him an open-palm gesture to go ahead.

"I won't go into my … my disgrace as a man with an addiction. Suffice it to say that I hit bottom and then I saw the error of my ways and came back to the living. I'm ten months clean. Unfortunately, my mother was a mean and vindictive woman who I think always hated me because I resembled my father. He left her after five years during which she made his life a living hell." He looked around the room. "Can I have a glass of water?"

"Of course."

Hollis poked her head out the doorway and asked Tiffany if she could bring in a couple of bottles of water.

Sitting down again, she folded her hands and waited for him to continue.

"That house is mine. My mother turned my daughter against me. Susan, Shelby's mother, was a good woman. We loved each other until the day she died, and I love her still. But my mother hated the fact that Susan loved me and wouldn't go along with her."

Tiffany returned with the water and left.

Hollis couldn't help but ask, "Mr. Patterson, if your mother hated you so much, why would she give Shelby, your stepdaughter, her house?"

His little laugh was soft and off-putting. "I wondered that too. My mother was shrewd. I was a disappointment to her all my life, but especially after I got caught up in drugs. But even though I beat that and made sure my kids did too, she never would forgive or forget." Darol, who had been clenching and unclenching his fists, finally folded his hands. "She knew it would torment me to have my stepdaughter turn against me."

Thoughts swirled around in Hollis' head. This apparently simple matter was becoming increasingly complicated.

"Shelby doesn't want to hurt you." She bit her lip. "But she's intimidated, and can you blame her after the harassment?"

His eyes turned ice cold. "What harassment?"

For a quick moment Hollis flashed back to a similar reaction from Shelby. Were these abrupt mood swings a family trait?

"Shelby says she's been getting repeated hang-up phone calls and her car was vandalized."

"Shelby's in LA, so how could I do something like that? That's not me!" He was shouting, slamming his fists on table. Standing and towering over Hollis, he demanded, "Did she say it was me?"

Out of the corner of her eye, Hollis saw Tiffany take a quick peek inside the conference room window. Hollis motioned with her head that she was fine.

"No, no, she didn't say it was you." Hollis deliberately lowered her voice so he'd have to strain to hear her. "Can you think of anyone who would want to … to frighten her?"

Darol sat back down.

"You mean *my* kids? No, no … I don't know. They're grown,

they're adults. They travel back and forth between here and LA. Did she say they did it?"

"No, she doesn't know who's doing it. That's why she's feeling … a little afraid." Hollis remembered Shelby expressing more anger than fear, but she didn't want to get another flare-up out of Darol. "But I take you at your word, Mr. Patterson. I've been retained to secure your daughter's house and to liquidate the asset. I appreciate your situation but your mother's trust is valid."

" 'Liquidate the asset.' You mean sell it, right? Did she tell you that we live there? That's where we sleep at night. You're just going to kick us out?" His voice started to rise again.

Hollis rubbed her forehead. "Mr. Patterson, there is no need—"

He stood up and went to the door. "It's not going to happen." He pointed his finger at her. "You hear me? It's not going to happen."

He left, slamming the door behind him.

Hollis looked up at the ceiling.

And this is my first case.

CHAPTER 9

FOR THE FIRST TIME SINCE Hollis could remember, the Fallen Angels all arrived to a meeting early. Triple D's conference room was certainly more comfortable than the library and everyone acted curious about where she worked. Placing a bottle of water at each seat, Hollis closed the curtains that opened onto the firm's lobby. She had deliberately chosen six o'clock as the meeting time so that most of the attorneys and staff would be gone.

As she looked around the quiet room, she couldn't help but reflect that two weeks ago Jeffrey had been alive. Miller was finishing his first origami crane and Richard, deep in thought, twisted his bottled water on its coaster. With heads down, Gene and Rena were both clicking through their smartphones.

Hollis cleared her throat. "Why don't we go ahead and get started." She glanced at her notepad. "Brian Wallace wants us to help him check out his stepmother's activities leading up to Jeffrey's death."

Richard passed his hand over his bald spot. "He didn't say *us*, he asked you and Gene."

"No, he mentioned all of us," Hollis insisted. "He knows we

come as a package. Besides, I couldn't do it without you guys. I don't have your skills, Richard, for evaluating numbers, or Miller's research resources, or Rena's network of contacts."

Miller doodled on a pad of paper and looked thoughtful. "The police won't want us interfering in their investigation. I'd like to do something to help find Jeffrey's killer. Since it's too late for that, all I can do is help his son. I can live with that."

"Me too," Rena said. "Jeffrey played by the book. He put us all back on track. He shouldn't have died the way he did."

Gene cleared his throat. "When you think about it, working with Brian keeps us low profile. We can work behind the scenes, helping him, while we find out what we can about what happened to Jeffrey."

"Yeah, good point." Richard sat up. "It's probably best if you two are his main contacts, though. He doesn't have to meet with all of us."

"Don't worry, Richard." Hollis leaned in. "You've made it clear you want to stay below the radar."

Richard opened his mouth to speak, then closed it. He could see the looks the other Fallen Angels were giving him. He splayed his hand across his chest. "Don't get me wrong. I want to help, but I would rather not be out front on this. My wife—"

"Oh good grief, not her again," Rena said and took a swallow of water.

Miller demanded. "Who *is* your wife, anyway? Does she work for the president or something? What's her name?"

Richard turned red. "That's none of—"

"Come on, people, let's stay focused," Hollis intervened. "It sounds like we all want to do this thing with Brian. Is everyone in?"

Their eyes met expectantly, and everyone agreed.

Gene said, "Did you say he was willing to pay?"

"He's going to pay my firm a small retainer for my services as a co-executor. Actually the estate pays me, not him. As a group, I don't think taking money is a good idea." Hollis scribbled on her pad. "I would rather not be obligated to him for looking into the trust. Besides, we're doing this for Jeffrey."

"I'm with Hollis on that," Richard said. "Brian seems like a straight-up guy, but I'm doing this because Jeffrey worked long hours to keep his clients clean. I don't want that time and money wasted going to someone who doesn't deserve it."

They all nodded vigorously.

Hollis stood. "Good. I'll contact Brian and let him know. I'll tell him to send me anything he has on his stepmother and everything on the Wallace trust. Here are copies of the preliminary ME report." She handed out the pages. "When I get his information, I'll copy it for each of you, too. We should probably still plan on meeting next Thursday at the library."

"It's going to be impossible to evaluate the financial distribution if there's a trust," Richard said. "It's blind to the public."

Gene's fingers pulled randomly at the hairs in his eyebrow. "True, except I bet ol' Brian can get his hands on his dad's previous will and maybe even his tax returns. Don't worry; there will be something for you to start pulling apart."

"Good thinking, Gene," Rena said. "It doesn't sound like a lot of networking will be needed here, but once I see what's in the file I can help Gene with the background check on Frances, and maybe on Brian, too."

"Hey now, that is good thinking." Hollis smiled. "Okay, let's wrap this up for now. I'll tell Brian to send everything he can as soon as he can. Let's meet on Tuesday and lay out our plan."

After saying their goodbyes, they all gathered up their things to leave. Gene hung back to walk out with Hollis as she turned off the lights.

"What do you really think about all this?"

Hollis shrugged. "Between a disputed trust and an unsolved murder of one of the beneficiaries, we're in for a bumpy ride."

RETURNING HOME, HOLLIS WAS DRAINED, anxious, and on

edge. The message light on her phone blinked. Putting her purse down, she pressed the button.

John's lighthearted voice greeted her. "Hey, how about a drink tonight? Let me know one way or the other."

Hollis thought she might be oversensitive, but his cheeriness sounded a little forced. They needed to see each other, but it was too late tonight. She pushed the call-back button.

"Hey, I just got home, so no drink tonight. How about I fix you dinner tomorrow? It's the start of the weekend and we won't be in work mode."

She could hear John's smile as he said, "I was wondering how you were going to get back in my good graces."

She laughed, a little uncomfortably. "Do I need to get back into your good graces?"

His tone turned serious. "We need to talk. I know you're probably wiped out now, but tomorrow, okay?"

She searched for something more to say but all that slipped through was, "Okay."

She hung up and hugged herself.

HOLLIS LOOKED CRITICALLY AROUND HER dining room. The table centerpiece was a small vase of flowers and two large lime-colored candles. The setting was colorful, with pastel tangerine plates and pale yellow cloth napkins.

It looked too girly.

She removed the plates and went to the kitchen to swap in her everyday white plates. *Better.*

She was still debating on changing out the candles when she heard a key in the lock. She and John had exchanged keys only a few months ago. She had used his key only once, primarily because her place was cozier. Hollis never minded his access—except for the very first time, when she heard the key in the door and almost broke out in hives. Other than that, she thought she was handling things well. John entered with arms outstretched for a hug. In one hand he held her favorite bottle of Zinfandel from the Brown Estate Vineyards in Napa Valley.

"Thank you." She smiled. "It will go perfectly with dinner."

He looked at the table. "Everything looks real nice. I wasn't expecting the royal treatment." John took off his jacket and hung it up in the guest closet.

Hollis raised her lips for his light kiss.

"What royal treatment? I eat like this every night."

"You mean this isn't going all out for your man?" He eyes gazed into hers.

"You're so funny." Hollis laughed longer than the comment warranted and looked away. She motioned for him to take a seat at the table. "Do you know if they've found out anything more about Jeffrey's murder?"

John's jaw tensed. "What are you doing?"

"I was curious." She reached for the bottle of wine and began to open it. "And I'm getting ready to pour you a glass of really good vintage wine that my lover brought me tonight."

He put his hand over hers.

"Sit down. I'll repeat, what are you doing? I thought we could have one evening when murder, mayhem, nut cases and other assorted personality disorders from our work-a-day world didn't have to join us for dinner." John's gaze held hers.

"Just forget it. It was a simple question." She looked away. "I'm getting ready to feed you so we can enjoy the rest of the evening on a full stomach." Hollis slipped her hand out from under his and poured her own glass.

"The promise of later sounds great, but I would rather you be real with me, now," he said and took a sip of wine. "Mmm, this *is* good."

She went into the kitchen, calling out over her shoulder, "I told you it was." She went over to the counter and started putting away the cookbooks she'd used. "Now, I'll just—"

"No, wait." He held up his hand. "Sit down. We're not eating until we get things straight."

"Dinner is ready now." Hollis sat heavily and threw the

dishtowel on the table. "What do you want from me?" Then, as if hearing herself, she leaned back in her chair and let her chin drop on her chest. "Look, I don't know what the matter is. At first I thought it was Jeffrey's death, but it's not all about him, it's … it's … me."

"You mean *us*?" John looked at her struggle for words. "You want me to go?"

"No!" she protested. "No, I definitely do not want you to go."

He got up from the table and took her in his arms. "And I don't want to go, but we need to clear the air between us."

She clung to him. "This is where I want to be."

"Then what's the problem? I will be here for you, always."

She pushed him back, and in a shaky voice said, "You're asking me to take down a wall I put up to keep my feelings safe. Last time I didn't read the signs. No, 'sign' is not a strong enough word; it was a billboard. I let my ex-husband betray everything I held dear. I lost my way."

He tilted her chin to look into her eyes. "Listen, I love you. I love *us*. We can take it slow. There are other signs, too. But don't make up stuff to justify pushing me away."

She grazed his lips with her fingers, then murmured, "I need more time."

CHAPTER 10

"Hollis," Tiffany said over the phone, "Vince is here from the mailroom. He has a package for you." Her voice did little to hide her curiosity.

Hollis smiled to herself. "It's okay. Send him back to my office." She owed her cheerfulness this Monday morning to an enjoyable weekend with John. Once they'd gotten past their rough start, he agreed to give her the space she needed and not push her. She'd relaxed, and now she couldn't seem to stop smiling.

"Aren't you going to want me to date-stamp it in?"

"I'll bring it to you later. It's not time sensitive," Hollis said. "Tiffany, just send Vince back to my office."

A few moments later he stood in her doorway.

Hollis got up and gave him a hug. He stiffened, bent over, and patted her shoulder.

She took a step back. "Vince, you look good."

He was dressed in a new white T-shirt and his standard gray hoodie with a pair of dark slacks that had a worn sheen. Hollis didn't care. She looked into his eyes. He was clean, inside and out.

"Hi, Hollis, I wanted you to know I'd started work. I was here last week but I had to go to employee training."

"That's great news. Have a seat."

"I can't. I gotta get back. The U.S. Mail gets delivered at ten o'clock."

Hollis smiled to see him taking his job so seriously.

"I came to bring you this package. We're supposed to hand-deliver packages we're told to look out for."

"But I didn't send a hand deliver notice."

"I know. When I saw your name on the package, I just wanted to see you and let you know I was here." Vince added gravely, "Thanks, Hollis, for getting me this job. You won't be sorry."

She grinned. "I know."

BRIAN HAD SENT HER SEVERAL documents comprising about sixty pages. The before will and the after trust were included, along with several years of tax returns and a home refinance application. Hollis removed the staples and headed to the firm's high-speed printer.

She was finishing up when one of the new paralegals walked up to use the machine. "I'll sign out for you. What's the client code?"

Hollis gave her a smile. "Thank you, but, uh, I used to be a paralegal. I'll take care of it. This is a new case and I need a new matter number."

The young woman, who looked like a high school junior, waited patiently. "No problem. By the way, congratulations! I saw in the firm's weekly report you brought in a new client." She stacked an inch-high packet into the copier. "I'm taking the bar in four months. The part I dread the most is having to find new clients."

Hollis wondered when they started letting seventeen-year-olds take the bar. "It's not so bad; sometimes they seem to fall out of the sky." She turned to leave. "Good luck with the bar. Let me know if I can be of help."

She dropped the last packet in the overnight mail to the Fallen Angels; they should each get their copy the next day. She wanted them to have a few days to look over the material before their next meeting.

"Uh, Hollis," Tiffany said in a hushed tone from the doorway. "Sorry for the interruption."

"What's the matter? Come on in."

"I can't. I've to get back to the front desk." She looked over her shoulder and whispered, "There's a couple waiting for you in the main conference room. They don't have an appointment."

"They must be drop-ins. Why are you whispering?"

"You're starting to have a lot of drop-ins." Tiffany spoke in her regular voice but her expression was stern. "I'm sorry; I'm being silly. I know they can't hear us. But I want to be able to see your meeting from the lobby."

"Why? What's wrong? Who are they?"

"They said their names are Joy and Sonny Patterson. I think they're related to that other guy who came last week."

"Oh." Hollis got up grabbed a pad and pen. She steered Tiffany out into the hallway. "If it's who I think it is, they're brother and sister, not a couple."

Glancing into the conference room as she entered the lobby, Hollis could immediately see what had caused Tiffany's alarm. Shelby's brother looked like a coiled snake ready to strike. Hollis could even sense his glare from where she was standing. Joy, while less intimidating, wore her attitude of unease in the set of her jaw. They were both wearing jeans and sweatshirts that advertised a 2010 jazz festival. Joy was clearly her father's daughter—brown-skinned, attractive, tall, with piercing dark eyes. She paced the room. Her brother Sonny, who was slightly taller with acne-scarred cheeks, sat sullenly in a chair.

"Good afternoon," she said, not moving to offer her hand. "My name is Hollis Morgan. How can I help you?"

The young woman sat down and spoke first. "We're Shelby's brother and sister. I'm Joy and this is Sonny. We came to tell you that if Shelby sells our house, she still can live on campus, but if you take our house we won't have a place to sleep."

"I know this is unfortunate. I tried to get your dad to understand—"

"No, you don't understand." Sonny stopped slouching and sat up straight. "Shelby doesn't have to go to college now; she can get a job and go to college later. She doesn't need that house."

Hollis looked over at him with sympathy, but addressed her comments to Joy, who seemed the calmer of the two. "I've been hired to process a valid legal claim. It was your grandmother's house and she chose to give it to your stepsister. Shelby's not to blame."

Sonny jumped up and pointed his finger in Hollis' face. "Look, we're not gettin' out of that house. We can make her and you real sorry if you try to make us."

Hollis flashed back to her time in prison, where intimidation was an everyday tactic and standing up for yourself was the only survival option.

She spoke between clenched teeth. "Look, you slime bug, get your finger out of my face. You threaten me or my client again, and you'll find a home all right. You'll be checking into the rooms in county jail."

"Sonny, cut it out." Joy put her hand lightly on his arm. She led him back to the table and they both sat down. "He didn't mean anything. It's just that we're trying to get our own place and—"

"Don't be telling our business, Joy. She don't want to hear it," Sonny said in a much subdued voice. "She just wants her big-time lawyer fees. Let's go."

Joy looked at her brother, then Hollis. She sagged in her chair, pressed her fingertips to her forehead and nodded. They both stood, and eyes downcast, shoulders slumped, walked slowly out of the office.

Hollis slipped into a chair and closed her eyes.

Tiffany entered the room. "Are you okay?"

She nodded as a bead of sweat slipped down her back.

THE REST OF MONDAY WAS uncommonly quiet, and Hollis was grateful. The morning had been a little too active. She would leave early, which would give her time to stop off at the store to buy groceries for dinner. But before that, she had a few wrap-up questions that needed answers.

She spoke with one of the other attorneys in the firm who dealt with real estate matters and received confirmation on the legal steps required to file a proper trespassing action.

Next she'd find out the local law enforcement procedures for clearing out the Pattersons. Then she would try one more time to reason with Shelby and her father about reaching an agreement and explain the cost of taking formal legal action.

"Sergeant Grayson, this is Hollis Morgan. I don't know if you remember me. I used to be a paralegal with Dodson Dodson and Doyle, and you would sometimes give me Sheriff's Department help."

"Sure, I remember you, Hollis. What can I do for you?"

"Well, now I'm an attorney, and it looks like I still need help from the sheriff's office." Hollis propped the phone against her ear while typing on her laptop. "I've got quarreling family members who won't get off my client's property. She legally owns it and wants to sell."

"Let me guess. They currently live there."

"Right. So I might have to file trespassing charges. Will you help me?"

She could hear his laugh. "Glad to. What choice do I have? In your other life as a paralegal you helped me out many times. I'm going to email you a checklist of items I'm going to need. There's no criminal activity going on, is there?"

Hollis paused. "No, none that I know of."

He quickly went through the process. "Now, try and get the things on the list back to me by the end of the week. I'm going on vacation in a short while and it sounds like it would be better if I could get this wrapped up before then."

"You got it, and thank you." Hollis hung up.

She had one more call to make.

"Shelby, can you talk?"

Shelby hesitated. "Sure, Hollis, let me get comfortable. Rena's at work and the babysitter went to pick up Chris from pre-school. What's the matter?"

"Your father was here to see me last Thursday. He was understandably upset and he is unwilling to move out. Then today Sonny and Joy came to my office."

"I don't care about them. But what did Dad say?" Her voice shook and rose in volume.

Hollis held the phone away from her ear and counted to three. She used the same trick on Shelby as she had on her stepfather and lowered her voice. "Calm down. He talked about his relationship with his mother and gave his side of the story for why she left you the house."

Shelby sighed. "He just wanted you to feel sorry for him."

Hollis imagined Shelby's sullen expression. "I was surprised when I met your stepfather. He seemed totally rehabilitated from any addiction. He was very articulate."

"Yeah, well, he puts on a good act," Shelby said sarcastically. "Don't let him fool you." Then she changed her tone. "I mean he's not evil. He's clean now and he's my dad. We all just need to get through this. Did you believe him?"

"I don't have to believe him. You're my client. But he did say he wasn't leaving the house. It was the only place he and his kids have to live. Your sib ... I mean Sonny and Joy were equally confrontational."

"They're not really my brother and sister. I barely know them." Shelby was breathing heavily, but her voice was calmer. "You see, I knew this was going to happen. So you're going to have to evict them."

"Actually, you can't evict them because there's no landlord

agreement. You can have them removed for trespassing."

There was a silence.

Shelby finally responded. "Will they go to jail?"

"Not likely, but they could face a fine."

"Can we put the house on the market now?"

Hollis sighed. "Yes, I suppose. But Shelby, isn't there someone in your family who could speak with your father? This could get real messy. How would an agent be able to show your house if your father and his family refuse to let anyone in? And I assure you they will."

"No, no! They are *not* going to hold me hostage. My tuition is due at the end of July. That's less than two months away. Mrs. Patterson wanted me to go to college and I'm going to go." Shelby started to cry. "All my life my father tried to convince me how much he loved me and it was all talk. I admit it was uncomfortable to listen to his mother always complaining to me about Dad, but she said she would never let him hurt me. She was there; he wasn't."

Hollis could only imagine how that family dynamic played out, but she needed to get Shelby to face reality.

"Shelby, maybe Rena could talk to your dad. Do they get along?"

Hollis heard Shelby sob then sniff loudly. "I don't know, I guess so. They don't really know each other that well."

By now Shelby was almost wailing, which reminded Hollis that she was little more than a teenager. "Shelby, I can't talk to anyone about your case without your permission. Can I share our conversations with Rena and see if she is willing to get him to understand the circumstances?"

"N-no, not yet, maybe later," Shelby stammered. "Our family is already divided. I don't want to have to deal …. No. Wait, I don't mind you talking with Rena, but let Aunt Denise deal with Dad. She's his sister. Maybe she can make a difference."

"All right. Then I'll get back to you with the information about filing for trespassing and feedback from a real estate agent on the listing. Unless you have somebody you'd like me to use, I'm looking at agents with offices in the neighborhood. A nearby agent would be more likely to know that market. Oh, and text me your Aunt Denise's cellphone number."

"Sure, I'll do that now. And Hollis …." Shelby paused. "Thank you. I know I might be making things more difficult, but the house is all I've got."

"I'll be getting back to you."

GEORGE WAS OUT OF THE office when Hollis went to brief him, and she left him a note to contact her when he returned.

After a few calls, she made arrangements to retain a real estate agent, Kevin Gregg. They worked out the details on how he would get the keys to evaluate the house. He wanted to walk through it before recommending a listing price. She warned him about the tenants who might be there, but he said he'd dealt with unhappy tenants before. Relieved, Hollis said she would leave the keys with Tiffany.

She punched another number into the phone and got a message machine. She introduced herself and briefly went into why she was calling. "Denise, please give me a call tomorrow when it's convenient for you to talk about Shelby. I'm anxious to resolve the issues regarding your mother's house."

"What about Shelby Patterson? What issues?" George came in and took a seat across from her.

"George, let's meet in your office." Hollis got up and walked with him down the hall. "I never thought I'd say this, but I'm not sure I'm right for the Patterson case."

Instead of sitting in front of his desk, she chose the upholstered side chair. His corner office was three times the size of hers and had a comfortable seating area as well as a small meeting table. He sat across from her.

"Tell me what's happened."

Hollis told him about the conversation with Shelby as well as the visits from her family.

George frowned. "He threatened you?" He crossed his arms across his chest. "You're right. You're a probate attorney, not a family counselor or a street cop. Contact your client and send her a cancellation form."

"Still …." Hollis ran her fingers through her hair. "I hate to give up on my first client before I've had the chance to do anything." She sighed. "I might be overreacting; when I say it out loud to you, the situation doesn't sound as dire."

"If these people are violent—"

"They're not violent, they're just … loud." Hollis laughed. "It's true. I realize I'm all hyped up over loud voices. What's the matter with me?" She took out a pen and started writing a note. "George, forget this conversation. I'm fine. I've already made contact with the sheriff about the best way to handle this. I'll let you know how it goes."

George shrugged and stood. "Don't burn out trying to be an ace, Hollis."

"Who, me?" Hollis looked down at her hands. "Ah, George, one other thing … I kind of have another client I'd like to sign."

He leaned back in his swivel chair. "Define 'kind of.' "

Hollis went through the circumstances of Jeffrey Wallace's death, his trust, and her conversations with Brian.

"So, I'm not sure if he's technically a client. The Fallen Angels are in it together."

"Are you giving legal advice?" he asked. "Is he willing to pay you?"

"Yes, some amount, anyway, for being co-executor He says he doesn't have the money, so I would be limiting the legal work."

"If you're going to be talking to another attorney, I think you should write up a client engagement form. Also, the responsibility and liability will be with you, not with your book club members."

"I know." She sighed.

AT HOME HOLLIS PUT HER feet up on the bolster of her bed

and took a sip from her glass of Zinfandel. John was running late. He had to drive up the coast to Mendocino "to see a man." Hollis wondered if this was a typical Homeland Security assignment. It didn't matter; she wasn't a worrier. She used the extra time to clean out the drawers in the bathroom. The mundane task would help her to wind down her brain after a day with the Pattersons.

By the time John arrived an hour later, Hollis was reading and only mildly annoyed. They chatted easily over a reheated dinner.

"Spring cleaning a little early, aren't you?" John pointed to the full garbage bag in the bathroom doorway.

Hollis grimaced. "I had a difficult conversation with a client. This is my way of venting."

"Ah, this is good to know in case …." He stopped.

She looked up. "In case what?"

He reached down and brought her to a standing position. "In case we ever live together."

Hollis suddenly knew what it felt like to look panic in the face. "John, I … I'm …."

John pulled back and let her arms go. "I didn't say tomorrow." He stiffened. "But maybe it's never going to happen."

Hollis touched his arm. "No, no … I'd like us to live together … sometime. It's just that I … I'm … I'm not there yet."

He kissed her on the forehead. "I know."

CHAPTER 11

TUESDAY WAS STARTING OUT A lot calmer than the day before. From the package of information Brian sent over, Hollis reviewed Jeffrey's separate will and highlighted the parts that spoke to his personal wishes. She was almost finished when the phone rang, jarring her.

"Hollis, this is Denise Patterson-Hoyle. I got your message about Shelby. I guess we need to talk. I called her before I called you, and she explained what you're trying to accomplish."

Like her brother, Denise sounded educated and professional. Hollis took out her notebook. "Yes. To be frank, I called to tell you that I didn't think I'm the right attorney for Shelby's case."

"Oh, why not?"

"Well before we go further, since then I've had second thoughts, and I've decided to continue." Hollis cleared her throat. "However, in the last few days I was visited by your brother and his children. Both times I was very uncomfortable."

"Oh," Denise said quietly. "I'm sorry, real sorry, but Shelby is counting on you. I'm glad you changed your mind because if you won't help her, who would? I'll talk to my brother, but he doesn't always listen to me either. When Mama divided up her estate, she gave me her bank accounts and some jewelry. But she only left Darol some savings bonds."

Hollis knew this from reading Mrs. Patterson's trust, but it didn't address the issue of the occupancy of the house.

"Denise, I only took Shelby's case because Rena asked me to. I'm brand new at this. Disputed wills are not unusual, but this is the type of thing that can rip families apart. Are you sure you want to go down this path?"

"It's what my mother wanted. I'm not going to go against her wishes just because it's uncomfortable."

Hollis took a deep breath. "Okay, then I also want to point out that there are plenty of lawyers out there who are experienced in domestic er ... cases and would be much better at handling the issues facing Shelby. I'm still going to suggest to her that she may want to contact one of them. I don't want to waste her money or time. Email me and I'll send you names of at least two attorneys who specialize in ... in family probate and domestic disputes."

"But if we still want you, what happens next?"

"Shelby is my client; I've spoken with her and said the same thing I'm saying to you now: I need your help. I have to show that we went overboard trying to give Darol and his family notice. If I'm to continue, I need you and your family to contact Darol, Sonny, and Joy and tell them why they must leave and what the consequences will be if they don't."

There was a silence on the other end. Hollis waited.

"Okay, tell me exactly what you want me to say," Denise murmured. "It's not going to be easy."

THIS TIME HOLLIS WAS THE last to arrive at the Fallen Angels' meeting.

She had tried repeatedly to reach Shelby to arrange a date for her to accompany Hollis on a visit to the house. But she had not returned her calls. She would try her again after the meeting.

Quick greetings came from around the room as she sat at the head of the table. Each member already had the preliminary medical examiner's report and the compilation of Brian's information she'd mailed out. She passed around copies of the final ME report. The library's community room grew quiet as everyone began reading through the material. Gene, pulling at his eyebrows, looked up. "Did you notice that the original will had only one beneficiary—Brian? He might have an ulterior motive for wanting his stepmother out of the picture."

She nodded. "I thought that too. Remember, I'm only able to give you copies of the trust because he authorized me. In that vein, I think we need to make sure that Jeffrey didn't have any other relatives."

"He didn't, I checked." Miller was already working on his second origami crane. "Besides, it's not as if it's that large of an estate."

"Good thinking ahead," Hollis said and pointed to his paper art. "Miller, I've always wanted to know what you do with all the cranes you make. You must have thousands by now."

He gave her a shy smile. "My niece is an artist. She forms them into huge paper sculptures for a pediatric ward. So they serve a dual purpose: stress relief for me and they bring joy to some kids."

Hollis was moved. "I had no idea."

"Me neither," Gene said.

Rena patted his shoulder. "That's real nice."

"Yeah, dude, I'm impressed," Richard said. Leaning in, he added. "Look, I hate to bring us back to our task at hand, but I did a little pre-checking of my own." He picked up a stack of pages from a folder in front of him. "I went through the tax returns Brian gave you. They included the two years before Jeffrey was married and the year before he was killed. And they're pretty interesting."

He had everyone's attention.

"Well?" Hollis prompted.

"Prior to meeting the current Mrs. Wallace, Jeffrey earned a typical civil servant salary. It was his only income source. He didn't own any other property." He paused.

Hollis sneaked a peek at the others. They reacted the same as she did. It had hit them all at the same time that this was Jeffrey Wallace they were talking about. This was their former parole officer whose life they were poking around in.

Richard cleared his throat.

"Ahem, he didn't own any other property." Richard was warming to his subject. "He and Frances Wallace filed a joint return in 2008. That year the couples' income is reported as triple what Jeffrey had filed prior to the marriage."

Rena straightened in her seat. "Wow, what does she do for a living?"

"She lists her occupation as 'consultant,' " Richard put on his glasses and picked up an Excel worksheet. "But my best guess based on last year's tax return is, ol' Frances makes her real money as a gambler."

Gene and Miller sat up in their seats.

Gene reached for Richard's copy of the tax returns. "You're kidding me."

"Are you sure?" Miller picked out the tax return from his packet. "Jeffrey doesn't … I mean *didn't* strike me as someone who would be attracted to a gambler."

"Maybe it wasn't just the money he was attracted to," Hollis said.

She had left the tax returns to Richard to plow through, but now she read her copy of the most recent return. Three separate reporting dates totaled a five-figure income from the Lucky Spin Casino.

Richard had prepared a worksheet and now he handed copies around the table "Hey, guys, you're just looking at one year. When you dig into the schedule, there are fourteen instances of declared gambling proceeds from previous years offsetting twice that number of gambling losses."

"You are kidding me," Gene repeated.

Rena lifted a single well-arched eyebrow. "Are you telling us Jeffrey was rich? I'm sorry, but there's something wrong here. I don't believe it."

Hollis frowned. "We all put him on a pedestal, but he's still human. Besides, having money or even being a gambler doesn't make him a criminal."

"Hey, he was honest enough to report their gains on a tax return." Miller smiled. "You've got to give him credit for that."

"He doesn't need our credit," Hollis snapped. "Is that all, Richard?"

"Hey, don't shoot the messenger." He straightened his papers into a small stack. "Maybe you could ask Brian to hunt around for Frances' old tax returns. Then we would know for sure she's the shark."

Gene nodded. "Let Hollis and me see what we can do. Did you find out anything, Rena?"

"Well, Frances doesn't circulate in any social circles I'm familiar with. I'm checking with some friends to see if she has made any significant fundraising or charitable contributions. But now—knowing she hangs out with a whole different crowd—I'll check some other sources."

Richard smiled. "You know any mobsters?"

Rena didn't smile back. "Maybe."

"Okay, let's focus," Hollis chided. "We're pulling in all these pieces about a man's life. But what does it have to do with Brian's hunch that Frances is up to no good?" She rubbed her forehead. "Miller, see what you can find out about their vacation last year in Hawaii." She handed him a sheet of paper. "Here. Brian provided a copy of their reservation. It's a real long shot that anyone will remember them—"

"Actually, I know someone who heads the Hawaiian hotel trade association. They might be able to give me a contact with the hotel staff." Miller pulled out a highlighter and underlined the hotel name and date.

Hollis smiled. "That's good. I'm going to see if I can speak with the attorney who drew up the trust. He might have insights that he'd be willing to share."

"And I'll keep digging," Richard said.

The next morning, Hollis' first call was to Brian Wallace. She was relieved when he agreed to sign a client form appointing her co-executor, although at half her hourly rate. Still, George was right to insist she sign him. Now she'd have access to Triple D's resources and the clout of the firm's name when she contacted the trust attorney for the Wallaces—her next call.

The firm offices of Sloane & Stivers weren't far from Hollis' own. When she reached Anthony Stivers over the phone, she could tell that he wasn't wild about speaking with her.

She thought she heard papers shuffling as he spoke. "I'm not sure what I could tell you about the trust. The contents speak for themselves. It's clear the family didn't want to continue with my services."

Hollis understood his reluctance to brief someone he perceived as stealing his client.

"Yes, I could tell it was a well-written trust, but I represent his son, who is the executor. My questions are not about the trust itself. I won't take a lot of your time."

Shuffle. Shuffle.

"I have an opening at two o'clock this afternoon. Will that work for you?" he said.

Hollis smiled to herself. "That will work just fine. See you then."

She marked her calendar and then tried again to reach Shelby. No answer. She left another message on her cellphone.

Hollis took out Jeffrey's trust and took detailed notes on a separate pad. It was a boilerplate revocable trust with

Frances having use of all the assets until her death, at which time the remainder would pass to Brian. Both Frances and Jeffrey had separate pour-over wills, which specified that assets not included or known at the time of the original trust would become assets of the trust upon the party's death. It also allowed specific bequests to be made outside of the formal trust. Hollis knew that clients used it primarily for personal items they wanted to go to specific beneficiaries. The trust was very straightforward. She flipped through the pages of the wills.

Jeffrey had bequeathed all his separate and personal possessions to Brian. The remainder of his estate, if Frances did not survive him, would go to Brian while he was alive, then to the Public Library Foundation.

She read on. Frances' will paralleled Jeffrey's, except that all her personal items went to a sister in Oregon.

For a brief moment, Hollis thought of her own possessions. Did she have anything of value to leave behind to someone who would care? Just as quickly she put the thought aside. She hadn't spoken to her family since before the trial. Her sister had emailed her after it was over to say that the family was embarrassed by her involvement but relieved that Hollis wasn't implicated.

She squared her shoulders. No one in her family had responded to her letter indicating she had passed the bar.

Anthony Stivers didn't have a corner office, but he had a real fireplace and an expansive sixteenth-floor view of the San Raphael Bridge. More importantly, he validated parking. All these advantages gained him high marks from Hollis. His firm was located in a recently renovated early 1900s bank building. The original structure had only five floors. A UC Berkeley architectural student had won a national contest for the best reuse design, allowing the building to retain its historic interest while gaining eleven new floors. The original façade treatment was carefully integrated, giving the landmark a new life.

Stivers' appearance matched the building. He wore a crisp white shirt, gold cuff links, button-down navy sweater vest, navy bow tie, and gray slacks. He looked very early 20th century. Hollis couldn't help but glance at his desk, expecting to see the kind of green eye shade worn by professionals in the early 20th century to protect them from the glare of the newly invented light bulb.

"Water? Juice?" His wiry Ichabod Crane frame moved stiffly, and gestures were almost robotic.

Hollis declined.

"Very well." He came from around his desk and sat in the adjacent chair. "What can I tell you about the Wallace trust?"

Hollis had her opening. "Does the client meeting stand out in your mind at all? Do you remember Jeffrey and Frances Wallace?"

"When you called, I remembered them only slightly. Since then I reviewed their file and re-read their trust documents." He picked up a pair of glasses, put them snugly up against the bridge of his nose and opened up a green legal file. "I remember them well. It's hard to believe Jeffrey is dead. Do they know who did it? He didn't really want a trust—too expensive for his tastes. Like most people, he thought a will would be sufficient. Fortunately, he left all decisions on finances up to his wife, who was very financially savvy. Jeffrey Wallace, except for his favorite charity and one side matter, left everything to Frances and Brian. After that he didn't want to get involved."

"What kind of person did Frances seem to be?"

"She seemed quite charming. Like I said, she was the one I dealt with most. She made arrangements for him to be notarized because he didn't want to find time to come into the office."

"So, no red flags went up?"

"No, why would they?" He took off his glasses "Ms. Morgan, I don't know what the current financial holdings are in the estate, but we were not talking a large estate here—more like a moderately funded estate."

"Call me, Hollis." She gave him a small smile. "Did you have any indication that Frances Wallace was a gambler?"

He snapped his fingers. "That's what I was trying to remember." He flipped through the file until he found his notes. "During the only time Mr. Wallace was actually here he kept making teasing comments about his wife's trips to Las Vegas, and could he get custody of her frequent flyer miles. Only she didn't laugh."

It sounded like Jeffrey might not have been pleased with Frances' gambling habits.

"Mr. Stivers," she paused to give him time to say she could call him by his first name, but he didn't, "did Jeffrey and Frances appear happy? I mean did you get the impression that everything was all right in the relationship?"

He thought a moment. "Yes, yes. I would say they seemed fine. At least they didn't seem hostile in any way. In fact, I remember them being somewhat affectionate with each other."

"Yet three months later Frances was talking divorce," Hollis said.

"Hollis, you've got two phone messages from a Denise Patterson-Hoyle." As Hollis passed through the lobby, Tiffany handed her two pink call-back slips. "She said she also left a message on your phone."

Hollis frowned. Something must be wrong. She filed her notes from her meeting with Stivers.

She was ready to push the voicemail button, but decided to call Denise instead. She picked up on the half-ring.

"Shelby is missing."

"Missing?" Hollis closed her eyes and leaned back in her chair. "Tell me what happened."

"That's just it. We don't know what happened." Denise's voice quavered. "I went to meet her at the airport this morning, but she wasn't on the plane. She must still be in the Bay Area."

"When was the last time you spoke with her?"

"Day before yesterday. I tried to reach her all day yesterday to confirm her arrival time. Did you tell her that unless I spoke with Darol you would leave her case?" Denise's tone was accusatory and she sounded exhausted.

"First of all, I didn't say I would leave her case if you didn't speak to her father. Second," Hollis tried to keep the worry out of her voice, "I've tried to reach her myself with no success. Have you called Darol?"

"Yes, this morning from the airport, but I couldn't get him. I think his cellphone might be disconnected. He doesn't always pay his bill on time." Denise choked. "I've been calling and calling her. What do we do now?"

"Keep trying." Hollis tried to keep the concern out of her voice. "And since it's been forty-eight hours, I'm going to contact the police."

THE SAN LUCIAN POLICE DEPARTMENT was composed of two uniformed officers and two detectives. If they needed more personnel, they had a contract with the County Sheriff to provide assistance.

Hollis sat in an interview room just off the main lobby with a young officer who was taking her statement.

"So you represent Shelby Patterson and you're reporting her missing?"

Hollis nodded. "I've confirmed with her family in Southern California that no one has heard from her in the last three days. I spoke with her by phone around the same time."

"Are you aware of any reason why she would disappear?" He did not look up from his laptop.

"She's not a magician. She didn't disappear. She's missing." Hollis bit her tongue. "I'm sorry. Shelby is only eighteen and she's been having problems with her family."

"Do you think she could be a victim of domestic violence?"

"I don't know, maybe." Hollis sighed. "I think you should question her stepfather and his son and daughter."

"We will. But for now why don't you tell me what you know."

Hollis took the next few minutes to recount her encounters with Shelby and her family.

"Give me their full names and the address of the house. I'll see what we can find out. Is there a problem letting them know you've initiated a report?"

"Er … no, it's okay."

"Fine. I'll get back to you if we find out anything. But there is a very good chance, from what you told me, that she may want to diss … drop off the grid, until you've handled the dirty work."

Hollis was not ready to concede that possibility. "Just let me know if you hear anything."

CHAPTER 12

⟨⁓⟩

HOLLIS CAUGHT UP TO GEORGE the next morning in his office and told him Shelby was missing.

"I'm not surprised," he said, sounding nonchalant. "From what you told me, she's a little immature and fully capable of running away and hiding." He kept his attention on his paperwork.

She was a little taken aback by his response.

"The police think that's a possibility, too."

He looked up. "Are you sure you still want to represent her?"

"If she wants me." Hollis shrugged. "I'm certainly not ready to throw in the towel."

George closed the file he was reading. "Okay, then keep me informed with any updates."

SHE WAITED AN HOUR TO check back with Denise, who let her know that she still hadn't heard from Shelby's father. The police had gone to the house and talked with Joy and Sonny. They both said they knew nothing about Shelby's going missing. There was little more Hollis could do than wait.

She worked a little later than usual that day, waiting for her phone to ring.

Where was Shelby?

HOLLIS PUT HER CONCERNS ABOUT Shelby on the back burner as she ran Frances Wallace's name through PeopleSearch, an information database. By submitting a bare minimum of personal information, you could access an individual's public records, and a short time later, pages about their life would scroll out like a dossier.

While she waited for the search and download, she called John.

He'd left a message earlier that day extending an offer to cook dinner for her. She called him back to accept his invitation and to ask for the name of the detective assigned to Jeffrey's case. Even though he was transitioning to Homeland Security, he was able to find out that the Wallace case was being worked out of the community policing office near Lake Chabot and assigned to a Detective Mosley.

"John, I forgot to ask, can I bring anything to dinner?" she said.

"Nope, just your smile," he said. "I didn't bring anything for dinner when you cooked."

"How's the new job going?"

"I can't go into any detail right now, but I'm doing okay. We can talk about it tomorrow. How about you; how's the search going?"

"I don't have any revelations. But Brian has raised some interesting questions. Maybe I can meet with Mosley sometime tomorrow afternoon."

"Hollis, remember, we have a deal," John cautioned. "If you come across anything that could help out Homicide—without doing any detecting—be sure and tell them."

"I'm an attorney. I think I would know that." Hollis knew her irritation was evident. "I've got to get a client letter ready.

Sorry, gotta go." She hesitated, "And no, I haven't forgotten. Talk to you later."

She could hear his protests continue as she hung up. She was in no mood to be lectured. She turned her attention to the stack of pages on her printer.

Frances Wallace was one busy lady. As Hollis paged through the printout, she wondered if Jeffrey had done a background check before he'd married her.

He should have.

Prior to Jeffrey, Frances had been married twice. Born in Carson, Nevada, she went to college in Reno but didn't graduate. Cross referencing dates and names, Hollis discovered she'd married the first time during her junior year. Her first husband died four years later. She married again eight years after her first husband's death. The second husband died in a stateside military hospital after they'd been married three years. Hollis felt a chill.

She took her time reading the rest of the report. One thing was clear. Frances was a survivor—literally and figuratively. Detective Mosley likely knew all the facts by now and Hollis was more than curious about his take on them.

She finished making notes to the Wallace file. She was ready as she could be for Mosley.

Once again, she tried to reach Shelby. No answer.

"Ms. MORGAN, GOOD TO MEET you. Let's go into my office."

Ted Mosley led her to a room off a hallway. The man was unimpressive in every way. He'd make an excellent undercover cop because no one would ever be able to describe him: average height, average build, brown eyes, and brown hair. Unremarkable and unassuming. Hollis took the seat he offered her.

They made small talk for a few minutes.

"Is there anything you can tell me about how the investigation is going?" Hollis asked.

"We're making progress, but it's going slow. It seems like the guy was well-liked. We can't find anyone who might want him dead."

Hollis frowned. "I can't imagine you would. He was one of the good ones."

"Well, somebody didn't think so." He shook his head. "I'm sorry. When was the last time you saw Wallace?"

"About a year and a half ago. I needed a recommendation from him."

"A lot can change for a man in a year and a half," Mosley said, his demeanor solemn.

Hollis sat up. "What do you mean? Did something happen to him? Is there more than the murder?"

"No, of course not." He shook his head.

He's lying.

Hollis prided herself on her internal lie detector. It was a gift she'd exploited since childhood, and it served a dual purpose: she was adept at telling lies and just as adept at detecting a lie as soon as it left a person's lips.

Hollis peered at him more closely. "Brian Wallace has asked for assistance in determining the circumstances surrounding the Wallace trust."

"I don't understand. Assist him in determining what?"

"His stepmother may not have been entirely upfront about the assets in the estate. Brian is the executor, but Frances Wallace controls the estate."

"We checked into the money motive. His estate is modest. There doesn't appear to be enough to risk a prison sentence."

Hollis persisted, "Brian seems to think that his father and Frances were divorcing. She'd initiated proceedings. Obviously now it's moot."

Mosley leaned back in his chair and made a note on a pad. "Really? We interviewed Frances and Brian, and neither brought that up."

"There may be another money motive. Brian wants us

to make sure the trust isn't fraudulent. I'm sure he plans on bringing this up with you."

"Who's this 'us'?"

Hollis mentally kicked herself. "I have a couple of friends he knows."

He looked at her with skepticism. "Anything else?"

"Are you aware that Frances Wallace's first two husbands died? It appears from natural causes, but …."

It was Mosley's turn to frown. "What law firm did you say you were with?"

"Dodson Dodson and Doyle," Hollis said. "The reason I'm here, Detective, is to find out if there's anything you can tell me about Frances' financial situation. I can't subpoena her bank records, but I thought you might have."

"If I could, and I can't, why would I share them with you?"

"Because I'm an ace researcher, and I bet your departmental budget has been cut back and now you have few resources to do any deep research. And I would be willing to share anything I find with you—for instance, the name of Frances' two former husbands."

Mosley chuckled. "How long have you known Faber? Word around the station is that he's starting to date again."

Hollis paused at the switch in topics.

"I've known John for a while." Ignoring his question, she said, "So do we have an agreement?"

"Yeah, I'll tell you what I can. But I expect you to tell me any and everything you know that could influence this case." He leaned in. "Faber, or no Faber, I will bring you up on obstructing justice and withholding information charges if you don't."

Hollis bristled. She could feel a blush warming her cheeks. "You don't have to warn me twice."

She handed him a sheet of paper with Frances' information. It took all her restraint to keep from making a smart retort, but she needed Mosley to trust her.

"Thank you, Ms. Morgan. Check back with me in a few days. We hope to have this wrapped up by then." Mosley opened the door for her.

Back in her office, Hollis tried to reach Shelby. No luck.

Out of frustration she contacted the Sheriff's office, and using the checklist from her friend, initiated the trespass action. The woman on the phone, who was clearly multitasking, eventually informed her that she could go forward and have the locks changed.

A few minutes later, she briefed George on her progress. He wasn't very encouraging.

"There's no backing out now," George said. "She's your client. You need help? Are you sure you're ready to deal with domestic disputes?"

"I won't know until I try." Hollis sighed. "Let me know if you think I'm missing a step, but it worries me that we can't find her."

Her paralegal arranged for a locksmith.

Hollis explained the situation to the locksmith and told him a process server would accompany him with the legal papers. Evidently used to such assignments, he seemed unfazed. He agreed to change the locks mid-morning on Monday, when it was less likely anyone would be home. Hollis should have her process server meet him there.

Now she needed a process server.

She called Mark. His law firm had a large real estate section. Attorneys usually had a list of reliable contractors, so hopefully he could refer her to someone.

She left a message. "Mark, I need a huge favor. Give me a call back as soon as you can."

He rang back within a few minutes.

Mark Haddon was a true friend. He had stood by her through the many dips and curves in the road to getting her life back. He'd helped her elimination as a murder suspect and saw her through her pardon. In return, Hollis had introduced him to Rena. Lately their contact had been infrequent because he was busy building a "legal eagle" reputation, and she was busy getting her career back on track. They hadn't spoken since that evening when she'd convinced Rena to join her in finding Jeffrey's killer.

"Hey, Hollis, what's going on?"

After the social amenities and a brief explanation, she ended with, "And on top of it all, I'm missing my client. Mark, can you help me?"

"Ugh. I hate evictions, so I know you're in a tight spot." He thought a moment. "Our firm keeps a process server on retainer. How about I contact her and give her your number?"

She smiled. "I will be forever grateful. And a woman—that's great. We've been giving contracts to non-traditional vendors to give everyone a chance. I'll file the paperwork with the court. Our firm will reimburse you."

She gave him the locksmith details to pass on to the process server.

"How are you and John doing? Rena tells me that you guys might be getting serious."

"Yeah, we're doing real well. I'm not sure how you would define 'serious,' but we're not seeing anyone else."

"For you, seeing anyone, let alone not seeing anyone else sounds serious. Let's set up a lunch or dinner and catch up."

Hollis smiled at the confident tone in Mark's voice. He was like a younger brother who was finally coming into his own. When she'd first met him he was an awkward, self-conscious and overly cautious associate attorney. Now he was a junior partner and on his way up the ladder in one of the largest law firms in the world.

"How about next Friday for lunch? The door locks will have been changed by then and surely Shelby will have turned up."

"Great. No, wait, let me get back to you. I'm working on a corporate merger."

"Then it's your treat."

Her next call was not as pleasurable.

"Denise, have you heard from Shelby? She still hasn't returned any of my calls." Again, Hollis strove to keep the concern out of her voice. "I filed a missing persons report, but the police seem to think that Shelby may have gone off on her own."

She could hear a deep sigh on the other end.

"I was praying that you would have good news. No one here knows where she might be." Another deep sigh from Denise. "Hollis, do you think they have her in that house?"

Hollis grimaced. "I really don't know. Do you have any family members who can talk with Darol? Or, anyone who has a relationship with Joy or Sonny?"

"Of course. It's just that we don't have anyone in Northern California. I suppose I could get one of the family members to fly up but …." Her voice trailed off.

Hollis cleared her throat. "I arranged to have the locks changed on Monday. If we need to, we'll file a trespassing complaint. Meantime the agent will do a complete walk-through. If Shelby is there, he'll know."

For some reason that possibility cheered Denise. Hollis began to think it was because someone was taking action—and responsibility. Or, closer to the truth, she was beginning to sense that they were all afraid of Darol.

Denise said, "What exactly are you getting ready to do? I'll pass the word on to the family."

Hollis explained the strategy and gave her the contact numbers for the locksmith and process server. She agreed to contact Denise as soon as she got word that the locks had been changed.

HOLLIS WAS IN A PENSIVE mood, sitting and sipping a glass of white wine in John's kitchen at his insistence she limit her role to that of guest. He moved about efficiently, if not hurriedly.

He refused to disclose the menu, but she had a pretty good idea. He only had one complete meal in his cooking repertoire.

For once she didn't mind not being part of the process. She was tired. It had been a crazy week. If it took this much energy to carry just two cases, she was going to be drained in no time. This must be why some lawyers burned out so quickly.

For the second time she offered to help with dinner.

He rushed to rinse the salad greens. "No. I invited you to my place. I'm in control here."

Hollis put her chin in her hand and took another sip of white wine. "Er ... okay. But just answer me this one question: why are steaks sitting in the microwave?"

"They were still partially frozen when I put them in the broiler." He paused, and his shoulders slumped. "I didn't take them out in time to thaw. I didn't expect them to brown so fast, and they were really raw in the middle. So, I thought right before we were ready to eat I'd—"

"Oh, I see."

She poured herself another glass of wine and smothered a smile.

Twenty minutes later, dinner—although less than stellar—was edible. Once the steaks had finished cooking in the microwave, she'd showed John how to prepare microwaved baked potatoes. Either that or they weren't going to eat that night.

John shook his head. "How can a restaurant customer order a baked potato if it takes over an hour to cook? They'd be there forever."

"I think they bake their potatoes ahead of time and just keep them warm."

"Oh. That makes sense."

Afterwards, as they sat on the couch, Hollis, curled up with her cup of green tea and his head in her lap, was tempted to tease him about dinner. But once she sensed his anxious mood, she held back.

"Okay, what's wrong?" she asked.

"I talked to Mosley." He sat up. "And before you start to complain, it was for a completely different case. But … he told me about your visit."

Hollis pushed away. "It didn't involve police business."

"I know, I know," he said hurriedly. "But it did sound dangerous."

"It did not." She stood. "I helped him out. Did he tell you that? I gave him more information than he offered me."

"Yeah, but a missing person and a potential domestic dispute … either one can get out of hand real fast." He held her hands. "Listen to me," he said. "I can't change who you are. I don't want to. But—"

"But … but …."

He motioned to the kitchen with his head. "The main reason I wanted to cook you dinner was to show you that I can be domesticated … eventually. I think, if we were under the same roof, I would know what you were up to, and I wouldn't worry as much."

Hollis kept her expression neutral. "You said you'd give me more time."

"It's been four days."

She chuckled, then slowly her smile vanished.

"No, I'm sorry. I'm not ready yet. I care for you. I love you, but …."

"But."

CHAPTER 13

HOLLIS WANTED TO HAVE MORE information to take to the Fallen Angels, but the weekend was over too quickly, and in deference to John, they'd spent some solid quiet time together. On Monday morning there were no messages from Shelby or Mosley. She was tempted to call him, but it was too soon. She'd picked up the phone several times, only to click it off in each instance. He wouldn't appreciate being hounded.

She was going for a second cup of tea when the phone rang.

"Ms. Morgan, Detective Mosley. Sorry to bother you, but I knew you would want to know that we've arrested the killer in the Wallace murder."

Hollis sat back down in her chair. "What? Who did it?"

"We arrested Brian Wallace yesterday evening. He was arraigned this morning."

"Brian," Hollis said in disbelief. "Why would he kill his father?"

"I don't have the time to go into it with you now."

"Can I see him? He's my client too."

"Yeah, you can go to his home. He made bail an hour ago."

Hollis was silent, trying to grasp the recent events.

Mosley's voice was brusque and papers rustled in the background. "I'm on my way to an attempted homicide," he said. "You were good enough to share what you knew, so I'll make time for you. I'm available tomorrow around this hour. You can come and see me then."

Hollis held her head in her hands. While she was talking with Mosley she had gotten two more calls on her message machine. She knew there was trouble.

"Hollis, this is Brian, where are you? Give me a call as soon as you can."

She hated it when someone asked a question in a message. What sense did it make? They wouldn't be able to hear her answer. She wasn't in any rush to call. She needed to think about what she would say.

She pushed for the next message.

"Mrs. Morgan, this is Top Notch Locksmith. Sorry to have to tell you this. I've left several messages. I turned your contact information over to the police. I went to the Patterson house this morning to change the locks with the lady process server you sent. We were both shot at from outside the house …."

His voice droned on, but Hollis wasn't listening as she tried to absorb what he'd said. She hit replay.

"She was standing next to me while I changed the locks. I finished, but then as we were leaving, I was just tellin' her it was good nobody was home. Then bang, bang. We weren't hit. Anyway, the cops still sent for an ambulance. They took a report and that's all I know. I'll send you the bill."

Numb, she went to the beginning and replayed the messages. She knew she should call the police, but she needed to fully absorb what was going on.

Finally, she punched her phone keypad.

"Detective Mosley, this is Hollis Morgan. Was that attempted homicide you were working on this morning in San Lucian hills?"

"I'm glad you called. I was getting ready to send a car out to your office," he said. It sounded like he was on his cellphone. "Right after you left, an officer brought me your name as a contact person for one of the victims. When can you come in?"

"I'm wiped out. Can I come in later today?"

"Make it tomorrow. No one was hurt. The two victims are making their statements now. I've got one school play and a soccer game to attend." She heard papers shuffling. "Say hello to Faber for me."

Before leaving the office, Hollis listed the calls she had to make. First, Mark. He was still at his desk and she rushed to explain what had happened at the Patterson house.

"Mark, I am so sorry. I had no idea it could put someone in danger," she said. "I feel terrible."

"Did the locks get changed?"

She smiled. "Yes."

"You have to know Clarice. She just wants to get the job done. She's been shot at before. In fact, I think she's actually been shot before."

Hollis was surprised. "Really?"

"Yeah, that's why we keep her on retainer. She's the best." He paused. "Rena tells me that things are also moving pretty fast with Jeffrey Wallace's murder."

"Yes and no. The police have arrested his son. But I don't think he did it."

"Be careful, Hollis. You've been down this road before. Just let the police do their job."

"If one more person tells me that, I think I'll scream."

"Scream, I don't care," he said. "I just want you to listen to me."

She grunted.

They said their goodbyes and she picked up the phone again. Brian wasn't home and Shelby didn't answer. She slammed the phone down.

Detective Mosley was running late.

Hollis had fortunately brought a book and tried not to become impatient. Brian wasn't home, so she left him a message. Then she tried to reach Shelby. Still no answer. She went back to her book, but she couldn't concentrate.

"Ms. Morgan, I apologize for keeping you waiting." Mosley rushed forward with an outstretched hand. "We were following up on that attempted homicide this morning. Come on back to my office."

"It seems you're destined to deal with me, Detective." She sat down. "First, Jeffrey Wallace, and now my client, Shelby Patterson. It was her house where the shooting took place."

"Yeah, so I found out." He offered her a bottle of water. "Tell me what you know about the process server, Clarice Adams. What was she doing for you?"

"I don't know her at all. She was a referral from a friend. I needed someone to go with a locksmith to change locks on the door of the home of a client who was under a trespassing action and possibly, domestic violence."

"Top Notch Locksmiths?"

"That's right. I got their name from the Internet. It was the firm's first time using them. My client's name is Shelby Patterson. She inherited a house full of disinherited relatives who refuse to leave."

"Did you get the sense they were violent?"

Hollis thought back to her visitors. "I got the sense they could be. They're definitely intimidating. Is Miss Adams still upset?"

"No, not at all. She's back at home." Mosley smiled. "Our division is very familiar with Clarice Adams. She's been around a long time and very good at what she does. She has a license to carry a concealed weapon, which she'd already drawn when the locksmith got the door open. But they were shot at by someone outside the house—maybe even someone returning to the house."

Hollis frowned. "Let me tell you what I know about the Pattersons."

She proceeded to give Mosley the details of the past week and a half. He wrote down the names of the family members. He also wanted their descriptions.

She resisted pointing out that she had already given the same information to an officer when she filed the missing persons report. She glanced over at his wall clock, but Mosley didn't appear to be in a hurry.

He caught her glance.

"Do you need to be somewhere?" he asked.

She shook her head. "No, no, I'm fine. It was important that we meet. Now, what can you tell me about the Jeffrey Wallace murder and Brian's arrest?"

He reached down to a small refrigerator under his credenza and made another offer of bottled water.

She declined.

"Okay, here's what I can tell you." He reached for another pad of paper covered in notes. "Co-workers heard Brian and his father arguing the afternoon of the killing. Apparently Brian came to his father's office to get him to sign some papers. Brian admits being there. His version is that his father originally agreed to sign but later changed his mind. Brian was heard threatening to make him regret it, and then he left." Mosley paused.

"Unless Brian confessed, you know the evidence is weak," Hollis said then stopped.

She shrugged a 'sorry' when Mosley's scowled at being interrupted.

He continued, "He returned that evening. Someone recognized his car in the parking lot. Three hours later Wallace was found dead by the cleaning crew. Even though Brian Wallace likely ditched his clothing, we found evidence of gunshot residue on his shoes."

"There are several logical reasons why that could be present that don't indicate his guilt. What does Brian say?"

Mosley smirked. "Yeah, well, he lawyered up when we arrested him and refuses to speak."

Smart man.

"What did he want Jeffrey to sign?"

Mosley looked at his watch. "We're pretty sure it concerned some money Brian Wallace thought he was due." He started to pack up papers.

Hollis rubbed her chin. Now things were starting to fall into place about why Jeffrey would let someone in. *But Brian*?

"Well, I'll let you get back to your work, Detective. I really appreciate your meeting with me this morning." Hollis went to the door.

"Ms. Morgan, you're new at this." He leaned over his desk. "I've been at this job for many years, and my gut tells me we got our man."

HOLLIS RACED THROUGH THE REST of the afternoon, arrived at the library early, and waited, toe tapping, for the Fallen Angels to join her. She was anxious to get the latest updates.

Everyone arrived on time except Rena.

"We can tell something's up from looking at your expression," Gene said. "You don't have to wait for Rena. Let's get started."

Miller nodded. "Yeah, you've got me sitting on the edge of my seat."

Hollis was about to speak when Rena rushed in.

"I know. I'm not even going to bother apologizing. Except… I'm sorry."

Rena tossed a folder on the table and quickly took off her jacket.

Richard looked at his watch. "Okay, Hollis, talk."

She took a deep breath. "I've got a lot to tell, and nothing to tell." They were all staring at her expectantly. "The biggest news is that the police arrested Brian for Jeffrey Wallace's murder."

Shock was evident on everyone's face.

Richard recovered first. "You're kidding me. That kid?"

"I don't believe it," Miller said. "What's his motive?"

Hollis shrugged. "The detective in charge thinks it was the

result of an argument between father and son over money."

"That's nuts. If Brian killed Jeffrey, why would he hire us to go after Frances over a routine trust?" Gene scratched his head thoughtfully. "He'd have a lot of other stuff on his mind."

"Maybe he killed Jeffrey for his inheritance," Rena offered. "Any inheritance, no matter how small, is still an inheritance. He may have only discovered later that his stepmother had it all coming to her first."

Hollis started to pace. "No. He was the executor. He'd seen the trust. He knew Frances was first in line. He wasn't questioning the validity of the trust, only Frances' recent behavior."

She stopped and looked at each of them in turn.

"That's all I got. Does anyone have anything substantive to report?"

"Yes, ma'am. That's why I was late." Rena handed out copies of a sheet of paper. "A friend of mine put the word out with a few of his friends about Mrs. Frances Wallace. I found out the lady has an account with one of the biggest bookies in Nevada. But not under the name Frances Wallace. She uses Frances Cole, her maiden name."

They all quickly read her handout.

"Who's your friend, Al Capone?" Richard nudged her with his elbow.

"Big Al is dead, Richard," Rena shot back. "It was in all the papers."

Gene ignored them both. "Hollis, what did you find out about Frances' background?"

Hollis knew her smile wasn't a pleasant one. "Frances' previous two ex-husbands are dead."

"What is she, a black widow?" Richard sucked on his tooth.

A universal "wow" registered on the other faces, along with a few double takes.

"You need to tell the police. She must have—"

"I did. And, as I told you, they still arrested Brian. She must have an alibi." Hollis folded her arms across her chest.

"Could she have hired someone?" Miller asked. "Maybe Jeffrey found out about her sideline. No, wait, he signed the tax returns."

"Quick, check the signature, Richard." Gene moved behind him to look over his shoulder.

Richard, glancing down at the page, shook his head. "If it's a forgery, it's an excellent one."

Gene plucked at his eyebrows. "Her name doesn't show up in any of the past news wires. Miller, did you find out anything from the hotel in Hawaii?"

"I talked with the on-duty desk clerk. After some prodding, he finally remembered them. Jeffrey got a bad sunburn and had to be taken to the hotel clinic." Miller pulled out a slip of origami paper and started to fold. "He said the couple appeared okay. Each day they went out walking to the grocery store or the beach, and they took one or two of the hotel tours."

Hollis held her head in her hands. "It looks like we need more background details about their finances before we can figure out where to go next."

"Can we meet next week? I'm busy the first part of the week," Richard said. "And this is moving kind of fast."

Rena nodded. "Yeah. Fast in the wrong direction."

"Are we so sure of Brian's innocence?" Gene asked. "I mean what do we really know about him and his relationship with Jeffrey?"

"We're not sure of anything," Hollis said. "But he's Jeffrey's son, and I want to give him the benefit of the doubt. I'd like to know what he has to say about that night."

"Will they let you see him in jail?" Miller asked.

"He's home on bail." Hollis shifted in her seat. "Look, people, he's paying my firm to review the trust, but he's not paying you. This could get intense. If you can't take the time, it's understandable."

"Stop right there." Gene held up his hand. "I'm here because of Jeffrey, not Brian and not you, and certainly not for hope of any money."

Everyone nodded in unison.

"I can meet anytime Thursday afternoon," Miller said.

Hollis smiled. "Are we all good for one o'clock?" She waited for their confirmation. "Great. I'll reserve the community room. See you all then."

THE NEXT MORNING HOLLIS OVERSLEPT. This was as rare an occurrence as it was common for her to be late for the firm's staff meeting.

The gods were with her. When she walked into the lobby, Tiffany told her the staff meeting had been cancelled because of an accident on the Bay Bridge. The managing partner was stuck in traffic.

In her office, Hollis pulled out her growing file on Jeffrey Wallace's estate and punched in Brian's number on the phone. She wanted to arrange for a time to visit and hear what was going on with him directly from his lips.

Brian answered. "I'm glad you called. I know you called me back, and I was going to call you, but I've been occupied … the last few days. How soon can we meet? I've got important news."

He's been 'occupied.'

"I can meet you whenever and wherever you choose. In fact, I'm free now." Hollis paused. "Er … Brian, I know you were arrested."

"Oh," he said. "Then, can you meet with me in an hour? I can come to your office."

HE WAS PROMPT.

This time they met in the firm's conference room with the panoramic view of the Bay. Brian walked over to the window and stared out. He had dark circles under his eyes and his suit appeared slept in. Still, even in his current state of disarray she noticed how much he resembled his father.

She pushed a mug of coffee across the table. He took a seat.

"What's going on, Brian?"

"My lawyer won't let me talk about my case, but I will tell you this: I did not kill my dad." He took a much longer sip of coffee.

"I'm your lawyer too." Hollis sat down opposite to him and folded her hands. "Do you know who did?"

"I have a good idea. But I can't prove it." He studied the coffee as if it and not Hollis were speaking to him. "What have you found out about my stepmother?"

Her thoughts flashed on Brian's short-term mourning style. Also, her lie-detector told her he was holding something back. She hesitated a moment, then brusquely brought him up to date on the club's discoveries.

As Hollis spoke, he glanced around the room and finally focused on her. His eyes held hers. "You've got to find out what she's hiding. What if she's in with the mob? Maybe she owes them money. That's why she's got to process the trust as quickly as she can."

"Uh, Brian, I don't know that it's the mob, or even if there is a mob. But did you hear what I said about the two dead husbands? Now she has a third," Hollis said. "Frances could have a very good motive for killing your father. Is there any way you could get your hands on her old tax returns? The ones she filed before marrying your dad."

"I don't think so. I didn't know she was using another name. I should have thought of that." He was staring out into space now, eyes unfocused. "She didn't disclose that in the trust."

"Brian, you're still not hearing me about the bigger picture. You have bigger problems than the trust right now. You've been arrested as the prime suspect in a murder." She was careful not to mention that the police had told her about his argument with Jeffrey. "I would think the trust should take second stage."

He flinched at her words. "I won't be a suspect much longer. My attorney is taking care of that." He got up again and walked over to the window. "But I can't hold off processing the trust much longer. You have three weeks at the outset."

"I'm not sure—"

"Be sure."

Hollis bit back a retort. He not only looked like Jeffrey, but he was sounding like him too.

John's voice was grave. "I was wondering if you were going to call again."

"I was wondering if you were going to take my call," Hollis said quietly. "What is going on with us? We've started tiptoeing around each other. I don't like it."

For the past few days, she'd thought of them as a couple, a real couple. The idea of living together took her back to her first marriage, the fraud and her loss of judgment. She couldn't do that again. She wouldn't be able to recover the next time.

As if reading her thoughts, John said, "I hate talking on the phone about this and I'm trying to ignore this loop of emotions you're stuck in because I know it has to do with your ex. But I'm not him. If you're not going to give me a chance, then we don't have a chance."

"I know. I just need more time. But I don't want you to go away."

"I'm not going away. You're pushing me away." He sighed. "Look, take the time you need. I've got to go to an out-of-state training starting Wednesday. I'll be gone for a week. I think the separation might be just what you need to think things through."

A defensive protest was rising in her chest, and her heart seized up in fear.

She choked out, "This whole thing with Jeffrey's murder … his son being arrested. And at work … this afternoon George gave me three more matters." She paused. "I need you to bounce things off of. I don't need time to know that I love you and that I want us to be together."

"I know. I love you too," John said. "But I don't want to be just your boyfriend. You need time to think about that."

"Did you just remember you had out-of-state training?"

He hesitated then responded, "They give me date options. I just decided to take the next one scheduled. I leave Monday."

She heard the quiver in her voice. "Will I still see you tonight?"

"I'll be there at seven."

Hollis exhaled. She hadn't realized she'd been holding her breath. She held her head in her hands for a few moments, then reached into her inbox and picked up the next file.

CHAPTER 14

———— ❧ ————

THE PHONE WAS ALREADY RINGING when Hollis entered her office the next morning. She turned on the lights and answered.

The caller hung up.

She slammed the phone down.

Less than a minute later the phone rang again. Hollis snatched it up this time without speaking.

"Hollis, it's me."

Shelby.

"Where are you? I've been crazy worried. Your family is worried sick. Are you okay? What's going on?" Hollis could hear anger creeping into her voice, replacing the concern.

"I'm fine. I know you're mad and I'm sorry. Can I come to see you this afternoon?"

"I'm here until twelve thirty." She didn't try to muffle the irritation in her voice. "Or, you can come by after three."

"Let's make it three."

For the second time that morning Hollis slammed the phone down. She pounded her desk with her fist. Shelby was clearly alive, well, in good shape, and from the caller ID screen, in Northern California.

Shaking her head, she gripped the phone and punched in a phone number. She spoke with Denise, letting her know about Shelby's call.

"You mean she's been all right all this time?" Denise asked, perturbed.

"She didn't say she wasn't. I'm meeting her later today."

"Tell her to give me a call; I have a few words for her, too."

THAT AFTERNOON THE LIBRARY WAS relatively lively; the San Lucian librarians were readying for a weekend book sale. In contrast, the Fallen Angels sat solemnly in the community room.

"It doesn't feel like we're making much progress," Richard said, "other than helping the police arrest our client."

"He's not our client." Miller pulled out a sheet of origami paper. "Obviously Brian thinks he's going to be cleared. But what I don't get is why he's so confident he's going to get off, and that his stepmother is in the clear. In my book, she's the stronger suspect."

"That may be true, but she's got that strong alibi," Rena remarked. "What did he say when you asked him about the argument with his father?"

Hollis gave a small wave of dismissal. "I didn't tell him. I didn't want him to know we have a two-way pipeline into the department and that we aren't relying on him as our sole source of information."

"So, what's next?" Gene asked.

Hollis looked down at her notes. "He's given us three weeks. Then he has to process the trust. Whatever gains or assets Frances is hiding will be hers."

"Three weeks is not a lot of time," Richard said. "Did you ask him for her pre-marriage tax returns?"

Hollis nodded. "He said he would see what he could do."

Gene waved a hand to get her attention. "I don't know, Hollis. It seems like we're not really helping Jeffrey. The reason we got back together was ... not to avenge him, but to make sure that his death was ... wasn't a waste." He drummed his fingers impatiently on the table. "Now we're embroiled in an inheritance dispute that seems more and more like a greed issue."

"Yeah," Rena said with a grimace of disgust, "Brian is beginning to sound like a jerk."

They all looked at Hollis for a response. She stood up and glanced around the room, trying to collect her thoughts. Finally she said, "I agree. This isn't what I wanted to do to help Jeffrey. But I don't think we're that far off. Did you ever think the trust could be a link to why Jeffrey died?"

Richard straightened. "What do you mean?"

"I mean the thing that keeps hanging me up is the timing. Here's a couple that appears to be getting along fairly well. They make out a standard trust. Each makes the other the administrator slash beneficiary." She drew a slash in the air. "Three months later Frances files for divorce." Hollis sat down again and peered at her notes before continuing, "I've been in probate for a number of years. A final divorce decree would require reviewing all the assets, even in a trust."

"Everything should be fifty-fifty, right?" Rena asked.

"Maybe," Hollis said. "Depends. I'd want to see how the trust was funded." She saw no understanding in their blank faces and went on to explain, "I mean that I would want to know how much money was in the Wallace's bank accounts, savings, and investments. If she put in more than half, then a divorce might mean she would lose up to twenty-five percent of her contributions. For a gambler, that could be a lot of money."

Miller frowned. "Just out of curiosity, could her gambling debts go into the trust?"

"Yes, maybe," Hollis replied, scribbling a note to herself on her writing pad.

"So it seems like Frances wanted to break the trust for some reason," Richard said. "Well, I guess, *not* break the trust because it's already in effect with Wallace's death."

"Just the opposite," Hollis said. "She wants the trust filed as soon as possible. We just have to figure out why."

Richard raised one eyebrow and folded his arms across his chest. "It has to be about money."

Hollis tapped her pen on the table. "Someone once told me, it's always about money."

"I bet it has something to do with her filing for divorce," Rena offered.

"We need to know more about their relationship," Hollis said. "Gene, it's your turn to meet with Brian. Find out what you can about the marriage. Do your reporter routine. Could Frances have been after an asset we don't know about?"

"Got it," Gene said.

"Rena, go back to your street er ... connections and find out if Frances is in good standing. Find out what's she's been betting on lately. Has she approached them since Jeffrey's death?"

Hollis faced Miller. "Miller, we could use your help with checking on non-public information to cover one loose end—Brian. Find out what you can about him. The police probably already have a full file, and it might be one reason they arrested him and one reason why this trust is so important to him."

Miller took notes. "Not a problem. Research is my business. The library has access to numerous databases—not so much for individuals—but I'll see what I can do with that and a few other resources I can tap into."

"Wait," Hollis said. "Let me send you a printout from our firm's database. I ran a public records listing. Hopefully it will help speed up the angle you're working on."

"Absolutely," Miller nodded.

"What about me, El Capitan?" Richard mocked her with a false salute.

"I'm hoping Brian will come up with those additional tax

records," Hollis said. "Until then, is there any way you could pull bank records?"

Richard looked thoughtful. "Not easily, but there just might be somebody .... Yeah, there just might be somebody I know who could get the information for me."

Hollis began packing up her papers. "All right. Let's meet back here Monday at our regular time to share notes. Miller, I'm going to get you that printout. And then I'm going to pay Frances a visit."

AFTER TRYING THREE TIMES WITHOUT any luck to reach Frances Wallace by phone, Hollis still chose not to leave a message. She wanted to deal with Mrs. Wallace face to face.

She began to get ready for her meeting with Shelby Patterson.

Shelby arrived on time. Tiffany informed Hollis that she'd already brought her a coffee. When Hollis entered the conference room, Shelby, her body language distressed and penitent, was clutching her cup of coffee with both hands and staring into it. She wore a tweed jacket over jeans and a white turtleneck sweater. Her hair was pulled back in its standard ponytail. She looked well put together. There was nothing to indicate that she had been having a rough time.

"Where have you been?" Hollis asked, taking the chair next to her.

"At a friend's."

"Does your friend live at the South Pole, where they don't have phone service? Because I find it very hard to believe you couldn't answer any of my calls or receive messages."

"Look, I know you're mad. And I don't blame you." She rubbed her forehead wearily. "But I knew Dad wouldn't like me telling him to leave, and Joy and Sonny ... well, let's just say they're wired tight. I ... I'm afraid of them." She backed her chair away from Hollis.

Hollis propped her elbows on the table and cupped her chin in her hands. "I'm not buying it. You couldn't text me? I was really worried." She was trying to contain her anger. "I think it's best if you find another attorney. Someone was nearly killed trying to assist me so I could help you, and you don't have the courage to even call."

"Hollis I—"

"I really don't want to hear this."

"Then I don't have anything to lose by talking," Shelby said. "I sincerely apologize for being so self-centered, but I was scared. I wanted to hide to protect myself."

"Do you realize that while you were off with your head in the sand, a locksmith and a process server got shot at on the front porch of your house?"

Shelby hung her head. "I didn't know. Did they tell the police?"

"Of course they did." Hollis peered down at her, her exasperation evident.

"I'm a coward. I let other people fight my battles for me," Shelby said. She looked up at Hollis, her eyes pleading. "But I do need the money from the house to pay for my tuition. My grandmother wanted it for me." She laid her head down on the table and looked up at Hollis like a woeful Bassett hound. "Where my family is concerned, I don't have a backbone. I need you to be my backbone. You see what they can get up to? Shooting at people, for God's sake."

Hollis said in a calm voice that surprised even her, "I do understand your family situation, but I can't work with a client I can't trust—a client who won't even communicate with me. I'll find you an attorney who can be a better advocate for you."

Shelby's eyes filled with tears. "I understand. But if you give me a second chance, you won't regret it. Please." She reached over to touch Hollis' hand.

Hollis closed her eyes and opened them to look into Shelby's pleading ones. She closed her eyes again and opened them with resolve.

"Okay, all right. I'll stick with you." She held up her hand when Shelby started to reach over to hug her. "But if you pull another act like this again or decide to play some other game, that will be the end."

"Understood."

"Be here tomorrow, I'll text you the time. The locks have been changed, and no one should be living there now. I'll have the real estate agent meet us here; his name is Kevin Gregg. He needs your signature to take the listing on the house."

"Understood."

"Have you called your family? Especially your Aunt Denise."

"Okay, I will. I—"

"While you're calling them, I have to call the police and tell them you've returned."

"Can I hug you?"

Hollis stiffened. "No."

ON THE DRIVE HOME HOLLIS felt the tension in her body ease. She wasn't surprised at the way the conversation with Shelby had gone. Even though she'd threatened to walk away from Shelby's case, she was a sucker for giving people second chances. After all, wasn't that what saved her?

Waiting in commuter traffic was the break she needed to shift her thinking to the evening ahead with John. She loved him, of that she was sure. But the commitment he wanted was too much and too soon given her past experiences with trusting people. She pulled into the driveway and blinked a few times, trying to make sense of the scene in front of her. She got out of the car and walked up the pathway to stand in front of John.

"What are you doing out here on the front steps?" She kissed him lightly on the lips. "Did you forget your key?"

"I don' need no stinkin' keys." He laughed and held her close. "I'm fine. I just wanted to see you drive up. I'm going to be gone a while. This is the picture of you I wanted to keep in my mind."

She gazed at him in surprise. His sentimentality caught her off guard. "I didn't know you were such a romantic. Let's go inside before my neighbors bring out their cameras to make a YouTube video."

"What's for dinner?" he asked as he followed her upstairs to the bedroom.

"John, I know I said we would have a quiet dinner here, but I had a really hectic day. Can we eat out and come back here?"

"Sure, that works for me." He sat down at the top of the steps and waited for her to change shoes and check her phone. He raised his voice so she could hear him. "What made your day so hectic?"

"Oh, you don't want to listen to the dull details of my little day," she called back. "Your day has got to be more interesting than mine."

"You can stop playing the sweet little partner." He leaned back against the wall, a smile playing on his lips. "I know Brian Wallace is out on bail. Mosley told me about your meeting."

Hollis stood next to him, hands on hips. "I hope he told you that once again I shared some critical information and didn't press him for any of his."

"He did indeed." John pulled her into his lap and kissed her. "Let's go before we forget we're hungry."

They chose a favorite neighborhood restaurant. It wasn't crowded, just a few familiar regulars. They settled into a booth and ordered quickly.

"Are you all packed and ready to leave?" Hollis asked, playing with the stem of her wine glass.

"Not really. I have some last-minute running around to do. My flight leaves at seven in the morning on Monday. There's a layover in Chicago. I'll get into DC early evening."

"Will you give me a call when you get in?"

"Yeah, if you want me to." He looked over his shoulder then back at Hollis. "Look, I don't know what phase we're going through. I'm not sure I like it. I think we need this little break—not for me, but for you."

She dropped her gaze to her hands. "John I—"

"Hear me out. I think you know where I stand. I want you in my life. But it's not a one-way street. Use the next week to figure out where you stand. I know you love me, but I need to know that you want me in your life." He picked up his fork. "Now, let's eat. I'm starving."

Hollis smiled slowly. "So am I." Her face turned somber. "I really do love you."

He looked at her. "I know."

THE NEXT DAY, HOLLIS PREPARED for the meeting with Shelby and the real estate agent. Listings were income for Kevin, and a listing for a home in the desirable hills of San Lucian was rare. She was able to get a hold of Shelby without any problem, and she agreed to be there on time to sign the papers. Hollis had ordered two more sets of keys made. She gave one to Shelby, another to the agent, and kept the third.

Kevin came with the papers for Shelby to sign and left with the understanding he would do whatever it took to get the house sold quickly. He promised to be at Hollis' beck and call and left them like a man on a mission.

"Shelby, you and I need to check out the house before it goes on the market," Hollis said. "When are you going back to LA?"

"I'm not—not until the week before classes start. I've decided to stay with my girlfriend in San Lucian. Her place is where I … I was before. Rosa and I went to school together. The location is more convenient than Rena's and hopefully my house will sell quickly. I'll go back to Rena's later on to get my things."

"When can you go to the house for a walk-through?"

"Can we make it next week? I want to go to Santa Cruz this weekend. I'll be back late Monday. I can meet you there on Tuesday morning."

"Okay. See you there at eleven o'clock."

Hollis gathered her papers and went back to her office.

She punched the number for Frances Wallace, who answered before the first ring ended.

Her voice was warm. "Yes, Ms. Morgan, I remember you from the memorial and from my husband talking about you."

"I was hoping to speak with you sometime in the next couple of days about Jeffrey." Hollis had chosen her words with care. "He started our book club—"

"Yes, I know. It was an achievement he was proud of." She paused. "I'm going out of town for a few days. I know tomorrow is a Saturday, but I'm available to speak with you then."

Hollis took her address and agreed to see her mid-morning.

She spent the rest of the day preparing briefs on cases George had left for her assessment. She found herself warming to the task. It was satisfying handling matters that could be resolved quickly and unemotionally.

It was a few minutes before five when Hollis gathered her things to go home. John was making final preparations to leave for his training program. She felt an ache in her chest. She was going to miss him.

She pushed the down button on the elevator. If she timed it right, she could go downstairs and check on Vince before he left for the day. She hadn't seen him since he started his GED prep classes.

"Vince, are you down here?"

The layout of the firm's mailroom defied logic. It was a small maze of open white-plastic boxes along a series of tables that twisted in adjoining L-shapes next to a large bin where the mail was dropped off by the postal service.

"Hey Hollis." Vince came from a small hallway with his jacket in hand. "I was just getting ready to leave. Is everything okay?"

She reached out to give him a hug, but at the last moment remembered his aversion to being touched. Instead she held out her hand and he grazed it with his own.

"Everything is fine. I came down to see how things were going with you. We're getting great mail service upstairs and I wanted to see the man in charge."

Vince blushed.

"Thanks," he said. "I'm really trying. I like it here."

"How's your mom?"

He frowned. "She was doin' real good until a couple of days ago. She was real happy we was gettin' an apartment. I found this one near the airport. It's only a converted motel room and it's a little noisy, but it's better than the shelter. I'll have the money for it with this next paycheck. Anyways … anyways, one of the people at the shelter made her mad and she … she used a little."

Hollis hoped her face didn't reveal her disappointment.

"That's why I've got to get back to her now. Nighttime is really rough for her. If I'm with her, she's stays straight. She wants to stay clean."

Vince turned off the lights and they walked toward the elevators.

"What about you?" Hollis asked. "How's the GED going?"

"I knew you were going to ask me that," he said, shaking his head with an almost-smile.

Hollis realized that when he finally let himself smile, he was going to be a good looking young man.

"Yeah, and so? What have you got to say for yourself?"

"I'm taking these classes at the adult school over in Oakland. Well, just one class right now until we move. There're five subject areas, you know: math, social studies, writing, science, and reading." Vince was walking backwards, waving his arms with animation. "The test for all five is about six hours. But they said it shouldn't take me too long because I have a lot of high school credits. I can take the test at any time; I just need to brush up."

They'd reached the lobby, and Hollis walked with him to the doors leading to the street.

"Vince, I'm glad for you. If you get stuck, just get in touch with me. Don't forget to let me know how things are going." Hollis left it at that and waved as she hurried away.

She continued to watch him. Halfway down the block, Vince turned and looked at her over his shoulder. He gave her a wave, with another almost-smile.

CHAPTER 15

HOLLIS DIDN'T KNOW WHAT SHE expected to see when she drove up to Jeffrey's home. His office at work was decorated simply, with minimum furniture, no family pictures, and the only adornment being a single plastic-encased poster of a cat clinging to a tree branch.

His home was completely different. Located in a modest but gated community, the Mediterranean single-story house was nestled in a cul de sac of similar style homes. Lush green lawns and boxwood shrubs marked the boundaries of each property. The Wallace house was a soothing ochre color with climbing purple and red bougainvillea. The curved walkway to the wooden front door was cobbled and interspersed with small mounds of moss. A 'for sale' sign stood solidly next to the walkway.

Very nice.

Frances Wallace greeted her at the door. Her sleek white-on-white jersey pants outfit suited her perfectly. She was a striking woman, and Hollis couldn't help but wonder what had attracted her to the rather ordinary and not at all flashy Jeffrey.

A great guy, but one who few would describe as handsome or charming.

"Thank you for coming out on a Saturday." Frances directed Hollis toward the living room.

Hollis declined her offer of coffee or tea. "But water would be nice."

Frances quickly returned with a pitcher of water and two glasses containing ice cubes and lemon slices.

"You have a lovely home," Hollis said, looking around at the tastefully decorated open space living and dining room.

She smiled. "Thank you. I did it myself. Jeffrey didn't care for … for …." She dabbed at her eyes with the sides of her hands.

"I'm sorry," Hollis said, looking around for a box of tissues.

Frances pulled one from her sleeve.

"No, *I'm* sorry. Usually I'm okay, but every once in a while…. Anyway, how can I help you?"

Hollis poured a glass of water. "Your stepson Brian asked my firm to help him get your trust processed. He was concerned that his … his suspect status might cause a delay." She paused. "So I agreed to assist."

Frances straightened her back. Tears dried, she put on eyeglasses and from behind a sofa pillow pulled out a tablet and pen. "Good. I want the trust filed with the death certificate as soon as possible. I have the numbers of our bank accounts and the policy numbers from the insurance." She handed Hollis a sheet of paper.

The transformation in five seconds from grieving widow to business administrator threw Hollis, but for only a moment. Her years as a paralegal had prepared her for a wide range of reactions from family members. Frances had run the whole emotional gamut right before her eyes.

Hollis looked down at the paper. "We have a hearing date within three weeks."

"No sooner?" Frances asked.

Hollis ignored her question. "Do the police really think Brian killed his father?"

The question had the effect she'd been aiming for. Frances looked as if the cold water had been poured over her head.

"Why ... why I ... I know. It's crazy, isn't' it? Brian couldn't have killed Jeffrey. They always argued. I told the police. I mean the police seemed to think it was done with violent intent. But Brian couldn't have, don't you think? I try not to think about how Jeffrey died." She used her tissue to dab her forehead and reached for a glass of water.

Interesting.

Hollis took a sip.

"I don't think this will be an issue, but I understand you filed for divorce about three months ago," Hollis said quietly.

"Er ... yes. That doesn't affect the trust, does it? I mean timing wise." She took a long drink of water and appeared to gaze out the bay window overlooking the backyard. "We loved each other, but we were different people. He helped me during a bad time and I fell in love with his sincerity. But it wasn't enough for the long game."

Hollis pretended to look at the file she brought with her. Her thoughts focused on speculating why Frances felt the need to lie, especially since she was so bad at it. "So, you've put the house up for sale?"

"Yes .... I did put it on the market. It's way too much house just for me. I might move to Nevada. It's cheaper to live there and your money goes further."

I bet it does.

Hollis looked down at her file again. "Well, I guess that's all the questions I have for now. Can I call you again if something else pops up? I know you want this settled as fast as possible."

"Yes, yes, please do what you can." Frances picked up the tissue but didn't use it. "It's very lonely here without Jeffrey."

"Yes, I can imagine," Hollis said. "Do you have any questions for me?"

"This might sound terrible, but I don't know anyone else to ask." Frances licked her lips. "If Brian is convicted, does he still get his share of the trust?"

Hollis looked her in the eyes. "If he's found guilty and a reason for the murder …." Hollis swallowed. "If a motive for the murder was to benefit from the estate, then no."

Frances sat up a little straighter. "Then let's hope things turn out for the best."

Hollis nodded, but she was pretty sure she and Frances would disagree on the meaning of 'for the best.'

THE WEEKEND WENT BY SLOWLY. Hollis and John spent a quiet weekend reading, doing laundry, eating in, and watching the *Doctor Who* marathon. Then it was Monday morning, and she missed him the moment she knew his flight had taken off. He called her from the airport while she was still at home, and again after she had just arrived at work. The calls were welcome but their conversations felt awkward and stiff. The last one was an improvement.

"Good luck with the training," she said.

"Good luck to you, too."

She whispered, "I love you."

"I know."

MOSLEY HAD LEFT A MESSAGE that the tracer he put on her phone hadn't come up with any results. The caller was definitely using a throwaway phone.

Hollis wasn't as much afraid as she was annoyed. She was pretty sure the calls were being made by Shelby's siblings. If they thought they could intimidate her the same way they meant to intimidate Shelby, they were going to be sorely disappointed.

After working steadily all morning, she made herself a cup of tea. She had a little time before meeting with the Fallen Angels, and her thoughts drifted to Frances' comment about

Jeffrey helping her out of bad times. Hollis wanted to know what the bad times were.

She punched in Brian's number.

"Hi, Hollis, thanks for calling. Gene and I had lunch yesterday, and he told me you were going to meet with Frances. Did you learn anything?" he asked.

"Brian, do you recall Frances' situation before she and your father were wed?"

"Not really. I didn't know he had met someone until just before they got married. I was still in high school." He was silent for a moment before adding, "She was working at another job. She quit about two years ago to start her own consulting business."

"She said your father helped her through bad times. Do you know what she was referring to?"

"No."

Hollis took a deep breath. "Brian, what did you and your father argue about that day?"

He didn't respond right away, then he said, "That answer is going to take a while. Look, I've got to get ready for a meeting with my attorney in an hour. How about after that?" There was little emotion in Brian's voice, as if he was making an effort to maintain his cool, but she could hear him breathing heavily.

"I've got a meeting after that. How about late afternoon?"

"Okay. Do you mind coming here to the house? I haven't been feeling well today."

"Sure, not a problem." Hollis looked at her watch. "I'll come by right after my meeting. Will five o'clock be all right?"

"See you then." He hung up.

THIS TIME HOLLIS WAS THE first to arrive at the library. She spread out her notes in the middle of the table and was in the midst of making small stacks when Gene walked in.

"Do you think we have any kind of handle on this thing?" he asked, sitting next to her.

Hollis shrugged. "I honestly don't know. Greed and opportunism are not crimes. It's sad to think that this is Jeffrey's legacy, but people have killed for less."

"So you think Brian did it?"

She frowned. She had avoided asking herself that question. "I don't know."

Richard and Miller arrived together. The mood in the room was subdued.

"Why the glum faces?" Rena dropped her purse and a stack of papers on the table. "I'm not that late."

Everyone chuckled.

"You seem pretty perky," Gene said. "What's that about?"

Rena pulled out a piece of blue paper.

" 'Cause I gots news."

Gene smiled. "Do tell."

"If you remember, my assignment was to find out if Frances was in good standing with her gambling debts." Rena glanced at each of them in turn. "Well, not only does ol' Frances have excellent credit, she's talking to some people about buying into a casino."

Richard sucked on his front tooth and started going through the stack of pages next to him. "You're kidding me. I read over those trust papers and tax returns. There isn't *that* much money." He tossed the papers in the middle of the table.

Hollis frowned. "When did she start talking to these people?"

Rena nodded, "About three months ago."

Three months—that time period again. Hollis flashed to a conversation she had with Brian about how Frances had filed for divorce three months ago.

Hollis looked over at Richard. "Were you able to get access to their bank accounts?"

Richard nodded. "Nothing special. About fifteen grand in the savings account, a substantial government 401k for him, and a modest investment portfolio in her name."

"How do you find out these things?" Rena asked.

"I got the account numbers from the trust and asked a friend to get me the balances." Richard took off his glasses.

Miller had already started on a sea green origami crane. "How big is Jeffrey's insurance policy?"

Richard replied, "Five hundred thousand. It's a lot, but it doesn't seem enough to finance a casino. They still have a mortgage." He raised one eyebrow. "Of course, depending on the policy, it could climb to one mil."

"I've got to think that the insurance beneficiary would have been the first place the police would have looked for a suspect," Gene said. "They arrested Brian, not Frances."

"Gene, how did your meeting with Brian go?" Hollis asked.

Gene shrugged. "He either has academy award winning acting potential or he is sincerely trying to find out about his father's estate. Either way, he doesn't seem too concerned about being accused of murder. He also doesn't seem that interested in finding out who did kill his father."

"I noticed that too," Hollis said.

Rena rubbed her forehead. "What's his background?"

"He's a supply manager for a wholesale company," Gene said. "He graduated from San Francisco State and is at the same job he took right after college. He has a longtime girlfriend. He said they're thinking of getting married next year. Pretty ordinary, actually."

"That it?" Richard asked.

"Yeah, but I learned something interesting." Gene frowned. "There was one odd moment. I asked if Frances had any children from her former marriages. She didn't. Then I said something about growing up Jeffrey's only child and he said he wasn't. He has an older brother who left home when he was a teenager."

"What was so odd about that?" Miller asked. "Although, he didn't show up for his father's funeral."

Gene jutted an index finger into the air. "Exactly. I think Brian was holding something back."

Hollis straightened. "What about?"

Gene shrugged. "I don't know, just a sense. I'm not as good as you are with lie detecting."

"Interesting," she said. "I have a meeting with him this evening. I want to talk to him about his argument with Jeffrey. I never thought about doing this, but maybe I should run PeopleSearch on Brian." Hollis was talking to herself more than the others. She wondered why she hadn't considered it at their last meeting. But until now it hadn't occurred to her that a public records search could possibly turn anything up. "It could answer a few questions."

Richard stopped slouching and looked up. "It couldn't hurt."

"I agree, but where do we go from here?" Rena asked. "I've got a buyer's trip coming up for the store, and I have to prepare. Are you going to need me for the next couple of days?"

Miller put away his origami papers. "Yeah, I need to get ready for our quarterly board meeting."

"We have a little time before Brian wants to file the trust," Hollis said. "Other than a lot of curious and suspicious findings, I don't think we have any reason not to let it go forward."

Richard gathered his folders. "Maybe there's nothing to find."

Hollis frowned. "On the other hand, there is just too much smoke."

"Well, we're running out of time," Gene added.

"Okay," she said. "I'm going to go to the police with our random puzzle pieces. They may have some of their own." She started putting on her coat. "I'll visit with Detective Mosley and see how the investigation is going. Since you guys seem to be busy, we can wait until next week to get together. If I discover anything new, or if any of us thinks of anything new, we'll arrange to meet earlier."

Gene gave his briefcase a pat. "Sounds like a plan," he said.

CHAPTER 16

———∾∾———

HOLLIS GOT BACK TO HER office with an hour to spare
before her meeting with Brian. She logged on to her
computer, called up PeopleSearch, and entered a public records
request on his background.

While she waited, she called Mosley and got him on his cell.

"Detective, would it be possible to meet with you tomorrow
about the Jeffrey Wallace case?"

"What about it?"

"I'd rather talk to you in person," she said. "There's a good
chance you haven't arrested the real killer."

"And you think you know who the real killer is? Do you have
any solid information or is this just speculation?"

Hollis hesitated. It wouldn't do for him to classify her as a
pest.

"I'd like to share with you what we've stumbled across," she
said. "You can decide if it's solid information, but it may throw
some new light on your investigation."

"Okay, make it in the afternoon. I'm out all morning."

BRIAN LOOKED PALE AND AGITATED. Dressed in sweat pants

and an oversized T-shirt, he hadn't shaved and his hair appeared to be finger-combed.

They were standing in his living room, now cluttered with the addition of his father's office furniture and stacks of boxes. Jeffrey's wall poster leaned against the wall. A few open boxes were sitting on a side table, and Hollis could see papers, folders, and probably more personal effects from his office. The fireplace mantle was covered with pictures and trophies and what looked like an empty beer can.

Brian proceeded to pace back and forth.

She made room on the sofa to sit, after moving a soiled paper plate and napkin onto the coffee table.

"Coffee?" Brian offered.

"No, thanks. I drink tea," Hollis said.

"I don't have any tea. What about water?"

"No, thanks. Really, I'm fine. Brian, you said we could talk about your argument with your dad. What was it about?"

He ignored her question.

"I've got to get to the office. Since the arrest I've been going in after hours. I don't want to talk to anybody about my situation. I'm really behind on my paperwork. My boss keeps leaving me these notes." He picked up a sheet of paper and read, " 'I know this is a difficult time but we need your report.' " He ran a hand through his hair. "He doesn't know the half of it."

Hollis nodded. "Then you should probably start talking to me, so you can get back to work."

Brian looked at her and nodded. He finally cleared catalogs from an overstuffed chair and sat down. "Ever since I was a kid, Dad was a stickler for rules. He had a rule for everything. He made them up as needed." He rubbed his forehead with his fingers. "You knew him; he could be a real hard nose."

Hollis nodded again, trying not to show her impatience.

"So, anyway, I needed money to get married. I had asked him for a loan." Brian got up and started pacing again. "He said if I needed a loan to get married, it probably meant I should wait."

I agree.

Brian looked up at her as if he could hear her thoughts.

"He reminded me I hadn't paid him back for the money he gave me for my car. I told him that I was waiting on a bonus check to come through. Gloria—that's my girlfriend—and her family had already started making reservations and stuff."

Hollis said quietly, "So the argument was about money?"

Brian looked sheepish and couldn't look her in the eye.

She squinted. "No, wait a minute, your argument with your dad wasn't about him writing you a check." Hollis sat up. "The argument was about the trust. You wanted one of the assets out of the trust."

Brian shrugged and nodded. "He had five Sebastian Torneo first editions. I never heard of the guy, but they had been given to Dad by some rich family grateful for his getting their son through his parole. They knew about Dad's love of books."

Hollis had never seen a first edition Torneo. Clearly Brian didn't share his father's 'love of books.' Torneo was one of her favorite adventure authors and she would love to take a peek, but she didn't think this was the time to ask.

Brian continued, "Anyway, Dad had set them aside for my older brother."

"Your older brother?" Hollis said.

"I know, I know. I told Gene yesterday that my brother went away, and for our family he did. I don't know why I hedged about him. I guess because Dad died a little inside when Todd went to prison. We all just put him out of our lives—at least I did. I hate to say this, but he was an embarrassment."

Hollis grimaced. Her family had treated her the same way when she had done her time in prison. The momentary reminder brought an old spark of pain.

She held up her hand. "Wait a minute. Stop right there and don't go any further. Tell me about this brother."

Brian leaned back in his seat. "Todd is serving five to ten in a facility near Corona for armed robbery. He's already served five years. He's about to get out on parole."

"Have you ever gone to visit him?"

"No, he refused to see any of us."

Hollis squinted at Brian. She had to gather her thoughts and sort through the questions zipping through her head.

Brian was lying, but what was the lie?

"What happened?"

For a third time, Brian stood and began to pace. "Todd was smart in school, but he liked to play more than he liked to study. Even so, he and Dad were close. Dad always gave him a break even when he didn't deserve it. Then, several years ago, he and some friends stole some computers from a school and were going to sell them to a fence. Only they didn't get that far. One of his friends had a Taser gun." He swallowed. "They were caught, after a policeman was wounded."

Brian stopped pacing and stood contemplating the view out the window.

Hollis finally asked, "Did you get word to him about your dad?"

Brian nodded. "He knew."

"They wouldn't let him come to the funeral?"

"Ah, sure, but he didn't want to come. He sent word that he didn't want to see Dad that way."

Hollis understood the rationale, but she wasn't sure that if the circumstances were flipped, she could have stayed away.

"Brian, the language in the trust is pretty standard. Jeffrey left everything to his heirs. But you're his executor. Did he want Todd to get the first editions? Is that why he left them out of the trust?"

He hesitated before answering. "Yeah, he said Todd would need money when he got out. He wanted to be able to give him a nest egg to get back on his feet. But Dad expected to be alive when Todd got out."

"Oh, now I get it. The reason why you went to see your Dad that night." Hollis closed her eyes, letting the pieces fall into place. "You needed money *now*. Jeffrey knew his other son would one day come home. He was always preparing for that future."

Brian stood over her, his arms crossed at his chest. "But I was the son who was here. I was the one who needed help now." He threw up his hands. "So we argued and I left him ... alive."

"Did he say anything before you left?"

His eyes glistened. "He said he knew how the father of the prodigal son felt."

Hollis nodded. "Do you own a gun?"

Brian choked back an answer. "Yes, but it wasn't where I thought I left it. I think Dad took it because he was always after me to put it away after I came home from the shooting range. I might have left it out and he found it and hid it." Brian shrugged, unable to meet her gaze. "He'd do that to make me ask him for it." His eyes flitted back and forth.

He was *definitely* lying.

Hollis frowned. "I thought you lived here."

"I do. I just moved in the week before Dad ... before Dad was killed."

"Let me guess: Jeffrey was killed with your gun?"

Brian nodded.

"Does Frances know about your brother?"

"Oh, yes."

"Does she know about the first editions?"

"Yeah, she wanted them for herself. But Dad was adamant; she couldn't move him either." He turned away from her and scratched his neck with his index finger.

He can't stop lying.

Hollis looked at her watch. "It's getting late and we've both have a busy day."

She stood and Brian walked her to the door.

He stopped on the doorstep. "You need to step up the processing of the trust; we don't have much time."

Hollis looked out onto the street. The lights were coming on. "We'll do what we can. But if I were you, I'd start worrying about being the only murder suspect."

CHAPTER 17

AFTER SHE GOT HOME, HOLLIS picked up a message from John, who said he missed her and would call back the next day. She liked knowing he was somewhere out there missing her, but having him on the other side of the country still felt isolating.

After bolting down a dinner salad, she remotely checked her office answering machine. Shelby confirmed she would meet her at the house in the morning and apologized again for going missing.

Hollis picked up a book and headed for bed. After an hour she put it down. She couldn't concentrate. There were too many loose ends with Jeffrey's trust. On its surface it was no big deal. The man was not rich, first editions or no first editions. Yet everyone seemed to have a secret. Now Jeffrey had his own—another son, a felon. She would run him through PeopleSearch tomorrow. And what was with Brian's lies? It was clear to Hollis' internal lie detector that their whole meeting was riddled with his half-truths. Brian's lackadaisical attitude about being arrested for murder was inexplicable. And Frances, who clearly was inching to get back to the gambling tables, definitely had something hidden going on.

She sighed deeply. It didn't seem as if anyone missed Jeffrey. His parolees cared more about his death than his own family.

And then there was her client, Shelby Patterson.

Another "it's all about me" family drama. She would be glad to get the house on the market and sold. Shelby's tuition was due soon and if they had a bit of luck, Shelby would be on her way to UCLA in plenty of time—family drama permitting.

Resigned that she wasn't going to be able to solve it all this night, she turned over and went to sleep.

IT WAS A BEAUTIFUL SPRING morning and the drive to San Lucian hills was pleasant. Hollis had only seen photos of the Patterson house, but she recognized it immediately when she turned onto the street. The grass was overgrown, and the shrubs were untrimmed. A green hose angled snake-like along the entry path to the front door. Shelby, who appeared to be driving a rental, was already parked directly in front of the house. She got out of the car as soon as Hollis pulled up.

"It's a mess, isn't it?" she said. "You don't suppose we need to be worried about getting shot at, do you?"

"No, I don't think so. Besides we can't let them scare you away." Hollis moved up the steps. "The work you see is only cosmetic. Kevin Gregg will hire a gardener to bring the yard up to speed before he markets the house. You ready to go inside?"

Hollis used her key. The door creaked loudly and opened onto a darkened room. Even though the drapes were pulled back, very little light penetrated the dark, wood-paneled room. She could see out the large rear bay windows that the shaded backyard had a large weeping willow in the middle, with a column of smaller shade and fruit trees along the fence line. As with the front yard, everything was overgrown.

Hollis tried the light in the dining room. It came on. Someone was still paying the electric bill—or at least it hadn't gone unpaid long enough for the power to be shut off.

Shelby entered tentatively, as if afraid of being noticed. She went to the mantle and ran her hand over a picture of an older, stern looking woman and a sterner looking man standing on the steps of the house.

"This is my dad's mother and her second husband." She put it back. "I loved her," she said quietly.

Hollis waited for Shelby to join her, and they walked quickly through the living and dining rooms. The rooms were still full of furniture but it was clear that the recent residents were not as neat as the original owner. A few fast food wrappers dotted the dining table and a dollop of ketchup had squeezed out and dried. The kitchen was dated, but relatively clean. A week-old *San Francisco Chronicle* was folded neatly on a chair.

Shelby followed Hollis like a shy child as they went upstairs. There was a long hallway lined on either side with closed doors. Hollis stood aside and nodded for Shelby to take the lead.

"This was the guest room." Shelby opened a door and went in.

The room was dark, with pulled curtains. Clothes were scattered on a chair and the floor next to it. It appeared to be a man's room.

They turned to leave, shutting the door behind them. The next room was adjacent, and as before, Shelby went in first.

"This was Gram's sewing room."

The small room had natural light that gave it a cheery atmosphere. It was orderly. A mattress was on the floor and the bed was made up. On a closed sewing machine cabinet were makeup bottles. A table full of catalogs and patterns stood in a corner.

Shelby led the way out. They passed a yellow and white tiled bathroom with two sinks, a tub, and a separate shower. Towels were folded neatly on the dual racks.

The last room faced the hallway entrance. The entryway had double doors, and Hollis nodded at Shelby to open them.

The girl took a step backwards. "I can't. This was Gram's bedroom." She stood to the side and pointed. "Me and my cousins used to come in here and jump on her bed. Then, when my mother died and I was sent to LA, I only came back a few times … but the room didn't change." A faint smile lifted the corners of her lips.

Hollis gently touched her shoulder, opened the door and went in. Shelby followed slowly behind her.

They stood in a small vestibule that opened onto a sitting area with two overstuffed chairs and a small coffee table. Opposite the sitting area was a queen-sized bed tucked into an alcove beneath a large draped window. A faux marble fireplace was centered on one wall, and across from it appeared to be the door to the master bath. A widescreen TV sat on a dresser in the middle of the room, facing the bed.

Shelby walked around the room. Shoes under the bed and casual shirts tossed on the chairs pointed to a masculine presence. Shelby opened the closet door and gasped.

"It's Gram's clothes. He just threw them on the floor so he could hang up his own."

Hollis put her hand on Shelby's shoulder and peered at the stack of clothing in the corner of the roomy closet. It was almost as high as the clothing pole. In contrast, a man's clothing was hung neatly at the other end.

"Shelby, I know this must be hard for you. Do you want to wait in the car? I can go through the rest and check things out. I've had to go into many houses and evaluate the assets, and sometimes seeing the personal belongings of the owners can be upsetting."

Shelby mustered up a smile. "No, I'm okay. I had some good memories here, too."

Hollis led Shelby back into the main room. "Despite the upset, the house appears to be in good shape. It shouldn't take long to ready it for the market."

Shelby was silent as they began to make their way back down the stairs.

A door slammed.

Hollis wanted to kick herself. They hadn't locked the front door. They both rushed out into the hallway.

"What the hell are you doing in this house?" A scowling Darol Patterson, wearing jeans and a navy T-shirt, waited at the bottom of the stairs, blocking their way.

Hollis could sense Shelby's growing panic as she stepped in front of her and faced Shelby's father. "Mr. Patterson, I needed to see the house to evaluate its condition before we put it on the market."

He ignored Hollis. "Shelby, I asked *you* what you're doing in this house."

Shelby stood behind Hollis on the stairs, looking down at her feet. Her shoulders were shaking. Hollis picked up the girl's hand and urged her to follow her down the steps. They tried to move past Darol, but he refused to budge.

"Mr. Patterson, please let us pass. I'd hate to call the police." Hollis stood as tall as her small frame would let her.

He ignored her.

"Shelby, what are you doing? We came to get our things. Are you going to kick out your family and send us to the street?"

Shelby stood silently, and a tear dropped on the hand Hollis held.

Hollis took a step closer. "Mr. Patterson, you should have gotten your things out of here. You—"

"Lady, could you please let me talk to my daughter? This is your job, but it's my life!" he shouted. "Shelby, talk to me. Even during my ... my bad times, did I ever hurt you? Can't I just talk to you for a minute?"

Shelby said nothing, but Hollis caught the slight shake of her head.

Hollis let go of Shelby's hand and dug into her purse for her cellphone. She held it up. "Mr. Patterson, I have a 911 speed dial. If you do not move from blocking our movement, I will have you charged, along with other felonies, with kidnapping and trespassing."

Darol Patterson glared at Hollis and took a step forward, causing Hollis and Shelby to step back. He gave them a tight smile and then moved to the side in an obvious attempt to intimidate.

Hollis glared at him and led Shelby by the elbow down the rest of the stairs.

They had made it to the bottom step when the front door opened and slammed shut again. Hollis could feel Shelby stiffen under her grasp.

Joy and Sonny came into the room and stood on either side of the entry.

Hollis stiffened. She glanced at Shelby, who had finally raised her head. Her eyes were wide with terror.

"What the hell is going on?" Sonny asked. "What are they doing now, Dad? You said we could get the house back."

Now Darol was silent and Joy spoke up.

"But we're not, are we, Dad?" Joy said, not taking her eyes off the intruders. "Shelby, you're so spoiled. You don't fool nobody with that Miss Sorry act you have."

Darol Patterson passed behind Hollis and Shelby and joined his children. They stood together, forming a wall. Hollis considered her exit options. Her first goal was to get out of the house with Shelby in tow. She could call the police, but they would not welcome a domestic call that had yet to involve any real violence. She didn't think just having a bad feeling would endear them either. She decided to go for option two.

She said, "Look, I know this situation is unfortunate. But this is Shelby's house, not yours. Your mother," she said, pointing to Darol and then to Sonny and Joy, "and your grandmother gave it to her, not to you. It will be sold, so take this opportunity to collect your things. I'll have someone come back to change the lock again. But you cannot stay here. You are trespassing."

She slowly edged her way down to the last stair with Shelby at her heels and stood at the corner to the entry hallway.

"Trespassing!" Sonny shouted. "Are you kidding me?"

Darol had not taken his eyes off his stepdaughter. "Shelby, Shelby, I am so disappointed in you. Things didn't have to end this way. Well, you can't say I didn't try to take care of you. I wonder what your mother would think of you now."

Shelby drew an audible intake of breath.

Hollis was beginning to feel very uncomfortable as she moved determinedly past Darol. He didn't budge an inch, but he didn't try to stop her. She breathed a sigh of relief when she and Shelby emerged onto the front porch. They weren't followed as they headed to their cars.

Shelby walked quickly and stood next to Hollis. She wiped at her eyes with her sleeve and squinted into the morning sun. "Get them out of my house."

In amazement, Hollis turned to face her.

"Shelby, why didn't you say anything to your stepdad? He needs to hear how you really feel about selling the house," she said. "I'll set things up with a real estate agent, but he won't have the conversation you need to have with your stepfather either. If your father or siblings give him a hard time, you're going to need to see the sheriff."

"But that's why I can't face them. They scare me until I can't speak." Shelby slid into her driver's seat.

Hollis recognized the conflict in the child-woman in front of her. At times she acted like an adult, and other times like a scared kid.

"Okay, I understand, but this time you've got to stand up for yourself." As Hollis moved toward her own car, she said, "I think if you sat down and talked with them, it might save you a lot of time and your family a lot of money."

"If I sit down with them, will you sit with me?"

"No ... well, maybe. But *you* need to talk with your family. This isn't a legal matter and lawyers can be very expensive when used for family counseling. I don't think your step-grandmother would want her hard-earned money going to strangers." She got in behind the steering wheel. "Call your Aunt Denise, or have her call me."

Shelby frowned. "Hollis, please don't give up on me. I know you think I'm leaving you holding the bag, but I don't mean to. I ... I just ...." She started to tear up.

Hollis closed her eyes. "I will do everything I can to get your house sold as quickly as possible, but I'm probably not the person you'd want to negotiate a diplomatic solution. As for bringing people together, I'm not very good at it."

Shelby sighed. "All right, I'll call Aunt Denise." She went to her car and pulled out onto the street.

Hollis glanced back at the house. Her heart thumped loudly in her chest as she caught Darol and his offspring looking out from the bay window with triumphant sneers on their faces.

RETURNING TO THE OFFICE FROM the Patterson house, Hollis was mentally exhausted.

It was only a bit after one o'clock. Everyone in the firm was in a staff meeting, but she didn't want to disrupt it by coming in late. She would have to rely on George to bring her up to date.

Shelby and her family had drained her thinking resources. On one hand, Hollis was sorry for the young girl trying to pay for an education. On the other hand, Shelby Patterson, like many of her teenage peers, sent mixed signals of passive compliance coupled with self-interest. She couldn't wait to file this case away.

It was time to leave for her meeting with Mosley.

AS USUAL, MOSLEY WAS WAITING for her. Hollis was waved through security, and three minutes later he was handing her a cup of green tea.

"You remembered. I'm touched." Hollis smiled.

"I discovered we have tea drinkers here." Mosley took a seat across from her. "So, what have you got for me, Ms. Morgan?"

Hollis frowned. "Do you ever think you could call me Hollis? You make me feel like we've never talked before."

He gave her a mirthless smile. "Old habits die hard."

"Yeah, I guess so." She pulled out her notepad. "You probably already know this, but Jeffrey Wallace has a son in prison. I don't know what kind of relationship they had, but he didn't come to the funeral. A lot of favors can be arranged in prison if you want something done on the outside." Hollis noticed Mosley taking a note. "I know it was likely Brian's gun that killed Wallace, which is what led to his arrest. But you need to look deeper into Frances' motivations. She pushed Jeffrey into getting the trust, then three months later filed for a divorce. She has gambling connections and wants to move to Nevada as soon as possible. Brian did not kill his father, but I bet the real killer is glad you think he did."

Mosley didn't look up. "Todd Wallace is out on parole, and he has an alibi for the night his father died."

"What?" Hollis said, startled.

"You wanted to meet to share and compare what you discovered with what we know … and what I can tell you." Mosley leaned back in his chair. "Todd Wallace was released on parole two months ago. He's living in the East Bay, and according to his parole officer, has held to all his restrictions. On the night of the murder, he was peer coaching at an AA meeting."

Hollis tossed her pen on the table. "Well, that doesn't mean he couldn't have had someone else—"

"Todd was not Jeffrey Wallace's natural son. He and his first wife adopted him as a child. It appears they had a close father-son relationship. It was Jeffrey who worked to get Todd out on early parole and find a place for him to live. Todd asked Jeffrey to keep his efforts secret from Brian and Frances. Now he says he's still dealing with a lot of regret and guilt. He wanted to have a chance to prove himself to his father."

Yeah, I bet.

"So, you don't think Todd has a motive?"

"Do you?"

Hollis ran her fingers through her hair. She knew she sounded more confident than she felt.

"Detective, you didn't know Jeffrey like I did. He was a good man. Brian's motives don't rise to murder. And the real killer is getting away. There must be more viable suspects than Brian Wallace."

"Ms. Morgan, I'm not going to get engaged in a guessing game with you. In fact, you assured me that you were not planning to interfere with police business and were only pursuing probate issues surrounding the descendant's estate." Mosley cleared his throat. "Right now, it's beginning to sound like you're playing shadow detective—and I don't need a shadow."

Hollis paused. "I came here in good faith to tell you what we've discovered."

"You came here to pump me for what we have on Brian Wallace."

"I'm just trying to be an effective co-executor." She put her notepad away. "Is there anything else?"

He chuckled. "I've gotta hand it to you: you don't give up." His face was instantly sober again. "Brian Wallace is our man. It was his gun and he had opportunity. We found GSR—that's gunshot residue—on his shoes, which proves he had recently fired a weapon. He and his father had been at odds for some time. Where the trust does come into play is that Brian thought he should have gotten an inheritance outside of the trust—and that's his motive. Finally, Frances and Todd have solid alibis and no motives. One more thing: Brian has a few debts of his own, so I hope his fiancée did a credit check."

Hollis didn't comment but she did barely suppress a groan. They hadn't run credit checks on their suspects.

Mosley tossed his pen on the table. "Now that's everything else."

CHAPTER 18

HOLLIS HAD TWO MESSAGES, AND she steeled herself before playing them back. The first was from Kevin Gregg, the real estate broker. He would be holding a broker open house on the following Tuesday. Knowing the Pattersons, that ought to be fun.

The next message was from John.

"Hey, can't talk. Just checking in. I miss you."

I miss you too.

For once she wanted to share an update on the Pattersons and get his reaction about the appearance of Todd Wallace on the scene. His message gave her a little energetic push and left her with a goofy smile on her face. She left a similar message on his phone.

George had left two files in her inbox with the note: "Let's talk." Hollis skimmed through them and immediately saw what was needed. She drafted the legal letters and tucked them in her drawer. At least she was able to get a jump on something.

She wrote notes on her Patterson family encounter and the status of the estate. She was ready to file them in a folder when George appeared in her doorway.

"We missed you at the staff meeting."

"I didn't get back until after it had started. Anything I need to know?"

George leaned against the doorway and took out a small pad. "No, there are some office procedural things that are changing. Ask Tiffany about those. Oh, and your friend Vince got a few compliments. Everyone is happy with the mail service. Finally, our billables are up for the year and Ed is very pleased."

"That sounds great." Hollis could barely muster a smile.

He let the pad rest on his leg then folded his hands behind his neck and gazed at her. "What's the matter?"

"I said 'great,' " she said. "Nothing's the matter."

"You look stressed and…." The closer he looked as her, the more she stiffened. "Is Shelby still making you crazy? Or is it the Wallace case?"

She sighed. "Maybe a little of both, but I'll be fine. Once the Patterson house is sold I won't feel so anxious."

George nodded slowly. "All right. How was the trip to the house with Miss Patterson?"

"Very interesting. Here are my notes. Don't read them now; wait until tomorrow." She stood. "I'm going home."

George took the pages and stood as well.

"Now that's an idea. Get some rest. What are your next steps?"

Hollis glanced at her calendar. "I met with Detective Mosley and he gave me some facts that could really impact what we know about Jeffrey's dea … I mean trust."

"We?"

Hollis shook her head. "I meant *me*." She smiled sheepishly. "I was using the queen's 'we.' "

She talked George through the highlights from the meeting with the detective.

He turned to leave. "I know you're not happy with this outcome, but at least it sounds like the drama is coming to an end."

"Maybe."

RATHER THAN LEAVE EARLY, HOLLIS stayed a little longer at work. Fortunately the day ended quietly. Hollis was now caught up with her case assignments from George, and she was able to assist another attorney with research on another matter. It was a relief not to have any interest in the legal outcome.

When she got home she quickly finished her household chores, freeing up the rest of the evening to finish a book she'd started weeks before.

Early the next morning, after a rare jog around the neighborhood, she returned home to get ready for work. Hollis smiled to herself. She was more than happy *not* to have any messages on her voicemail.

She sent John his daily text.

Even with the short morning workout, she was in the office before everyone else. Feeling as if her batteries had been recharged, she arranged to meet Stephanie for coffee. Thinking of her friend brought a smile to her face. They were much alike, and Stephanie, in her capacity as a forensic technician, had proven herself more than just a friend, but a life-saver.

"You should have called me last weekend," Stephanie said. "If I'd known John was out of town, I'd have asked you to the movies."

They were sitting in the police department cafeteria. The room was half-filled, with a few children running about and two or three tables of adults holding muffled conversations.

"I had a fantastic weekend by myself." Hollis picked at a blueberry muffin. "John has been putting pressure on me to move in with him. I needed time to think."

"Whoa, lady." Stephanie put her food down. "You never told me you two were contemplating Defcon two. We need to have a long talk."

Hollis smiled. "That's why I needed time alone, to contemplate."

"You don't sound very cheerful." Stephanie stared at her friend.

"I am. I … I just don't know …. I'm not sure." Hollis sat hugging herself, her hands gripping her upper arms.

Stephanie gave her an encouraging smile and nodded in understanding. "Then you're right to take your time."

Hollis said, "So, how is Aurelia? Any psychic revelations?"

"Not since we last talked." Stephanie took a bite of her bran muffin and chewed thoughtfully. Covering her mouth, she said, "I'm not that reliant on her. Although, I think you might be able to figure the John thing out better if you had a psychic session."

Stephanie swore to the authenticity and accuracy of Aurelia's predictions. Hollis was less impressed and the two friends agreed to disagree.

"I'll pass. I've stumbled along this far." Hollis wiped her mouth and checked the time. "What I need to figure out concerns my two clients. Both are atypical cases and both are challenging."

"Hmm, as often as you come here for meetings with the detectives, I take it that at least one of those cases involves law enforcement."

"Both do. When I was on parole, I knew that if I never saw a police department again, it would be fine with me." Hollis' smile was bittersweet. "But ever since I got off parole this place has practically become my second home. Go figure."

"Maybe you should go into criminal law."

Once Hollis was back at her office, she made a call to Richard.

"This must be important. I don't ever remember getting a call from you," he said.

"I apologize for bothering you at work, but I couldn't wait until our meeting. I need you to run a credit check on Brian— the kind the banks run with the FICO scores. I'll give you his social, and I've got his release to share info with the team."

Richard took down the number. "Got it. See you Thursday."

She made her next call.

"Gene, is there any way you can find out about Todd Wallace's prison sentence?" she asked. "I'm getting the legal party line, but I was thinking you might be able to come up with the street version."

She could imagine Gene pulling at his eyebrows. It was a wonder he had any left. She gave him a summary of her conversation with Mosley.

"I'll give it a shot," he said. "Jeffrey's son is out on parole?"

"And he's making it work," Hollis said. "The police are satisfied."

"But you're not?"

"Nope, I'm not."

Her last call was to Rena. They agreed to meet for lunch. After cursory air kisses, they dove into the menus.

"You know it's rare I have time to eat a social lunch," Rena said, scanning the long list of salads. "But we lucked out. One of our stores cancelled a meeting and it freed up my afternoon. What's going on with Brian?"

Hollis brought her up to date with her meetings with Brian and Mosley.

"There's something not right," Hollis said. "It's like looking for one of those pictures within a picture, but you can't see it because there is so much other clutter."

"Yeah, those things make me cross-eyed." Rena put the menu aside. "Are we really going to eat? Or is this just a micro Fallen Angels meeting? I'm starving."

"We're going to eat," Hollis said.

The server took their order.

Rena raised an eyebrow when she saw Hollis pull out a pad and pen. "I thought so."

"I hoped I could talk to you about two issues—Jeffrey and Shelby."

Rena nodded. "I was wondering what was happening with Shelby. I was afraid to ask. I haven't called her aunt in LA because ... because I hated to give them something else to worry about. They want so badly for her to go to college and succeed; they'd be discouraged if they discover she's acting up. Well ... I just wanted to see if we could work things out so I wouldn't have to make that call."

"Shelby is a typical teenager trying to find her way. She can be exasperating, but she's got good instincts. Now her 'step' family .... That's another story.

"That bad?" she asked. "Denise told me about the shooting and how Shelby has been acting irresponsibly."

Hollis' forehead creased. "Did you know that Shelby went missing for three days and no one knew where she was? I even filed a missing persons report."

Rena's brown eyes widened. "No, I had no idea. I take it she eventually surfaced okay?"

"Yeah, but I felt like an idiot—particularly with the police—when I found out she was deliberately hiding out at a girlfriend's. She only did it because she was intimidated by her stepfather and siblings, and on this point I understand her reaction. They want to stop her from selling the house."

Rena sighed. "Darol and his kids can be unsavory, but I don't think they would hurt her."

"They do a pretty good intimidation number, however. That's why I've had to change the locks—twice." Hollis held up two fingers for emphasis. She went on to explain about the shooting and what had transpired since. "Shelby was complaining of phone hang-ups and other harassing activity. I've been getting a few hang-ups myself."

"Oh, Hollis, I'm sorry. I had no idea. I didn't think—"

"It's okay, I'm getting used to them." Hollis put down her fork and let the waitress take her plate away. "We need to sell the house quickly. The longer this matter drags on, the more injured the Pattersons become. It's like a raw sore."

"What do you want me to do?" Rena asked. "I know Darol. I can try to talk some sense into him. Joy and Sonny I've only met a few times. They were raised by their mother."

Hollis frowned. "See if Darol will meet with you. Once I talk with Shelby I'd like you to bounce an idea off him. He could be given a portion of the sale proceeds for rent money—say for six months. If he still wants his kids to live with him, that's on him. But there is no more money after that. I have a fiduciary responsibility to make sure there is enough money to pay for Shelby's school and as much of her housing costs as possible."

Rena nodded. "Hollis, that's a great idea, but I thought you didn't want to get involved."

"I didn't," Hollis said. "While I may not have the patience or communication skills for a family counselor, I do know how to cut a mutually beneficial settlement."

"Do you think Shelby will agree?"

"I can only hope. But she knows I'm tired of her moods and inconsiderate behavior. Besides, she has to register soon for fall classes; and she'll want to move on. I'm pretty sure I can convince her. It's a fair deal."

"Okay, when I get your go-ahead that Shelby is on board, I'll tell Denise to get in touch with Darol."

"I'll let you know as soon as I need you to call."

Hollis pulled out her notebook. "Now let's move on to Brian Wallace," she said. "I need you to go back one more time to your friends and find out if Frances has put up her share for the casino yet. I don't think she has, but I want to make sure. Finally, I was hoping you could find out if Brian Wallace has any gambling debts, or any loan shark activity."

Rena took out a green leather monogrammed appointment book and jotted down a few notes.

"All right. I can handle that."

"I've got Rich and Gene doing some extra looking, too. I hope to wrap all these ends up soon."

"Great relaxing lunch, Hollis." Rena dabbed her mouth with

her napkin. "What are you going to do now, run a marathon?"

"Sorry." She made a face. "I'm off to visit Mr. Brian Wallace. It seems he neglected to mention a few things when we met a couple of days ago."

HOLLIS SAT WAITING FOR BRIAN in his living room. He left her alone while he finished a phone call. She took advantage of the time alone to take stock of her surroundings. There was a stack of unopened mail on the sofa table—at least the ones on top were bills, some envelopes in late-notice pink. She noted several glass rings on the walnut table where someone had let liquid stain the wood. On a side table was a white bag with a pharmacy logo. She read the bottle—a sleeping pill prescription.

She walked over to the cluttered mantel to look closer at a picture of Brian, Todd, and Jeffrey at a softball game. The brothers were still boys; Todd was in his teens. Todd was suited up, and Brian and Jeffrey grinned broadly. Evidently the ties of brotherhood weren't completely severed.

Brian walked into the room wearing a pair of navy sweats. His blond hair was slicked back.

Hollis put the photo back. "Happier times?"

"Er … yeah. That was a long time ago." Brian sat on the edge of an ottoman. "What's the urgency? Sorry I couldn't meet with you earlier; I had to meet with my other attorney. You said it was important to talk."

"Yeah, Brian, I think we're coming to a fork in our road." Hollis' expression was serious. "If we are to continue as attorney-client I need to take over as co-executor. Because of your status as a charged murderer, you really can't perform the due diligence that's needed. Granted, there's not much left to do. We're either going to find something on Frances shortly, or we're not. But I want to be able to close Jeffrey's estate."

"Actually, I think that's a great idea. But what do you mean I won't be able to perform?" Brian was starting to raise his voice, but he still accepted the sheet of paper Hollis pulled out, and without reading, quickly scribbled his name.

"What I mean is, why didn't you tell me about the results of the GSR test? The police found gunshot residue on you, which is damning evidence that you'd recently fired a gun. Also, just the day before yesterday you neglected to mention that your brother Todd was adopted and in fact no longer incarcerated—but has been out of prison for the past two months. I'm your attorney; you're supposed to tell me everything. And more importantly, you're supposed to tell me the truth."

Hollis moved to stand in front of him, and Brian backed away.

"You're my probate attorney," he mumbled.

Hollis looked at him a moment and sat down. "I won't even be that if you don't tell me the truth. I can't advise you if I don't have access to all the beneficiaries. I need to speak with your brother."

"I spoke with him a few days ago. He said Dad had found him a decent place to live that he could afford. Todd ... Todd doesn't want anything." Brian looked down at his hands in his lap.

Hollis was silent.

Brian looked at her. "Okay, honest, I didn't know he was out until a little while ago. It was between him and Dad. I know I should have told you when I found out. But I wanted to get the trust wrapped up, and he said he didn't want anything anyway. He wasn't even expecting the first editions."

"He'll have to sign a statement. Those first editions could be valuable, or they could just be old." She made a note. "We'll have to rush to get them appraised, and then have him sign a release."

Brian jumped up. "Why do we have to waste time and money getting them valued? Frances had it done a few years ago. Besides, didn't you hear me? He said he didn't want any part of Dad's estate."

Hollis deliberately lowered her voice. "He cannot sign away his rights to something when he doesn't know the value." She looked up at him. "He could change his mind."

Brian ran his fingers through his hair but said nothing.

"So tell me, what was the real reason you didn't tell me Todd was out on parole? Were you trying to keep me in the dark so you could rush the filing? Did Jeffrey tell you about Todd the night you argued?"

Brian's jaw tightened.

"Your silence answered that question. If he doesn't accept the books you'll be able to sell them and keep the proceeds for your wedding." Hollis peered at him. "Now answer this: why didn't you tell me about the results of the GSR test?"

He shrugged. "Why? What does it matter to the trust?"

"How did you get traces on your shoes?"

Hunching his shoulders and dropping his chin, he mumbled something incoherent.

"What did you say?" Hollis snapped, on the verge of losing her temper.

"I said, I came back."

"You mean, you argued with your dad, came back after someone killed him and then left him there for the cleaning crew to find?"

Brian fell on the sofa, sobbing hysterically.

Hollis shivered and looked at him with pity.

"I'll take care of your brother's paperwork." Headed for the door, she picked up her briefcase and purse. "I should be able to file the trust on time," she said over her shoulder as she went out the door.

CHAPTER 19

JOHN TEXTED HER THAT HE would call at eight o'clock that night, and he was right on time.

"I miss you so much—even more than I thought I would," she said, trying to keep the misery out of her voice.

"Hey, what's the matter? You sound upset."

"Not upset ... well, maybe a little. My first two cases involve terrible people and it's depressing as well as aggravating. I think I might be representing the bad guys." Saying the words out loud was forcing Hollis to face her worst fears.

"Hollis Morgan in distress ... now that's a first. What would Jeffrey say?"

She smiled weakly. "I can't believe he's been gone over a month, and thank you for your water in the face comment. Sometimes I need to hear how I sound to others."

"I miss you, too."

Hollis shifted the conversation to his training. It was going well. He was learning how another branch of enforcement operated and it added an intriguing layer to his own experience. He was also fortunate that his peers were dedicated professionals who—at least for now—weren't into power games and office politics.

"You'll be back Wednesday evening, right?" she asked.

"Right."

"I'll be glad to have you home."

HOLLIS GOT INTO THE OFFICE early to finish up some paperwork. Next she called Todd's parole officer for his contact information.

"How's he handling his parole?"

"Very well." His parole officer had a gravelly voice that sounded like he needed to clear his throat. "It's still early, but he has a job he's okay with and he's staying away from bad influences."

"What about his family contacts? Why didn't he go to his dad's funeral?"

"Like I said, he wanted to stay away from bad influences."

She moved on to the next item on her list. It took only a few minutes to get a PeopleSearch run on Todd. It wasn't very long. There was nothing about his natural parents. He was adopted at age three by Jeffrey and his first wife. He didn't start getting into any real trouble until after he graduated from high school. He was an accessory to the robbery and the mugging of a man who must have been the fence for their stolen goods. It landed him in prison, where he had resided for the past five years. Ready to meet him, she called and left a message on his voicemail.

It was while she was in the law library that Todd called and left a message on her phone agreeing to meet her for lunch the next day. From his clear and articulate voice, Hollis was re-arranging the picture she had painted of him.

SHE WAITED TO APPROACH GEORGE. He was leaving for four days to go to Los Angeles to argue a complicated probate case. Hollis wanted to update him on her two cases before he left.

"Hollis, you don't live a boring life, do you?" he said. "I would focus on wrapping up this Wallace matter."

"I have to admit they're an irritating bunch, but George, I know there's something I'm missing. Jeffrey's killing was personal, not random." She rubbed her forehead. "I thought my family was dysfunctional, but Jeffrey's is right up there. No wonder he understood where I was coming from."

George shook his head. "Just don't get sucked in. You're a probate attorney, not a criminal lawyer or a family therapist."

Hollis shook his words off. "Jeffrey Wallace was murdered. He's the only reason I'm an attorney. I can't walk away from him." Her voice drifted. "The problem is, we have too many suspects. Everyone has a motive, means and opportunity."

"Maybe, but the police don't think so. They think they have their man. Your job—although I do agree it's awkward with your client out on bail—is to process the Wallace trust. Unless you can point to some reason why that trust should not be filed, you have to do what you were retained to do."

Hollis nodded, even though she knew she wasn't going to take his advice.

"Now, about your Patterson case, I saw your note that the house goes on the market today. Are you expecting trouble from Shelby's relatives?"

"I asked the sheriff's office to send a car by every so often, but they couldn't give me a commitment. The broker is bringing an associate for safety in numbers. He'll contact me after he holds the open house to let me know how things went." Hollis flipped through her notes. "Shelby is staying up here with her friend until it's sold."

"Nothing else from her father?"

"After last week's meltdown? No, Dad and company may be ready to see the light." Even as she said the words, Hollis had her doubts.

But she could hope.

RENA STOOD LOOKING OUT OF the library's community room

window waiting for the rest of the Fallen Angels to arrive. Hollis saw her from the glass door and hesitated to interrupt her reverie. She paused a moment longer and then came into the room.

"Hey, you okay?" Hollis asked.

Rena blinked a few times and smiled. "Yes, I'm fine. Just remembering a conversation I had with Jeffrey."

"Yeah, I've been thinking about him, too," Gene said as he entered the room. He dumped a stack of papers on top of the table.

Miller followed him. "The only thing I've been thinking about for the past week is my branch. We're getting ready for a library merger. They're closing a smaller one and we're getting their books. We have to change the location codes on the books and in the system."

"Gee, Miller, that's fascinating," Richard mocked, taking off his hat and jacket. "What's with the papers, Gene?"

"Let's get started and I'll tell you," he replied.

Hollis sat next to him in a vain attempt to sneak a peek.

"If you all remember, my assignment was to find out about Todd's service time in prison."

Richard said, "So what's with all the paper? Did he have a pen pal?"

"No, he was a loner," Gene said, handing out pages around the table. "He got his college degree while he was inside. These are copies of the papers he left behind for his fellow prisoners to use in their pursuit of a higher education."

Hollis looked through the pages. "You said he was a loner, but did he align himself with any group?"

Gene shook his head. "Not that I could tell. He did his time and got out on good behavior."

"Well, unfortunately his good behavior didn't extend to his credit," Richard said. "His FICO score is the lowest possible. Interesting, but not really surprising, is the fact that he has collection accounts from the time before he was in prison."

Miller looked up from a paper crane. "Can you charge items from jail? Where do you have it sent?"

"Times have changed," Rena answered. "You can't use a credit card. But you can have an inmate account and it varies from prison to prison how much cash you can receive a month."

They all thought about that a moment, recalling their own prison terms.

"That might be the reason for the low FICO score." Hollis looked at her notes. "Rena, speaking of debt, what did you find out about Brian?"

"I ran out of time to check on Brian, but Todd Wallace appears clear. No one seems to know him. Now Frances, on the other hand, is another story." Rena cleared her throat. "Like we already knew, word is she's made it known she's coming into some money—enough to put up her share of a casino partnership."

Hollis frowned. "Did you find out when she began to negotiate a position as an owner?"

"About three months ago."

There was that three months, again.

Miller pointed at her. "Hollis what did you find?"

She recounted her conversations with Brian and Todd's attorney. When she got to the part about Todd walking away from the trust and maybe even the first editions, she pointed out that she didn't believe Brian's answers. "He starts to mumble when he lies or when he knows he's in the wrong."

"Your lie detector is pretty good," Gene said. "But why would he want to appear otherwise? It's not like he's in line to get a chunk of change. The first editions are only valued at around fifteen grand. I can see Frances grasping for every asset she can find. But the more we dig up, the more I have to agree with Brian: there's something more to this trust that isn't on paper."

"I don't know about you big spenders, but fifteen thousand would mean a lot to me," Rena said.

Miller reached across the table and gave her a high five.

"I think Brian's still thinking about it too," Hollis said. "It didn't sound to me like Todd was totally committed to walking away. I'll know more when I meet with him tomorrow." Hollis scratched her head. "Everyone in that family is hedging their bets—no pun intended. It's like a conspiracy to cover up or at least not to reveal the real truth—Frances wants it all, Brian wants it fast, and Todd insists he wants out. They're all in on it."

WHEN HOLLIS GOT TO THE café, she spotted Todd immediately. He was absorbed in his menu as if it were the *Wall Street Journal*. Dressed in tan slacks and a light beige V-neck sweater, he appeared modest and understated. He had blue eyes and sandy brown hair—on the longish side and shaped to his head. When he noticed Hollis approaching the table, he stood. He was tall; probably an inch or two over six feet.

They exchanged greetings and quickly put in their lunch orders.

"My lunch break isn't long," he said. "I agreed to meet with you because Brian said you wouldn't take his word for it that I don't want anything from my father's estate." He held his cup of coffee with two hands as if to warm them.

Hollis looked into his eyes. "I read the valuation done by Frances a few years ago. If the books are in fair to good condition, they could be worth up to fifteen thousand dollars—more if they're in excellent condition."

"I'm not going to lie; obviously I could use the money, but right now I'm thinking twice about claiming them."

"Why?"

"Dad and I had a deal. I broke the deal and went to prison for it." He looked past Hollis. "I'd feel like a hypocrite."

Hollis felt a pang of recognition. "I knew your dad, too. He was my parole officer for five years and then after that I'd like to think he was my friend." She frowned. "He would want to know that his estate … the things he gathered throughout his lifetime weren't squandered and gambled … er … tossed away."

Todd gave a short laugh. "I see you've met Frances." He turned serious. "Brian told me you were an ex-felon." His eyes narrowed and then he looked away. "I just want to put my time in for parole and get on with my life. As for what's going on between Brian and Frances … well, I just don't want to get in the middle of it."

"I know what you mean; I've been there." Hollis smiled as the waitress put their plates in front of them. After she left, she asked, "Did you see your father before he died?"

He stiffened. "Why are you asking me that?"

Hollis noted his reaction. "Oh, I guess because I would like to have visited him one more time before he died." She took a sip of tea. "Although you know how he hated sentiment."

"Oh, yeah … yeah, he hated sentiment." Todd took a large bite of his sandwich and swallowed before continuing. "Er … yeah, he and I talked before … before …." He took another bite and chewed hurriedly. "My prints weren't in his office. The police already questioned me."

"When was the last time you spoke with your dad?"

"The week before he was killed."

"How long—"

"Hi, Hollis, I saw you from the corner." Stephanie weaved through the scattered tables to stand next to theirs. Even in her lab coat with her hair pulled back into a bun, she looked professional and attractive. She bent down and gave Hollis a peck on the cheek, then looked up at Todd. "Didn't mean to interrupt. Just came by to say hello."

"No, no, stay." Todd stood and pulled out a chair. "I've got to head back to work. My lunch break is almost over." He reached out his hand. "My name is Todd."

Hollis smiled to herself. It was clear Todd wanted an escape route. "This is my good friend Stephanie. Stephanie, this is Todd. I'm helping his family."

"Oh, I'm sorry. I am interrupting." She smiled. "Call me when you get home. Nice to meet you, Todd."

She turned to leave.

"Do you come here often?" Todd asked hurriedly. "I mean I come here a lot. I haven't seen you before. I'd remember. I mean …."

Hollis looked at him with amazement as he responded to her curvy friend. Stephanie laughed.

"Todd," Hollis said, "don't you have to be at work? I'll be in touch about the papers you have to sign."

"Yeah, yeah, I've got to go." He stood and pushed his chair in. "See you around, Stephanie."

He wrapped the rest of his sandwich in a napkin, passed through the tables, and dashed out the entrance.

"Isn't he a little young for you?" Hollis asked with raised eyebrows.

"I'm younger than you."

Hollis smirked. "By seven weeks."

Stephanie rested her chin in her upraised palm. "You know, Hollis, I think I've seen him somewhere before. It'll come to me; I never forget a face."

"Let me know if you remember," Hollis said. She didn't think it warranted revealing that there was a mug shot out there with his face on it. "Did you want to get together this weekend?"

"Ah, John's still gone. Too bad! But I guess that means you're free to go out," Stephanie teased.

"No, you're wrong," Hollis protested. "John doesn't get back until Sunday night. But I'm still allowed to play with my own friends even if he's in town."

"Okay, that's all I wanted to know. There's a fashion show and luncheon this Saturday at Nordstrom."

"Okay, I'm game. I could use a diversion from work."

She signaled the waitress for the check and a to-go box. She wasn't hungry.

CHAPTER 20

"SHELBY IS MISSING AGAIN." RENA'S voice sounded strained, even on the phone.

Hollis looked up at the ceiling in disgust. "This is ridiculous. What happened now?"

"Darol called me," Rena said. "Since you talked them into that agreement, they've been trying to re-bond. She was supposed to pick him up from the doctor's office yesterday, but she never showed up." Rena paused. "It's not like her, Hollis."

"Rena, I've gone through this before. I foolishly believed her when she promised not to do it again." Hollis doodled a series of concentric circles. "Give it another two days. Then give me a call."

Rena sighed. "I don't blame you for not wanting to trust her, but there's more."

Hollis wanted to kick herself for asking, "What?"

"I spoke with Sonny and Joy and they said they don't know where she is, but I don't believe them. They sounded a little too … too … sugary," Rena said. "I think they are holding Shelby."

Hollis heaved a deep sigh. "Where do you think she is?"

"At the house."

"That's impossible. The agent is showing the house. Don't you think he would let me know if someone was being held captive there?" Hollis tried to think back to their tour of the house. Was there a place where you could hide a person? "Where are Sonny and Joy staying now?"

Rena said, "I'm not sure, maybe a motel. Sonny said they were getting an apartment in about a week if Shelby didn't allow them to stay."

"Call Sonny and see if you can arrange for you and me to meet with him, Darol, and Joy—today, if at all possible." Hollis tabbed through her contact list. "I'll call the realtor."

"When do you want to meet with them?"

Hollis said, "Later today; otherwise, first thing in the morning."

"Okay, I'll call you back with the arrangements." Rena hung up.

Hollis paused to clear her thoughts before punching in the number for the real estate office.

"Kevin, I was calling to check on the brokers' open. How did it go?"

"Ah, Hollis, didn't you get my message? I cancelled the brokers' open per your instructions. In fact, in my message I was letting you know that I have someone who might be interested in the purchase, and we might not need to have the open house."

Hollis shook her head to let the information sink in. "I didn't cancel the open house and I didn't get your message. Where did you leave it?"

"I didn't," Kevin said. "Your assistant said that you were ill and that she would forward my message. If the cancellation didn't come from you, then who—"

"I think I know who. Was my supposed assistant male or female?"

"Female. She called me two days before the brokers' open. I just had time to cancel it."

He paused. "What does this mean? I know you told me you were having problems with some of the family members."

Hollis hesitated before answering, "What this means is, I am not ill and I didn't cancel the open house. Probably one of the family members faked a call to you." She rubbed her eyes. "I may have to get an injunction."

"Sounds like you've got some real issues. Look, it may all work out anyway; my tentative buyer is out town until mid-week. So we have some time to get things back on track. But I'm going to need the new key," Kevin said.

"What? There's no new key."

"Well, the ones you gave me don't work anymore. I went by to take some pictures yesterday, but I couldn't get in."

Hollis could feel a surge of red creeping up her chest.

"Can you hold off until tomorrow afternoon? I will try to have things wrapped up by then."

"Sure, just give me a call."

Hollis looked up to see Tiffany standing in her doorway.

"Hollis, you had a call come through on our main line while you were on the phone. Here's the message."

She was afraid to read the slip of paper. *What else?*

It was from Rena. The gang of three would meet with them at Dolly's Diner at nine o'clock the next morning. Hollis was frustrated that they weren't meeting today, but she wanted to meet with the three together, and there was nothing else she could do. She just hoped that Shelby was okay.

Their story had better be good.

Tucked between small store fronts on Park Boulevard, Dolly's Diner was located in East Oakland near Lake Merritt. Hollis had never been there before, but after eating their lemon pancake special, she was ready to put it on her list of best breakfast places. She and Rena had agreed to arrive early and enjoy breakfast before their meeting with the Pattersons. They sat side by side on one side of the table to leave room across from them for the family.

The portions were large, the menu expansive, and the food divine.

"I hope they weren't counting on getting a free meal." Rena wiped her mouth. "I can't believe they changed the locks again." She raised her voice. "And I can't believe they're holding Shelby."

"I'd believe it." Hollis took a long sip of her tea. "I am more determined than ever to make sure Shelby sells this house and gets on with her life. But what I can't believe is that it's her own stepfather who is doing this to her."

They'd just finished their meal and ordered a second cup of tea when Darol, Sonny, and Joy walked into the restaurant.

Darol looked strained and the siblings looked distracted and nervous. As usual he was dressed nattily—in tan Dockers and a V-neck dark-green T-shirt. His children, on the other hand, look bedraggled. Their hair appeared finger-combed and their jeans and T-shirts were rumpled and stained.

"Ms. Morgan, Rena." Darol sat down and gave an almost imperceptible nod to his children, who sat on either side of him. "I wanted us to get together to talk this through before things got out of hand."

Hollis looked at him in amazement.

"Mr. Patterson, things are already out of hand." She was having a difficult time keeping her voice even. "First, Shelby is missing, the locks have been changed on the house without my approval, and the house sale has been stalled. I would most definitely say that things have gotten out of hand."

Rena folded her arms across her chest. "Darol, where is Shelby?"

He shrugged. "Don't look at me, Rena. Remember, I'm the one who called and told you she hadn't shown up."

Hollis sat back in her chair. "Let me put it to you this way. If Shelby doesn't contact me by the six o'clock this evening, I'm going to the police and I'm going to point them in your direction." She pointed at each of them separately. "Each of you."

Darol licked his lips. Sonny and Joy discovered a fascination with the edge of the table.

He reached out with open hands. "I'm telling you I don't know where she is."

Hollis nodded. "Great. You can tell it to the police." She looked at the Sonny and Joy. "What about you two. No idea where Shelby could be?"

They looked everywhere but at each other and vigorously shook their heads.

They were lying.

"Okay, I'm not buying it. Where is she?" she snapped.

"Nobody made sure that I could go to college." Joy's hands were shaking. "We only wanted to make her change her mind. We just wanted to get her to see how bad things were going to be for us."

Darol's face was contorted with anger as he turned to his children. "You mean you're holding Shelby somewhere? Even after I told you I had a plan to work things out, you defied me?"

Sonny straightened. "Dad, we couldn't just sit by and do nothing. We know you don't have any money. Then I lost the car wash job and Joy hasn't gotten her cosmetology license yet." He sighed. "So, we thought if we just had a little time with her ... talked with her ...."

"Are you two crazy?" Rena's eyes flashed anger. "Excuse me, but your excuses are really pitiful. Where the hell is Shelby?"

Joy's tears were already trailing down her face. "We're not making excuses. We thought it could be like the boy who cried wolf. She hid out on her own the first time, didn't she?" She put her hand on her father's sleeve. "Dad, we just wanted to stop things from going ahead so fast until we could get Shelby to see our side."

Darol shook his head. "I can't believe you defied me," he repeated.

Hollis could not contain her exasperation. "Where *is* Shelby?"

Joy wiped her eyes with the napkin and murmured, "In the house."

"I knew it," Rena said, shaking her head.

Sonny and Joy started speaking at once.

"She's safe and comfortable," Joy said, her eyes looking apologetically at her father.

"She's in the basement," Sonny said. "Remember that little room? We would hide and play in there as kids. There's a light, and I put an air mattress and a radio in there. We never left her alone, I mean in the house. One of us was always there. Except for now, 'cuz we're here."

Hollis couldn't keep the alarm out of her voice. "Wait, is she locked up?"

Darol looked in disbelief at his children and rose from the table. "Let's go."

Rena and Hollis paid the bill and dashed out to the car with Darol on their heels.

"Ms. Morgan, I didn't know about this thing with Shelby," his voice cracked. "I just needed a couple of more days. I think ... I thought we could work this out."

Rena gave him a stern look. "Darol, how did you think what you were doing was ever going to work out?"

Darol truly did not seem to know anything of his adult children's actions. Hollis read his resignation in the set of his jaw. Whatever his plan had been, he seemed to realize it had gone out the window. He quietly placed the house key in Hollis' outstretched hand.

Hollis wanted to reach Shelby as quickly as possible. Rena got into her car and Hollis moved away from the lot into traffic. Darol said they would meet them at the house. Hollis wondered if she should have insisted on them following, but it was too late now, and her first priority was Shelby.

HOLLIS AND RENA SPOKE LITTLE on the drive to San Lucian. Both were thinking of how frightened the young girl must be.

The new key easily fit the front door lock and they entered the darkened living room. Hollis turned on the lights.

"Over here," Rena said, walking toward the kitchen. She opened a door to a staircase leading down to the basement. She turned on the light. "I've been downstairs but I've never seen this storage area they talked about."

The basement was cluttered with boxes, old furniture, toys, and yard tools. Sonny and Joy must have blocked the entrance to the storage room.

"Shelby … Shelby, it's Hollis and Rena! Can you hear me?" Hollis shouted.

Rena yelled, "Shelby, where are you?" She began pulling things away from the wall.

They continued to call out but their efforts were met with silence.

Hollis' eyes traveled along the dimensions of the wall. A tall stack of chairs and small tables stood along the side of one wall, revealing tracks in the dust. She began to bring down the tower of cardboard boxes.

"Rena, help me. I think it's behind here."

They worked quickly in tandem, handing off the boxes one to the other until a door appeared.

It was locked with a deadbolt latch.

Hollis pulled back the latch and pushed in on the door. She hit resistance. "Shelby, can you hear me?"

Silence.

Rena came to her side, and they shoved at the heavy object blocking the door until Hollis was able to squeeze in.

Shelby's body lay crumpled and limp.

Rena stepped in and gasped, "Oh, my God, is she dead?"

Hollis bent over the young girl. She had a head wound that was bleeding, but her heart had a strong beat and Hollis could feel her breath against her hand.

"Rena, call 911."

Where were Darol and company now?

CHAPTER 21

THE PARAMEDICS HAD NO TROUBLE getting Shelby's vital signs back to normal. Two of them placed her on a stretcher and lifted her up the stairs to the outside.

The third medic pointed to an object lying on its side. "It looks like she fell and hit her head against that disconnected radiator. See? There's blood along the end panel. She's stabilized and we'll take her to emergency. The head wound will require an examination to assess the extent of the injury."

"I'm her family," Rena said. "Let me ride with her."

They all moved out the front door and onto the sidewalk.

Hollis noticed a uniformed police officer walking toward them.

"Rena, you go ahead with the ambulance," Hollis said, motioning. I'll speak with the police."

He came up to her. "Detective Lane, ma'am, were you the one who made the call? Can I have your name?"

Hollis gave him her name and summed up the situation. "So, we left her family and rushed here. They were supposed to meet us."

"I see. Can you give me their names and descriptions?

I'm going to need you to come to the station and give us a statement. I can have your car driven by a patrolman."

"The police already have their descriptions," Hollis said. "There's been an ongoing family dispute. And I can drive my own car."

"Yes, ma'am, but this could be the scene of a kidnapping. I would like you to ride with us for your own safety. There's another car arriving shortly to take you to the station. I need a few more minutes here to oversee processing the house as a potential crime scene. Then I'll talk with you at the station."

Not again.

Hollis knew there was little point in objecting.

AFTER FIFTEEN MINUTES OF ANSWERING questions and providing what information she knew to Lane and another officer, Hollis could feel the shift of her status moving from possible suspect to person with key evidence. Shortly after she arrived, Mosley entered with a slight smile and a shake of his head.

He handed her a cup of tea. She brought him up to speed with the events of the morning.

"Ms. Morgan, what was your impression of the Pattersons? They appear to have dropped off the face of the earth for the last couple of hours. There's an APB out for the three of them and their car."

Hollis' eyes narrowed. "The family seems pretty dysfunctional to me, and believe me I would know because I come from one." She bit her bottom lip. "They seemed desperate, illogical, and nervous. But … but I don't think they would have seriously hurt Shelby. How is she? Do you know?"

"As of an hour ago she regained consciousness for a short while. We told her where she was and then she blacked out again. She woke up again a few minutes ago and told us we could talk to you and Rena Gabriel about her condition. She was articulate and stayed awake longer than the last time, so the doctors don't think there's been any damage to her brain. But they won't know until she wakes up for good. It's just going to take a little while."

The door burst open, and a young female officer stood with a grin. "We've got 'em. They're bringing in the Pattersons."

Mosley stood. "Well, Ms. Morgan, I'm sure you're anxious to go check on your client. Your car is in the lot next door. With proof of identification, the attendant will give you the keys."

Hollis was anxious to go to the hospital. "Thank you, I'll check back with you for an update."

RENA, SITTING IN THE WAITING room, jumped up to give Hollis a hug when she came in and said, "I've been on the phone with the Patterson family. They're relieved that Shelby is okay and no real harm was done. Now they've got Sonny and Joy to worry about. I halfway regret bringing you into this mess, but the other half is happy it was you."

Hollis shrugged. "You brought me my first client. Years from now we'll shake our heads over a glass of wine, remembering." She glanced at the clock on the wall. "Any news from the doctors?"

"She released them to talk to us, and I told them I wanted to be apprised of her condition." Rena started to tear up. "They said she's still rolling in and out of consciousness, but she's staying awake longer each time."

Pulling out a tissue, she dabbed at her nose.

Hollis nodded. "The police are bringing in Darol, Sonny, and Joy now. How did they ever think that the way to work this out was by locking up Shelby?"

Rena tapped the arm of her chair with her finger. "Their logic, or lack thereof, is unbelievable. I can't get over this."

"You know, I don't think Darol knew. He seemed genuinely surprised at his children's plan."

"What's going to happen now?"

Hollis shrugged. "It's up to Shelby. If ... when she comes

through this, she can press charges, make sure her house gets sold quickly, and get on with her life."

"So they'll go to jail." Rena looked down at her hands.

"Maybe," Hollis said. "Worst case scenario is they go to jail for a very long time. Kidnapping is serious. But before we speculate, let's take it one step at a time. There's enough drama to go around."

They were both silent for the next few minutes until the door opened and a doctor came toward them, reading from a clipboard. He was short, with wire-rim glasses and a fringe of hair encircling his bald head.

"That's her doctor," Rena whispered.

"Miss Gabriel, your cousin is going to be all right. Her vitals are strong and right now she's resting. She'll have a bad headache for a few days, but we'll give her medication to relieve the pain. Does she live alone?"

"Er … yes." Rena faltered. "She lives at home in Southern California, but she can stay with me until she's better."

The doctor looked at his watch. "Good. We'll just need to watch her for a few days, make sure she's back to normal. There's no need to bring her back unless she has physical complaints. I'll send her prescription to the pharmacy." He turned to leave.

Hollis nudged Rena and motioned to the rooms.

"Oh," Rena said. "When can we see her? This is her attorney."

He paused and looked up at them. "You can go in now." He started flipping through pages on his clipboard again. "However, I had to inform the police that she was awake. They're on their way."

SHELBY WOKE LATER THAT AFTERNOON. Hollis and Rena were at her bedside while she gave her story to the police.

It seems that a basement door hinge pin was literally Shelby's downfall. When Joy locked her up that morning to leave for Dolly's Diner, Shelby banged on the door, slipped, and hit her head on a metal radiator stored in the room. Of course, the police took note that she was being held against her will, but Shelby insisted she wasn't in any danger—that it was a just a family quarrel. Besides, she wanted to get released to fly home to Los Angeles as soon as she could.

The good news was that Shelby seemed to have matured somewhat since the incident. She agreed to consider an agreement for letting Darol stay in the house. Hollis quickly emailed a draft to the Pattersons in LA so the family could advise Shelby.

Shelby beamed when the doctor said she was well enough to fly to Los Angeles and participate in the Patterson family meeting. It was to be a confab of aunts, uncles, and cousins. Denise promised to call Rena and Hollis as soon as it was over.

The weekend passed, and now it was Monday morning, and still no word.

Hollis distracted herself with two matters George had put in her basket. It helped to keep her thoughts from her two worrisome clients. She'd gone into probate because the law was clear and usually appreciated by all concerned. Instead she found herself with clients she wasn't even sure *she* appreciated.

She smiled at the slip of paper Vince left in her office mailbox. He was taking his GED general study tests today. Maybe, just maybe, she was having a positive influence on someone's life, and she liked the fact that it might be Vince. She wished him well.

It was close to noon, but she wasn't hungry. She didn't want to leave the office before she heard from Denise or Rena. She didn't have to wait long.

"Sorry for getting back to you later than I said, but it took forever to get these crazy people to come to an agreement." Denise sounded exasperated. "Go ahead and sell the house. Shelby will give a share of the proceeds to Darol to help him find a new place; maybe after he gets a job and back on his feet, he can buy his own home. Anyway, we need you to get as much for the house as you can."

"Wait a minute, Denise. Shelby is my client. I'll have to talk with her directly," Hollis said. "Is she there?"

"Er … no. I'll have to have her call you when she gets back." Denise hesitated. "Either way the house can go on the market. That didn't change."

"I'd rather give Shelby an update first. Just have her call me on my cellphone when she gets back," Hollis said.

"Sure … but …."

Hollis rolled her eyes. "What's going on Denise, where's Shelby?"

"She went for a walk; she said she wanted some fresh air." Denise cleared her throat. "We took a vote, and except for one person, we were all in agreement."

"Let me guess. That one person was Shelby."

Denise gave a restrained laugh. "Yes, but she finally caved. She's a bit miffed now, but she'll be okay. I'll tell her to get in touch with you as soon as she returns."

HOLLIS WENT BACK TO HER paperwork. The phone rang. This time it was Todd, who insisted on seeing her that afternoon. She agreed to meet him for lunch at the deli where they had met before.

"Todd, can you give me some idea what you want to see me about?" she said. "I'm ready to file the trust."

"I'd rather talk to you in person," he said. "I've discovered something I think you should know before you file the trust."

On that mysterious note, what could she do but meet with him?

AT THE DELI THERE WERE only a few tables filled with patrons taking a time-out. If Todd was irritated at her lateness, he didn't show it. He was wearing a pair of dark glasses and reading the paper. As she approached the table, he stood up.

"I'm so sorry for being late. The phone rang just as I was going out the door." Hollis breezed in and took the chair across from him.

"Hey, don't worry. It gave me a chance to catch up on the news." He waved the paper. "When you're in prison, you don't think about how much crime there is out here. There are a lot of criminals out on the street."

Hollis laughed at his dark humor. "It can be kind of scary sometimes."

"Look, I have to talk to you about Frances and the trust."

Just then his phone must have vibrated and he glanced at the screen.

"Sorry, I just got a call I need to return, and I think I drank one too many cups of coffee while waiting for you. Give me a few minutes. I won't be long."

"Go on. I can check my email and send a couple of texts."

Hollis settled in.

CHAPTER 22

―❧―

Todd got up and headed toward the rear of the café, asking for directions to the restroom along the way. He walked out of the restaurant's rear kitchen door into a graveled alleyway. Busy checking messages on his cellphone, he was only vaguely aware of a man talking into a cellphone and headed in his direction from the end of the street. Nor did he notice the second figure approaching from the exit door he'd just come through.

He clicked his phone and groaned. The text confirmation he wanted so badly hadn't come through. He was forced to leave a message. He scrolled down his contacts list to find the land-line number. No answer there either. He slid the phone back into his pants pocket and shook off the feeling of unease. This plan had to go through. If things worked out he was going to have his own car soon.

The first blow was a quick karate chop to the base of his head, and before he could slide down to the street, he was lifted by the second man, who stuffed his mouth with a dirty rag. They dragged him into a side alley between the buildings.

He had been beaten up before, in prison. Back then it had

been a noisy business, lots of yelling, swearing and jeering. This was different. The two men were silent, never saying a word as they kicked him several times in the groin and threw repeated punches to his liver and kidneys. Tears poured from his eyes. They stomped his legs and arms, breaking bones as if they were twigs for a fire. He could hear his own terrified screams, of course, but even they were muffled. The blows to his head came last, but they were welcome, because that's when he knew his torment was almost over.

CHAPTER 23

HOLLIS ORDERED ANOTHER CUP OF tea and looked at the time. Todd had been gone for almost twenty minutes. If it wasn't for the fact that she needed to know what he knew about the trust, she would have just left a note telling him they should meet another day. She called the waitress over.

"Have you seen my friend?" she asked. "He's supposed to be making a call in the back."

"Yeah, I did at first but then when I came back for an order he was gone. I think he went out into the alley."

Her heartbeat began to thrash in her ears.

"Which is the way to your rear exit?"

She pointed. "Just follow the doorways on the right."

Hollis left her jacket on the back of the chair and took her purse with her. She pushed down on the metal bar across the exit door, which opened up onto a row of garbage bins behind a row of businesses. She peeked tentatively out into the alley.

"Todd?" she called out.

She thought she heard a rustle of clothing or maybe just footsteps.

"Todd, are you out here?"

She bent down and moved a broken crate over to keep the door propped open. The noise from the restaurant was somewhat reassuring as she took small steps into the center of the alley. The smell was terrible. There was someone going through a bin at the end of the street with a cart full of plastic bottles. Across the way, a homeless man had parked his grocery basket next to another bin and was sorting through cartons of food and boxes. Neither was paying her any attention. She walked a little ways farther down the alley.

"Todd?"

"He's over there." The homeless man—without looking at her or pausing in his search—motioned with his head toward a darkened doorway about fifteen feet away. It was blocked by cardboard containers.

Hollis nodded a thank you and moved gingerly over to the boxes. She kicked one aside, too repulsed by the smell to use her hands. The largest box barely covered the extended bloody leg. She was mesmerized with horror. But she couldn't stop herself—even though she knew she should run away. She kicked away the remaining boxes to reveal Todd's tortured body, and that's when she heard herself scream.

HOLLIS' CRY BROUGHT NO ONE and only caused the alley's homeless visitors to vanish without a trace. She stumbled back into the café and yelled for help even as she was pushing 911 on her phone. The cooks and staff ran out and saw the mangled body and one worker lost his lunch.

She sat in the corner of the café in one of the larger booths. One of the servers brought her a cup of hot tea, and she sipped it absently. The patrons hung back, except for a middle-aged man who identified himself as a school security guard. He asked that everyone stay put until the police came. Most people listened to him, but in the chaos Hollis noticed that the dining area had a few empty tables where diners had been before.

Todd.

Within minutes the sound of sirens cut through the air, bringing a rush of paramedics that burst through the door and headed for the rear of the deli. A customer kept the door open for the equipment and stretcher. There weren't many customers, but the few tables in the way were moved over.

She had no interest in seeing what was happening in the alley. The paramedics had not returned with Todd and were likely waiting for the police forensics team. Then her attention was caught by another set of sirens and the entrance of Detective Mosley and two uniformed officers. One officer stood at the door. Mosley, without looking in her direction, moved quickly to the back along with the other officer.

Hollis slipped down in her seat. She pushed her tea away and waited. Fortunately she didn't have to wait long.

An officer carrying a small notepad came out and spoke to the group. "May I have your attention? There's been a homicide here. We're going to have to question each of you before you can leave." He looked down at the pad. "Does anyone here know a Todd Wallace?"

Heaving a long sigh, Hollis raised her hand.

She was directed to wait in the employee break room. From there she could see customers and employees going in and coming out of the manager's office, which evidently Mosley had commandeered as his interview room. In thirty minutes, the deli had emptied of everyone except the day manager and the forensic team processing the crime scene.

"Ms. Morgan, you do get around," Mosley said, flipping through his notes. "What are your dealings with Todd Wallace?"

"It's the same trust, Detective. The one associated with the Jeffrey Wallace murder. I have no idea why anyone would want to kill Todd."

"Why were you meeting with him?"

"He asked me to meet him here. He said he had something to tell me about the trust." Hollis took a few deep breaths before she added, "But he never got the chance to tell me. What happened? How was he killed?"

"He was beaten to death."

Hollis grimaced.

"Sorry." Mosley looked at her. "Tell me about this trust. What's in it? Why is it a big deal? How does it work?"

"Like any other trust." Hollis shrugged. "Families don't want to have their estate gutted by taxes or lengthy public probate court and fees, so they create a document describing how assets upon the person's death will automatically be distributed to a family member, or whoever, for their lifetime; then whatever assets remain are transferred upon their death immediately to other beneficiaries."

"Was he in the trust?"

"No, that's just it," Hollis said. "Jeffrey left Todd his own inheritance outside the trust."

Mosley stroked his chin, seeming to ponder this information. "So, who gets Todd's estate?"

Hollis paused. "I don't know off the top of my head. It depends on if he left a will or he could even have had his own trust, but I doubt it."

"How large is Todd's inheritance?"

He's looking for a motive.

"Maybe ten to fifteen grand," Hollis said. "Not enough to kill over. I guess he could have other assets I don't know about."

Mosley snorted. "Fifteen grand is a lot, if you're desperate. I've seen people killed for a whole lot less. But this is a little different."

"Why?"

"This murder occurred during the light of day, in a public place, and was a pretty brutal beating .... It is not a random killing. The killer knew he would be here with you and waited for the opportunity to take out Mr. Wallace. And one thing's for sure: he was a professional."

Hollis shivered under her coat.

"Ms. Morgan, did you notice the other customers when you came in? What I'm getting at is, did anyone leave after Todd Wallace went to make his call? Can you remember the people who were here? The server is too upset to help us right now."

Hollis tried to remember. "Is it a closed alley?"

"Yeah, but a few of the businesses are operating. We're checking to see if someone disappeared into one of the other buildings. Some exits were blocked with boxed canned goods—a health violation that will be dealt with later." Mosley's expression was grim. "Ironically, I wouldn't be surprised if the killer was counting on going out the back way but was thwarted by the code violations."

"I don't remember anyone specifically. I had to look around to locate Todd." Hollis tried to think. "There were four tables with customers. The one by the window had four women. The others were just customers by themselves. One man sat in the middle of the room. The other was a table over from Todd and I … there was a table with one woman. Oh, wait, five tables, and there was a couple sitting at the table close to the kitchen." Hollis closed her eyes, visualizing the room. "Yes, I think that's it."

"Nine customers." Mosley shook his head. "But there were only eight when we got here." He looked at her with sympathy. "Ms. Morgan, I have to ask you to come with me to the station."

Hollis nodded numbly.

She'd seen the killer.

CHAPTER 24

HOLLIS WAITED IN THE POLICE interview room for the forensic artist to arrive from downtown Oakland.

She called George, who was still in LA, and explained what had happened. Then she called John.

"You okay?" he asked. "Does Mosley have any crime scene clues?"

"If he did, it's not likely he would share them with me."

John paused. "You know what I'm going to say, don't you?"

"Ah … let me guess. Would it be, let the police do their job?"

"Hollis, promise me," he said. "This is murder, and from what you tell me, it sounds like a pro kill. I'm going to ask Mosley to give you protection."

"Oh no." Hollis was glad John couldn't see her evasiveness. "Now wait a minute, other people were there who didn't know they saw the killer. Anyone could identify him or her."

"But you're the only one who knew the victim."

THE POLICE ARTIST WAS A twenty-something intern who was studying on his own time at the San Francisco Art Academy, surprisingly clean-cut and free of tattoos for his age. He was evidently seeking a public sector career. Mosley had asked each customer to provide a description. After two hours of recounting every person she could remember from the deli, Hollis was drained.

"Don't force it. The computer is going to do the hard work," he said. "It's great you've got a talent for observation. We've gone through your first impressions. Go back and think about what they were doing, their mannerisms. Maybe you could hear their tone of voice. You'd be surprised at how much personal traits contribute to our visual output."

Hollis nodded. "Are you doing this with everyone who was there?"

"Yes, not just me. Two other artists have been brought in. But you got the best." He winked.

Hollis gave him a weak smile.

An hour later Hollis looked over the nine sketches scattered across the conference table. Some were partials—just hair and eyes, or in one case only the back of the head of a woman sitting in the corner. There were two full portraits—one of the man facing her reading the paper, and another of a woman. By recalling her laugh, Hollis noted her wide mouth and single dimple.

"How are we doing?" Mosley came into the room.

The artist nodded. "We're done here. She did good." He packed up his laptop, paper, and pencils. "Let me know when you want to meet to compare mine with the others."

Mosley commented to Hollis, "This is just routine. With computer software, we can do this in minutes instead of days. Don't go far. I want to get this guy today." He sat down across from Hollis. "Ms. Morgan—"

"Please, call me Hollis." She was tired and approaching irritated.

Mosley gave her an acknowledging smile. "Talk to me about Todd Wallace. If he wasn't in the trust and he was being taken care of by his father in his will, why were you talking to him? Why did you get involved?"

"I was 'involved,'" Hollis made air quotes, "because I'm a co-executor, and when you arrested Brian, he wanted me to … to wrap things up. My only connection with Todd Wallace was to verify that he knew the value of the first editions he'd inherited and was giving back."

"Did he change his mind?"

"No. That's why I was a little surprised to hear he wanted to meet with me."

"He said he wanted to tell you something was wrong with the trust?"

"No, I didn't say that." Hollis took a breath. "He didn't say anything was *wrong*, only that he wanted to talk to me about the trust."

Mosley nodded but didn't say anything. Hollis waited him out.

Finally he said, "So under normal circumstances, who would get the first editions?"

"Well, without a will saying otherwise, they would go to his spouse, then children, then parents, then siblings, then a whole line of relations before the law says it lands with the state of California."

"Did he leave a will?"

"I have no idea," Hollis said. "Look, I'm really tired. Can I leave now? I'd like to go home. You can reach me there."

"Sure, sure. You've had a rough day." Mosley pushed back his chair and stood. "But I would appreciate it if you kept me informed of anything you think of later that could be of help. I may need to speak with you again."

Hollis nodded. "Did you learn anything from Frances and Brian?"

He wagged his index finger at her. "You're to keep us informed, Ms. Morgan. Not the other way around."

HOLLIS SOUGHT RELAXATION, SINKING INTO a tub full of bath salts. A glass of Pinot Noir stood within reach on the floor and the bathroom light was dimmed to low. She closed her eyes and breathed in the lavender fragrance. Her brain felt like oatmeal, even as her thoughts shuffled through clues to the Wallace riddle as if trying to make sense of a partial deck of cards. Brian had not returned her call, but had instead left a message on her work phone saying that he and Frances were talking through Todd's funeral arrangements. He went on to say that the police hadn't released the body and that he would call her tomorrow.

Well, it appeared he and Frances could work together on something.

She took a sip of wine and closed her eyes. In moments the deli appeared in her head like a YouTube video. She scanned the visual for faces but nothing specific came through. She opened her eyes. Her cellphone was ringing. She reached for her phone, perched on the edge of the vanity.

"It's me. I hear splashing," John said. "You in the tub?"

A smile crept onto her face. "In all my glory." She paused. "How was your day?"

"It's interesting. I'm learning." He cleared his throat. "Are you nervous about being alone?"

Hollis sniffed. "No, not at all, but I'm really tired. It's another ten days to the probate hearing. If I sound like I'm dragging … it's because I am."

"Oh." He fell silent. "Okay, I'll say goodnight and see you tomorrow."

"Good night," Hollis said. "I love you."

She'd thought about telling him everything that happened, but he'd only worry. And he was in training. What could he do?

Out of the tub and dressed for bed, she poured herself another glass of wine.

Her home phone rang.

"Ms. Morgan?" Mosley's voice sounded like it was next door. "Sorry to disturb you at home so late, but we're going to need you to come down to the station first thing in the morning."

Hollis groaned. "Detective, I don't know any more than I've already told you. I've sat down with your artist; I've emptied my head of any possible leads. Please, I've got to get back to work and my life."

"Yeah, well it's about those sketches you came up with today."

"What about them?"

"When we compared them to the ones provided by the other customers, you're the only one who remembered Man Number Nine."

HOLLIS TURNED ON THE LIGHTS in the firm's lobby, but not before taking a moment to appreciate the sun's rays rising from behind the Oakland Hills and spreading its yellow glow over the silver-blue water of the Bay. She gave a nod to Mother Nature and went down the hallway to her office. She'd come in early before leaving for the police station to find her inbox filled with files tagged with yellow sticky notes from George.

Nothing she couldn't handle, if she could just spend some solid time at work.

There was a small stack of phone messages. Avoiding the temptation of interruptions, she continued to forward her phone to the receptionist desk. Most of the calls she'd already answered; however, a note from Tiffany caught her attention.

"Shelby Patterson came by. Please contact her as soon as you can." There was a number and a small postscript: "What happened to her head?"

So Shelby was in the Bay Area … but she would have to wait until later this morning. Hollis picked up the file with the least amount of research and completed George's assignment with ease. She put it in his inbox. It felt good to actually finish something. She glanced at the clock; it was time to go ID a guy.

MOSLEY WASN'T ALONE. TWO OTHER detectives whose names Hollis didn't catch sat at the table with fixed fake smiles. One was a middle-aged woman, who stared at Hollis with a combination of curiosity and condescension, and a male who didn't look up from his cellphone at all. Tea and water were offered; she declined both.

The sketches hung around the room like a rogue's gallery. Except for one, which only depicted the back of a head, they looked out into the room in silent protest.

"Ms. Morgan, again, thank you for taking the time to come in. I know this is not convenient, but we need your help. We need you to remember as much as you can while the details are still fresh in your mind." Mosley walked around the room until he stood next to the first sketch. "What we'd like you to do is describe the circumstances under which each person was engaged—when and where you saw them."

Hollis realized the sooner she gave them what they wanted, the sooner she could go back to her life. "I understand. For instance, take sketch number one; he was sitting toward the middle of the room. I only remember his eyes and red hair because he was reading the *New York Times*. I remember wondering if he got the paper that morning from the East Coast. He wasn't wearing a wedding ring and I couldn't see the rest of his face." She looked at the faces around the table. "Is that what you mean?"

They all scribbled notes on a pad.

Mosley smiled. "That's it exactly. Only one other customer remembered a man reading a paper, but he couldn't remember the color of his hair or the name of the paper."

He moved to the next sketch.

Hollis stood and walked over to the wall.

"This one and the next three were all sitting together. I couldn't see the face of the blonde with highlights, but the rest looked to me pretty much like you have them here." She pointed to one. "She was bragging about meeting a new guy who's a pilot. The conversation sounded pretty real to me."

Mosley nodded. "Yeah, they're the only ones everyone in the deli agreed on."

Hollis moved to the next sketch.

"This guy was with her." She pointed to two sketches, separated by a third.

Mosley unpinned one from the wall and put them next to each other.

"To me, they seemed fine. Just a couple meeting for lunch—no, make that coffee. They didn't have any plates of food in front of them." Hollis thought back to the day before. "He was wearing some kind of gray security uniform." She looked up. "He was the one who took over the … the scene, and told us he worked security for a school. We all listened to him." She frowned. "At least I didn't notice anyone taking off."

The three exchanged glances.

"What about his companion?"

"She was dressed casually in pants and a floral top. She had these really fancy nails, and she carried a large tote. At one point she took out lipstick and started to apply it." Hollis looked around the room. "Anyway, the server brought their bill and they were getting ready to leave when I went looking for Todd Wallace."

She moved to the next sketch.

Hollis frowned. "He was sitting at the table next to us. He was eating a hamburger and working his iPhone at the same time. He got up to get some napkins. Tall, about one-seventy to one-eighty pounds. He wore dark sunglasses the whole time. He was dressed like he worked in an office. I never heard him talk on the phone, but he did do some texting."

Mosley pointed to the sketch. "That works out. All the women could describe him, but none of the men." He crossed his arms over his chest. "Can you remember if he showed any interest in you and Todd? Did he stay in his seat when Todd went to the bathroom?"

Hollis closed her eyes and tried to picture the deli. "I don't know. I don't remember him getting up at all." She opened her eyes. "I do think he was one of the men who moved the tables back for the paramedics."

Mosley looked pointedly at the others.

He turned to Hollis and pointed to the last sketch. "What can you tell us about this man?"

Hollis squinted at the paper. "I remember him the least. He held open the door for the paramedics bringing in the stretcher. I think he was sitting across from the couple. He was medium build, brown eyes and hair, wore cargo pants and a fitted black T-shirt. He helped push the tables back, too."

Mosley said, "Excuse us a moment." He huddled with the other two.

Hollis sat and waited. Who were these detectives?

"Ms. Morgan," Mosley began, "this is important. No one but you could give a solid description of the last two men. Do you think you might recognize them in a lineup?"

Hollis shrugged. "Maybe. I could try."

WHEN HOLLIS GOT BACK TO the office, she was energized. The police would find Todd's killer, and if her hunch was right, Jeffrey's killer as well. If she could just get a little more information from Mosley …. She had a feeling that since she had proved to be helpful, he might return the favor and give the Fallen Angels the peace of mind they needed.

She picked up the phone and punched in Shelby Patterson's number.

"This is Hollis, Shelby. I got your message. What's going on?"

"Everything is okay, I guess." Shelby sighed dramatically. "I need to see you. Denise said she told you about the family vote. I need to know what happens next."

"I told her that nothing was final until you and I talked." Hollis looked at her calendar. "You can have anytime this afternoon." She glanced quickly through her messages. "I'm looking at an urgent message to call your real estate agent. So I should have some news for you."

They agreed on three o'clock.

Hollis picked through the files on her desk. She needed to

speak with George, but she wanted to be able to hand him a completed assignment first, so he'd be in a good mood. She chose one that was manageable, and an hour later she was done. It was close to lunchtime so she hurried to catch him in his office before he left.

"Good work," George said, speed reading through her legal opinion. "This is a creative treatment for a complex issue. Let me take time go over it in detail. We can talk about it after lunch."

Hollis nodded. "Not a problem, but I have a client meeting this afternoon I have to get ready for. Are you going to be here late?"

"I didn't want to be." George sat back in his chair and steepled his fingers. "Since you only have two clients, I assume it's Shelby Patterson. Brian Wallace doesn't seem to want to leave his house, and he's busy fighting for his freedom."

"You're right; it's Shelby. Her family decided that in order to keep the peace, Shelby would sell the house and give a percentage of the proceeds to her father to get a fresh start."

"How does her father feel about that?" George asked. "Is he willing to settle for anything less than owning the house?"

Hollis shrugged. "Who knows? I haven't heard anything about his reaction. I've been so caught up in the Todd Wallace murder that I haven't had time to check in with the Patterson situation. I'll know after my meeting with Shelby."

CHAPTER 25

⌇⌇⌇

Hollis worked through lunch. Later, she called Kevin Gregg, hoping the realtor had good news for once.

"Well, we had another open house. About fifteen brokers came through. Some weren't too happy with how dated the house is, but everyone was effusive about the views and the amount of backyard. I took the initiative to hire a gardener to clear the back so it can be presented in its best light. He actually took care of the yard when the old lady was alive. You know, I hadn't noticed there was a cottage back there. Once the yard crew got going, there it was—under the overgrowth of ivy and weeds. It doesn't take long for a yard like that to get out of hand—"

"Kevin, I'm sorry, I don't mean to cut you off. Well yes, I guess I do," Hollis said. "The owner is coming into my office shortly and I want to give her a brief report. How are things going with the house sale?"

"It's sold. Is that brief enough for you?" Kevin said. "Yesterday we got two offers, but only one buyer came in with an all-cash deal at five percent over asking price. He wants occupancy in two weeks. He'll accept the house in as-is condition."

"A buyer, yes!" Hollis' fist shot into the air. "That's fantastic. I'm sorry if I was abrupt earlier; it's been a rocky week. You can messenger over the paperwork. No wait, I'll send someone over to pick it up."

"Great. I'll let the buyer know. I'll arrange for the title company tomorrow."

"Who's the buyer?"

"A Darol Patterson. He says he knows the house from when he was a child."

Hollis groaned. "Are you kidding me? Kevin, that's the man who's causing all the trouble for my owner. He doesn't have any money."

"Now, are you kidding me? He seemed solid. Although he did tell me he would have to come back with a deposit check. It didn't register that they have the same last names." Kevin didn't hide the disappointment in his voice. "Well, there's still the backup offer."

"What does the backup offer look like?"

"Hold on, let me get the paperwork. I was so sure," he mumbled. Hollis could hear papers rustling. "Here it is. The buyer's name is Naomi Irving. Do you know her, too?"

Hollis laughed. "No, I don't know her. What's the offer?"

"She's an investor buyer. She's going to rent it out, then sell it when the market goes up a little higher. She gave a low ball offer—fifteen thousand under your asking price."

Hollis grimaced. "I'll have to take the offer to my client. There's no need to consider the first offer, but the second, I will definitely want her to think hard about. Scan me the offer, and I'll get back to you."

"FIFTEEN THOUSAND DOLLARS LESS! No way," Shelby said. "That's almost my tuition for a quarter. I want full price." She swiveled her chair to look out the conference room window with her back to Hollis.

Hollis raised her eyebrows in speculation. "It's up to you,

but who knows how long it will be before you get your asking price? Your tuition is due in six weeks. That means you have to close during that time to get your proceeds."

Shelby shook her head as if not to hear her. "And the family says I have to pay Dad's rent at an apartment, too. It's not fair. Gram gave the whole house to me. She never said I had to share the proceeds with Dad." She slammed her purse on the table. "I can't believe Dad tried to buy the house with no money. What was he thinking?"

Not very much.

"Okay, I understand where you're coming from, but I have an idea," Hollis said. "Push back a little on the investor's offer; tell her you'll take it contingent on her renting back to your father. See if she'll take a deep discounted rent for a good tenant. It's a win-win. She's got a tenant who cares about the place, and you don't have to pay your father as much."

Shelby was silent. Her brow furrowed as she weighed the pros and cons.

Finally, she said, "Hmm … that might work."

Hollis lowered her voice. "And Shelby, what do you think about not pursuing charges against Sonny and Joy? The police are cutting them a deal with firing a gun at the process server. They'll probably spend some time in jail or get a gazillion hours of community service anyway."

"Yeah, Dad told me. I'm not … I'm not sure. At first I thought about what you said about them not thinking straight. Not thinking at all is more like it. But Hollis, they locked me up to make me change my mind. Dad admitted that Sonny and Joy were responsible for the crazy hang-ups, the harassment, even my car in LA for God's sake. They told him they were only trying to help him, and they didn't show me any mercy."

"I know, but you weren't tortured. They fed you, and you were only there for one day. I'm not saying it wasn't the most idiotic thing I've ever heard of, but Shelby, you're getting ready to go to college. Let it go so you can move on."

"Move on. That's easy for you to say," she pouted. "Tell you what. If they apologize to me, not Dad, I'll tell the police I'm not pressing charges." She played with her purse strap. "Oh, Hollis, there's something I haven't told you."

Now what?

"I've always had this feeling that my Grandmother only showed me so much kindness and love to get back at Dad. He's right; she and I really weren't that close." Shelby's shoulders slumped and she said, "If I didn't need this money so much .... Anyway, I guess things worked out. It's just that she wasn't *for* me, she was *against* him. I don't deserve ... I mean ...."

"Don't dwell on it," Hollis said. "Life can be curious." She knew what Shelby wasn't saying or able to articulate. "I didn't know your grandmother. While she may not have been perfect, she was a strong woman, and in a way your stepfather sounds a lot like her. Accept her gift for what it is. I'm going to contact Kevin Gregg today and tell him to move forward as quickly as possible with the Irving offer and your counteroffer. Do you want to go through the house one last time? Is there anything you want to have of your grandmother's?"

"I didn't think of that. Yes, I'd like to find something to remind me of her. Maybe Dad will want to go there too."

After Hollis had Shelby sign a counter offer to the buyer, they agreed to get together the next morning at the house before Shelby caught her flight back to LA.

"If the buyer signs this, you can tell your father that he can return to his home, for a good while anyway."

Shelby gave her a weak smile. "He probably won't thank me for it, but it will be off my conscience."

BACK IN HER OFFICE, HOLLIS felt her shoulders relax as she put the phone down. Kevin had taken the changes to the offer in stride. He was confident that the buyer would agree to the counteroffer.

"We'll schedule a closing by the end of the month," he said.

"It was good working with you, Hollis."

Tiffany gave her a message from Brian that Hollis picked up with a certain degree of foreboding. It said he needed to talk to her. It was the word "needed" that got her thinking. "Needed" versus "wanted." Brian was becoming very needy. The stress of the murder charge must finally be weighing on him.

She picked up the phone again, but before she called Brian back, she wanted to have a conversation with his criminal lawyer, Matthew Kerr. Hollis was pleasantly surprised when he agreed to meet her in his office in a half hour.

"Ms. Morgan, it's good you caught me. I'm going out of town for a few days. What can I do for you and our mutual client?"

Hollis shook his hand and sat. "I'm just about done with the trust. The hearing is a week from today." She licked her lips. "Have you noticed that Brian has been acting more edgy and … and agitated lately? He left me a message today saying he 'needed' to see me. Is there anything going on?"

Kerr swiveled slightly in his chair. "No, things are starting to look up, but I do know what you mean. I've noticed it too."

"Have you found any evidence pointing to the real killer?"

He visibly bristled. "I'm not looking for the real killer. All I have to do is prove to one juror that Brian Wallace didn't do it."

Hollis let the chastisement float over her, but decided to recast her words. "Of course, you only have to worry about reasonable doubt. But in your efforts to defend your client, have you come across any other viable suspects?"

"Perhaps." He seemed to relax a bit. "The argument the police put forth earlier is the most damning—the fact that he owned a gun with the same caliber and had traces of GSR on his clothing. That said, there are at least two other of Jeffrey Wallace's parolees who he recommended be returned to prison. One had gotten the bad news that same week, the other the week before."

"That's good. I mean do they sound more viable than Brian as a suspect?"

"Doesn't matter. That's why I've let the police do their job. Unfortunately they don't feel they have enough yet to charge either one, so Brian is still the prime suspect."

Hollis wasn't as confident that life would sort itself out without some nudging. "It's good that Brian has you for his criminal attorney. I don't think I could leave the investigation in the hands of the police."

He frowned as if deciding whether she was being critical with a back-handed compliment. He stood when she did and stated, "Yes, it's best to work with them and let them do the heavy lifting."

BRIAN LED HER INTO HIS living room and motioned to the loveseat. This time it was clear of clutter. "Thanks, Hollis, for coming over. I haven't been feeling that well lately."

Dressed in sweat pants and a stained gray T-shirt, Brian had dark circles under his eyes and his hair needed a trim. Hollis took a moment to contain her surprise at his appearance.

The drapes were drawn, with only a thin sliver of light slipping in where the panels joined. Hollis again noticed Jeffrey's cat poster leaning against several boxes stacked in the corner.

She pointed to the rear of the room. "I've always hated that poster. I never understood your father's preference for it."

Brian's head jerked in the direction of the subject of her comment. His smile was sardonic as he responded, "Yeah, me neither." He got up and slid it behind the boxes. "Now we don't have to look at it. In a way, though, it says it all, don't you think?"

Hollis frowned. Sitting in the overstuffed loveseat she didn't understand his comment and didn't know what to think. "Brian, I'm sorry about Todd, I know that must be weighing on you."

"The police told me you were with him." He looked at her. "First Dad, now Todd. He'd just gotten out. My attorney thinks it was someone from prison who didn't like him." He wiped his eyes with the back of his hand. "I loved him. He was my big brother, and now my family is all gone."

Hollis reached over to the side table and placed a tissue box in front of him.

"I was curious why you had to see me right away. If you're not feeling well, you could come to my office almost anytime, or we could have talked on the phone."

"No, I don't go out much since …."

He didn't finish the sentence and instead offered her a bottle of water from a tray on the table. Hollis waved it away.

The silence was heavy between them. Hollis cleared her throat and said, "What's the matter, Brian? Why did you need to see me?"

He got up and walked over to the draped windows as if he could see out. "You remind me of my dad, do you know that?" He turned to face her. "I mean the words you use … what you say … the way you say things."

"I guess he rubbed off on me." Hollis furrowed her brow. "Jeffrey saved my life. He saved a lot of lives. That's why we're helping you."

He nodded rapidly. "Yeah, yeah, I know."

"It's getting late. Why did you need to see me, Brian?"

He ran his hand over his head. "What happens to the trust if something happens to me?"

She took a deep breath. For this he could have picked up the phone and asked her. "We've already been through this. There's a line of secession dictated by the state. As the co-executor I would make sure that the proper steps were followed. What are you really asking me?"

"I guess I'm just nervous about my criminal court hearing. Maybe … maybe I'll have to go to jail." He looked woeful. "What happens to the estate then, especially now that Todd is … is gone?"

Hollis thought a moment. She knew he didn't want to hear

the answer. "Brian, I think you know that answer. But I talked to your attorney. He's confident you won't be convicted." Hollis moved to the edge of the loveseat. "Besides, I know you don't care for Frances, but the trust holdings aren't that big. Even if … even if she is able to have the first use of the funds, there's just not that much."

"You keep saying that."

"That's because as estates go, your father's is on the low end." She paused. "Is there something you're not telling me?"

He shook his head. "No, I think it's Frances who's not telling."

CHAPTER 26

———— ⁓⁓ ————

HOLLIS SAT IN HER CAR in front of the Patterson house and looked pensively at the large residence, with its family stories and secrets. The fog was slowly beginning to burn away on the East Bay side but San Francisco was still fogged in.

She jumped at the tap on her car window.

"Morning, Hollis." Shelby smiled. "Thanks for meeting us here. Dad brought me. He got one of those throw-away cameras so he can take pictures."

Darol stood at the foot of the front steps looking at Hollis as if pleading for her not to bring up the events of the past few days. Then he turned away and took a picture of the house.

Hollis knew that she would never understand the ins and outs of this father-stepdaughter relationship. Its only consistency was its inconsistency. Shelby had agreed not to press charges against Darol but wasn't convinced that Sonny and Joy should not be held accountable.

Hollis got out and locked the car. "Good morning," she said. "Hello, Darol. We need to get going, Shelby. I know you have a plane to catch."

Shelby moved up the steps and opened the door.

Darol walked up to Hollis. "Er ... ah, I'm sorry for all the mess my kids created. I didn't know ... I mean I didn't think they would ...." He licked his lips. "I've done some real stupid things out of desperation—the real estate offer, I mean. She told me you talked her into giving me the opportunity to rent the house. Thank you."

"You're welcome." Hollis shrugged. "I'm glad it turned out to be okay."

They went through the house, room by room. It didn't take long. Darol took pictures, some with Shelby standing next to some memento, but most without her.

"Dad, look ... there's a shed in the back. I forgot it was there." Shelby stood, looking out the kitchen window. "Let's go outside."

Hollis followed behind the two of them. She had never really looked at the yard either. The gardener had cleared the overgrowth and trimmed the grass. The grass was brown and patchy but clipped and presentable. A small shed stood in the far corner of the yard.

"This used to be my mother's garden room," Darol said.

Hollis heard Shelby gasp when she entered.

"Oh wow, this is cool. Dad, look at this," Shelby said in amazement.

But Darol was already looking. The medium-sized room was filled with pictures and posters of him playing sports, receiving trophies, and posing with classmates. There was a tall shelf of toys and a stack of child-drawn pictures. Another held record albums, tape cassettes, and CDs. Against the wall was a coat rack containing a few clothes covered in plastic to keep the dust off. It was a shrine of pride built by a mother for her son. Hollis walked around to look at each mini exhibit.

Peering around the room, Darol was silent. Shelby snapped his picture.

"Dad, look at this! Did you play the saxophone?"

He nodded, but said nothing as he picked up what looked to be a class ring.

Hollis observed him moving slowly around the shed. His eyes traveled around the table tops, taking everything in, over and over.

Soon Shelby, noticing his silence, quieted.

"Dad, you okay?" She came and took his arm. "Grandmother must have loved you a lot to turn this into a space …. It's almost a museum, really, dedicated to you. All these … things … all these things that belonged to you when you were growing up." She pointed around the room. "While you're renting, you should take them out of here. I don't think we should leave them behind for strangers to throw away." She gently ran her fingers over a clay jar.

"I didn't know," he said, his expression solemn.

Finally he glanced at Shelby and nodded agreement. Then he gave Hollis a long look, tears brimming in his eyes, and walked heavily back into the light of day.

From her car, Hollis watched father and daughter embrace each other for a long moment. With irritation, she blinked away a tear attempting to form in her own eye, and as she watched them drive away, she knew one chapter was ending and another beginning.

CHAPTER 27

———

THE FALLEN ANGELS SAT RESTLESSLY around the library conference table.

"First Jeffrey and now his son—both gone in less than six weeks," Gene said. "Hollis, what's your read on why Todd was killed?"

She shrugged. "Probably for the usual reason; he knew too much. Or he stumbled onto somebody's secret."

Miller paused with a crane. "You think Frances killed him?"

"I don't know." Hollis frowned in concentration. "I don't think so. She doesn't strike me as someone who likes to get her hands dirty, but she's involved somehow."

"Well, does anybody have any ideas about what we're going to do about Jeffrey's killer?" Rena asked. "Where do we go from here?"

Richard sucked on a tooth. "Maybe we've got it all wrong. Maybe Jeffrey was killed by someone we haven't thought of—someone who didn't mean to kill him." He raised his hand to forestall the coming protests from his fellow Angels. "I know it was premeditated, but maybe it had nothing to do with the trust, and nothing to do with his caseload."

"Where are you going with this?" Gene asked with a hint of irritation.

"For instance," Richard said, "what if Jeffrey had a mistress?"

"Jeffrey?" Miller said shaking his head.

"There's no way." Rena gave him a high sign. "Not Jeffrey. He never struck me as someone who even cared about a personal life."

Hollis said with a raised voice, "And yet he married twice, raised two sons and lived a very real family life."

"Do you know that or are you just making it up?" Gene asked. "I mean about the family life. Neither of his two sons appear to be particularly warm, and while I don't know what his first wife was like, Frances doesn't come off as being particularly affectionate either."

"That's what I'm saying. Maybe he went elsewhere for companionship," said Richard.

"So, are we saying that his mistress killed him because they had a falling out or because he wouldn't leave Frances for her?" Miller finished another crane and added it to a small stack.

"Exactly," Richard said.

Hollis stood. "I think we're getting way off track. Let's just look at what we do know. Jeffrey is murdered. Brian hires us to check out Frances and the trust. A trust I shouldn't need to remind you does not rival the Rockefellers'; in fact just the opposite. Frances, while clearly able to hold back any feelings of grief, appears to have spent all of five minutes mourning the loss of her husband. She has moved on with her life with amazing speed to partner in a casino. Then the police arrest Brian, who seems convinced that he's not going to jail even though there are no other real suspects." She walked from one end of the table to the other and back again. "And that's another interesting point—why aren't there other suspects?"

"That's what I'm talkin' about. Jeffrey may have had a mistress." Richard responded.

"I'm sorry Richard, but I just don't get that feeling," Rena said. She sat back down and slapped the table. "I just had an idea. Suppose Frances owed money to her gambling buddies and they took it out on Jeffrey as a warning."

"That wasn't just a warning; that was the end," Gene said.

Hollis nodded. "I know, but maybe things got out of hand. And here's where I agree with Rena: they didn't mean to kill Jeffrey but maybe things escalated."

"Hollis, not that I doubt your deductive skills, but wouldn't the police have found something that points to a gang or mob hit?" Gene said. "And Rena, don't correct me. I know your contacts aren't necessarily the mob."

"Not necessarily," Richard said under his breath so that only Hollis could hear.

Rena added, "And you'd think a mob hit would not be a messy stomach wound; it would be a head shot."

Gene raised his eyebrows. "Good point."

Miller pushed his glasses up on his nose. "Do the police have any clues about Todd's killer?"

Hollis started to shake her head, but then shrugged. "Maybe ... I don't know. I promised not to interfere in police business, remember?" Her thoughts drifted back to that day in the restaurant. "Todd and I were talking and then he was gone. I still can't believe it, and I still can't figure out how the killer knew we would be there."

"But you yourself said you were able to help the police identify the potential killer," Gene said. "I think they owe you some information sharing."

Hollis sat down again and picked up her pen. "If we step back and put Richard's premise of a mistress on hold ... let's suppose whoever killed Jeffrey also killed Todd. Messy or not, maybe Jeffrey's messy killing couldn't be helped."

"So now the finger points to Frances," Richard said. "She definitely had motive, means, and—who knows?—opportunity. Jeffrey, and now Todd." He shook his head. "Seems a bit too much, but from what you've told us about her, I agree with you. My gut tells me she's just greedy, not homicidal."

"If all this is correct, wouldn't that put Brian in line for being knocked off?" Rena asked. "I would think that if Frances wants the trust processed as quickly as possible, he's the only one left in her way." She gestured a time-out with her hands. "I know, Hollis, it's not big enough to fight over, but it sure holds a fascination for a lot of people. And Brian wants to make sure Frances isn't up to something. Well, wouldn't Brian be a problem?"

"No, he wouldn't," Hollis said, "because Frances has use of all the proceeds for the term of her life; then the remainder passes to Brian. Brian was no threat to Frances."

"What about the divorce?" Gene asked.

"What about it?" Hollis said.

"Well, she was leaving him anyway." Gene held his pen as a pointer for an unseen board. "Did she agree to come up with the money for the casino before or after she filed for divorce— and more interestingly, before or after Jeffrey was killed?"

Hollis bit her lip and stared at him. "Gene, you're a genius." She turned to Rena. "Will you take me to your connections? I'd like to talk to them directly. I can't think of all my questions ahead of time."

Rena gave a small laugh. "My 'connections'? You make it sound like my connections are the criminal underground. It's just my cousin Nate. His business card says 'financial consultant,' but the family knows he's a bookie—a bookie, not a gangster."

"Okay then, can you set up a meeting with Nate?" Hollis asked. "Can you make it happen this evening or maybe first thing in the morning? The trust hearing is next Thursday."

RENA HAD SLIPPED OUT OF the Fallen Angels meeting, called her cousin, and asked him to meet them right afterward. Nate Gabriel's office was located at the back of one of the oldest and most popular barber shops in East Oakland.

As backroom offices went, Nate's was clean, orderly, and filled with enough electronics to make any Silicon Valley techie proud. He looked to be in his forties—he was starting to bald and beginning to show a bulging middle. Like so many in Rena's family, he had a smooth *café au lait* complexion. However, he had the build and stature of a linebacker.

Rena and Hollis entered the office from the rear of the building. Hollis wasn't clear if that was to shelter her from the eyes of the customers or the other way around. Nate and Rena exchanged hugs, and Hollis shook Nate's outstretched hand. The man towered over them both.

"Miss Morgan, good to meet you. Have a seat. Would you like some coffee?"

Hollis smiled. "Please call me Hollis. And no, thank you, I'm fine."

"Hollis drinks tea, Nate," Rena said. "Do you have any tea?"

He gave a small chuckle. "As a matter of fact, I drink tea too." He opened a small cabinet behind the desk. "Oolong, green, white, or jasmine?"

Hollis smiled broadly and shook her head. "I hate to say no to a fellow tea drinker, but really, nothing for me."

He motioned for them to sit and then took the seat behind his massive desk. "Well then, what can I do for you two?" He looked from Rena to Hollis and back to Rena.

"I'll start and let Hollis finish up," Rena said. "You remember I told you about my ex-parole officer and how he was murdered. You helped me get some information on Frances Wallace, and it helped us narrow down what she might be up to, but we still haven't been able to figure out exactly what she's got going on."

Rena and Hollis had just enough space between two computer monitors for them to see Nate's pensive look.

"What can I tell you?" he asked, crossing his arms over his chest. He looked at Hollis. "Frances is game enough to play with the big boys. I didn't really know her until Rena asked me to look into her gambling habit, and she has a nice one. But she keeps it together. I would say she's more of an investor than a player. She doesn't play against the house; she wants to *be* the house."

Hollis leaned forward. "But where does she get her money?"

Nate shrugged. "Remember, I said she 'wants' to be the house. Frances doesn't have any long money, but she's hanging out with people who do." He started to rock back and forth in his office chair. "You want my opinion? These people are tolerating her for now because it's not costing them. Frances is like an intern. She wants to learn and she has good organizational skills that are always needed in our business. And more importantly—"

Just then his cellphone trilled one of the latest pop hits.

Nate looked down at the caller. "Excuse me for just a moment."

They got up. He motioned for them to stay.

Rena and Hollis sat with their hands in their laps and pretended not to listen. They didn't have to pretend long. The conversation on Nate's end consisted of one word, "No." He clicked off.

"Now, where was I?" he asked.

Hollis smiled. "You were talking about Frances' aspirations and administrative abilities. But I have a different question. Could these business people get anxious enough to kill if they thought someone was standing in the way of Frances coming up with her share?"

Nate pursed his lips and he didn't say anything for a long moment. When he did speak, he spoke as if he thought Hollis could be wearing a wire. "I don't know anybody who does hits." He turned to Rena. "And I don't know much more than what I've already told you."

Hollis sensed his sudden reticence. "Nate, did Rena ever tell you how we met?" Hollis smiled.

"Er … no. She told me you were a lawyer. Why?"

Rena rubbed her mouth with her fingers in a vain attempt to hide her smile.

Hollis said, "I've served time. Rena and I shared that ex-parole officer she mentioned. And believe me, I know about the business."

"Well, well." Nate tilted his head and peered at her with a new speculation. "Okay then, we understand each other and the circumstances we're dealing with."

Rena leaned in. "Nate, if there was any question about Hollis, I wouldn't have brought her to see you."

He shrugged.

Hollis held her hand out. "Hey, I trust very few people, so I understand. Would it be possible for you to find out when Frances actually got involved with the casino deal in Nevada? We could use an actual date, or at least the week she started showing real interest."

He nodded. "Hmmm, sure, I can try to find out." He leaned forward. "But I can tell you that the deal is legit. I know some of the people involved and they are on the up and up. Despite what you read in the papers, these are solid businessmen who can't afford to be on the wrong side of the law."

He looked at Rena. "Check back with me in the morning, that is, if you don't hear from me tonight."

HOLLIS LOOKED OVER AT JOHN. His slight snore made her smile. He'd surprised her by coming home early from his training; she had only beaten him home by minutes. Dinner was her favorite takeout Chinese chicken salad. They both were tired and had almost fallen asleep at the table.

She touched his bare shoulder with her finger as if to make sure he was really there. He shifted slightly, but the snoring continued. She lay back and smiled. It felt good to have him in her bed, and she looked forward to their weekend together. She was glad their relationship wasn't defined by artificial conversation and could handle the intimacy of silence. She wanted to wake him and give him a big hug. She wondered if they lived together if it would be this comfortable, this much love every day. But no, she knew better. She'd been married before, in love before, betrayed before.

She couldn't sleep. Reaching for her robe and slippers, she slipped out of bed and went into the kitchen. She punched numbers into the phone.

"Hollis, what's wrong? Why are you calling me so late? It's after midnight." Stephanie's voice sounded sleepy and mildly irritated.

"I need your help." Hollis walked around her kitchen pulling out two leftover chicken wings from the refrigerator.

"Why are you whispering?"

"Because John is upstairs and he probably wouldn't …. I don't want him to know what I'm up to."

She yawned. "What are you up to?"

"First thing in the morning, can you find out what Mosley has on Brian Wallace?" Hollis crossed her fingers.

Stephanie howled, "Oh, no. How am I supposed to do that? This is an active investigation. I'm in the Forensics Division, not Operations."

"Listen, Brian is already arrested. I missed the initial arraignment when he was charged; otherwise, I could have gotten an idea of what the DA had. So, it's probably public information anyway. I just need to know what everybody else does."

Stephanie was awake now. "I heard about what happened to Todd Wallace from the other forensic team. Did you learn something the police don't know? Is there more going on?"

"Will you please help me?"

"Probably, but answer me this," Stephanie said. "Why can't you get this information from Brian's defense attorney?"

"You're my backup. He's my next stop."

EARLY IN THE MORNING HOLLIS found herself back downstairs in the kitchen. She made a cup of white tea and moved to sit outside on the balcony. The sun was just coming up. She sighed in contentment, taking a deep sip of the hot tea.

"Dollar for your thoughts?" John said, pulling out the chair next to hers, glass of orange juice in hand.

"They're worth at least five dollars," she said, smiling. "Say, I may be able to take off early today. I've got just a little paperwork to take care of and a quick meeting with another attorney. Why don't we play hooky? Let's make it a slow day. I'll be home early."

"That sounds like a great plan." John squeezed her shoulder. "I deserve the time off since I haven't been home for three consecutive days since I took this job. And there's a little paperwork I need to take care of as well."

"Let's meet back here when you're done," Hollis said. "Maybe this time I'll be back before you."

Hollis dressed quickly. John had already left before she had gotten out of the shower. She still made it to the office early and glanced through the case George left on her desk. This one was more serious. She was glad the Shelby Patterson house was fast on its way to closing escrow and she could close the matter. Now if she could just lay Jeffrey's murder to rest.

HOLLIS DIDN'T HAVE ANY TROUBLE confirming a second meeting with Brian's attorney. Matthew Kerr seemed friendlier toward her than during their last brusque encounter. He offered to take her to lunch so they could talk. When Hollis declined, he didn't seem bothered and offered to come to her office.

"I've never been in this building before," he commented, looking out the window at the Bay. "You've got a better view than we do."

Hollis nodded. "It's one of the great perks of this job."

She handed him a cup of coffee.

"Thank you for coming here," she said. "I won't take up much of your time. It's just that this seemingly simple trust has some big question marks, and now with Todd Wallace's death, well … I don't want to rush things. I may need a continuance."

Kerr nodded. "I can understand your caution. But Todd's death does a lot to point the guilt away from Brian."

Hollis frowned. "What do you mean?"

"Surely it must have occurred to you that whoever killed Todd, killed his father," Kerr said. "Todd was an ex-con, and Jeffrey Wallace sent a lot of people back to prison. They never found the gun. His son's killing was retribution and it was payback time."

Hollis leaned back in her chair and thought a moment. "But Jeffrey was murdered first. Wouldn't whoever was seeking retribution want him to be alive when they killed his son, so he could suffer?"

Kerr shrugged. "Or, it could be that the killer wanted Todd to suffer by seeing his father murdered first," he said. "Either way, I'm meeting with the DA to see about letting Brian go free. It's clear now that there are a lot stronger motives out there, and that their case against my client is weak."

"Has Brian shared with you his reasoning for having me involved in the handling of the trust?"

"Yes," Kerr said. "He told me about his concerns over Frances Wallace. We did some checking into her background and picked up on her gambling affiliations, but she'd already filed for divorce. Jeffrey Wallace was not contesting. There was no motive for her to murder her husband or her stepson. Then, of course, she withdrew the filing after the killing."

"That's all true," Hollis said. "Matthew, can I see the material the DA has against Brian? I think it could help me with the trust."

"How so? I don't see the connection."

It is a stretch.

"If I don't turn over every stone and find a reason not to process the trust, I'll have no other alternative but to file it next week."

He gave her a long, sideways look. "Your doggedness is

admirable. Irritating, but admirable. I really don't follow your line of thinking at all, but I'm confident that the DA will drop charges against Brian. So, if it helps you make our mutual client happy, I see no harm."

Hollis gave him her most brilliant smile. "Thank you."

"I take it you wanted it yesterday." Kerr got up to leave. "Tell you what—let's exchange information. I've looked at the trust. It's pretty standard. But whatever you've turned up in your own explorations might prove helpful if Mosley doesn't change direction from Brian. Send me your notes and I'll send you my copy of the DA file."

HOLLIS CONFIRMED WITH VINCE THAT he would deliver a copy of the Wallace trust and a summary of her notes to Matthew Kerr as part of his regular delivery run. He would then return with Kerr's copy of the police file material on Brian.

"How's the GED exam study going?" she asked.

Vince smiled. "Good, real good. I passed all the general study tests and I'm supposed to take the actual overall GED exam at the adult school next Saturday."

He'd cut his hair and sported a new olive-green hoodie. Hollis also noticed he'd added a couple of much-needed pounds.

"Best of luck." Again, she almost reached over to hug him but thought better of it when she saw him prepare to stiffen. Instead, she patted him on his arm and repeated, "Best of luck."

A flush crept across his cheeks. He took the large envelope and left.

Her phone rang. It was Mosley.

"Ms. Morgan, you've been a tremendous help to us already, but we could use your help again."

Hollis didn't bother telling him to use her first name. "What is it, Detective?"

"We think we have the men who killed Todd Wallace. We'd like you to come down and view a lineup."

Hollis had a flashback to several years before when she had

her first experience with a lineup. Only then, she was the one holding the card for witness identification. She also wondered if Kerr's plan to link the murders had gotten to Mosley. She certainly wasn't going to be the one to tell him.

"Yes, that won't be a problem. When did you want me to see me?"

"We will be ready for you at one o'clock ... and thank you."

Hollis was relieved she could still get home early.

It was clear that by the time Hollis arrived at the station that afternoon, Mosley had finally gotten the word about the Kerr/Wallace defense strategy.

He was not happy, and he seemed preoccupied.

"Please remain in the waiting room until we're ready," he said shortly, only briefly acknowledging that he'd inconvenienced her before going back behind the door to the office area and locking it behind him.

Hollis checked her phone for messages and decided not to return the one from John just yet.

But she was puzzled by the next two calls. They were both hang-ups. The last one, the caller stayed on the line for a long moment—she could sense, if not hear, someone on the other end. Then the hang-up.

But Shelby's case was over.

"Ms. Morgan, please come this way." A young female officer held open the door and gestured for Hollis to follow.

The line-up room wasn't quite like the one she remembered from her own participation years ago. It was narrow and dark. The almost full wall window opened out onto a well-lit section with a glaring wall of white containing height lines and placement numbers. Mosley was standing in the corner talking on the phone and gestured for Hollis to take one of the three front-row seats. The officer sat down with a pad of paper and pen.

"Okay, let's get started." He spoke into a mic on a desk at the far end of the room.

Out came seven unsmiling men, wearing casual clothing. Hollis peered at each one. Mosley asked them to turn, come forward, and step back.

"Well?" he urged.

"Detective, I've been on the other side of that plastic wall. I think I should take my time."

He grunted and sat back in his chair and waited.

"I recognize two men—number three and number seven." She was comfortable with her certainty.

"That's our guys. The sketches were right on," Mosley said with the first smile of the day. "Thank you, Ms. Morgan."

Hollis gathered her purse and briefcase. "Er ... do they have a motive for killing Todd?" She tried to make her question sound as offhand as possible.

Mosley picked up his folders and papers without looking at her. "Yeah ... yeah, we have a motive. Didn't you hear? Todd Wallace rubbed a few people the wrong way in prison." Then he mumbled some words under his breath.

"I'm sorry, Detective. What did you say?"

He looked at her and repeated, "Or so they want us to believe."

"But you don't believe it was a payback killing?"

Mosley slammed his binder shut. "No, I don't believe it. Why didn't they take care of him when he got out? Why wait until months later? And the link to his father's death is—"

"Todd's death can be linked to Jeffrey's death?" She hoped she carried off the look of disbelief.

"It's too neat," he said. "I don't like 'neat,' and in this case I don't believe in 'neat.' But Brian Wallace has himself an expensive lawyer. Don't listen to me, Ms. Morgan. Anyway, I've done my job. It looks like they're going to drop the charges against Brian."

Hollis thought it best to remain silent.

"Thank you for coming down and making a solid identification. I don't think we'll be bothering you anymore."

He opened the door for her to pass into the hallway.

She gave him a small smile. "You know, Detective, I don't like 'neat' either."

HOLLIS WAS JUST ABOUT TO leave for home when Rena called.

"I just got off the phone with Nate, He apologized for taking longer than he thought," she said. "Frances Wallace, using her maiden name of Cole, sat down with key potential owners about three months ago. Nate said it was the week before Easter. Evidently she hasn't come up with her share yet, but they are relying on her to step up soon. In fact, Nate said they're putting major pressure on her to deliver the bucks."

"Just over three months ago … that's also when she filed for divorce. This isn't making any sense."

"It sounds like this is the reason she wants you to hurry up and file."

"That I get, but where's the money … where?"

CHAPTER 28

~~~

THE AFTERNOON AND EVENING OF relaxed nothingness with an equally relaxed John was just what Hollis needed. They held to an unspoken agreement to avoid talking about the future of their relationship and simply enjoyed the day.

The next morning Hollis walked into her office and saw the thick manila envelope that Vince had retrieved from Matthew Kerr. She moved files aside, making room to pull out the contents. Most were the same pictures John had already gotten for her. A black and white photo of Jeffrey's office showed his desk covered with a few files and his bookshelf holding more certificates and memorabilia than books.

She froze when she came to the photo of Jeffrey's figure, face down on the floor and outlined in white chalk. Memories of their conversations—more like his lectures and her protestations—came flooding back. Still, she knew he was proud of her and she had grown to care for him. She skipped over the close-up pictures of the wound.

There was a hefty police report that included more pictures, but Hollis was more interested in the narrative. It was evident why Brian had been arrested so quickly. Although it had not been found, the gun that killed Jeffrey was the same caliber as Brian's gun on file. Based on the spray of gunshot residue, Jeffrey had allowed the killer to come close—almost face to face. And like Mosley said, they hadn't found any GSR on Brian's person, but they did find some on his shoes. The police report pointed out that he had plenty of time to shower and get rid of or clean off any residue.

Fortunately Brian had not agreed to answer questions without his lawyer. In Kerr's notes he commented that Brian had misplaced his gun, and he had worn the shoes to the gun range the day before the police came to arrest him.

There were also interview notes from Kerr indicating that Brian's employer stated that up to the time of Jeffrey's death, Brian was a fine employee. His good character was confirmed in interviews with Frances and Brian's neighbors and friends.

When Kerr questioned Brian about the argument he had with his father, Brian's responses seemed plausible. He recounted their conversation matter-of-factly. He said his father agreed to help him get a house if he stayed on a budget. Jeffrey knew that Brian wanted to get married, and didn't have a problem with the young lady. After Brian and his fiancé located a house, Brian went to his father to ask him to sell one of the first editions, and evidently Jeffrey had reneged.

Hollis frowned.

Jeffrey never reneged.

The notes went on to explain Brian's alibi. He was working out of his house, preparing for a big sales presentation to a major customer. Hollis flipped through the medical and psych exam Brian's attorney had ordered. She had to agree he had a strong case for Brian's innocence. It was clear the police were fishing and just wanted to have someone on the hook. She could easily see why the arrest wouldn't stick, especially now that they had two more likely suspects.

Hollis leaned back in her chair, rocking slightly, and looked out her window to the high rises that filled her view. Her thoughts went back to the report, reviewing the facts and the assumptions. She stopped rocking.

Jeffrey never reneged.

"Richard," Hollis held the phone to her ear with her shoulder as she shuffled through papers, looking for the correct page in the police report. "Can you run a credit report on Brian Wallace?"

"Our client?"

"Yeah, and is there any way you can get a copy of his bank statements? He's made or is trying to make an offer for a house. He banks at East Bay Valley."

"I'm not sure about the bank statements unless he's released them for his credit check."

"Do what you can and get back to me as soon as you can."

"Of course, *mon capitaine*."

"Very funny."

SHE WAS BEING WATCHED, NOT stalked, but she felt someone was keeping tabs on her. A face she had seen in the lobby was now at a table across from her in a café.

FOF … Friends of Frances.

It was all part of some intimidation game, but clearly those involved didn't know they were picking on the wrong person. She looked at her cellphone. She'd agreed to meet Brian at his home that afternoon, but she was following up with meeting Stephanie for lunch first.

"You're treating, and I want everything on the left side of the page," Stephanie said, folding the menu back in place.

Hollis nodded. "All right."

Stephanie frowned. "Wait a minute; you're not protesting. What's wrong?"

"Nothing. You've been good enough to do me a big favor, and I'm just saying thank you."

"Hmmm … well, maybe we should eat first before I tell you what I found out." Stephanie went back to the menu.

Hollis held back her curiosity because she knew it would do little good to rush Stephanie. If anything, Stephanie would hold out longer, knowing how eager Hollis was to hear her information. They chatted about their jobs and Hollis and John's relationship.

"That's what I want to manifest—a committed relationship." Stephanie wiped her mouth and pushed her empty plate to the side. "Aurelia says he's coming toward me now."

For a second time Hollis held her tongue and quick retort. "You deserve to have a good man."

"Okay, that's it." She laughed. "I've made you suffer long enough. Now, Hollis, I can't leave this information with you and no, before you ask, I can't make any copies, but I can point out some things to you that I found ... interesting." She brought out a thin folder from her purse. "You know that Jeffrey Wallace was shot in the stomach at close range. But there is something I found curious—his office wasn't tossed. Why not?"

Hollis shrugged. "I get it. Somebody's going to toss an office because they're looking for something or there's been a fight, or as Mosley insists, out of a burst of anger."

"Right." Stephanie nodded. "Second, there's a lot of pressure from on high for the Deputy DA to put this case to bed. Because the proverbial runs downhill, he in turn is putting the screws to Mosley. I've read Mosley's notes; he's convinced Brian did it."

Hollis sat back in her seat. "Stephanie, I think Mosley is going to let Brian go. He's got two suspects in the Todd Wallace murder that they've linked to Jeffrey's killing. I wasn't so confident that a link existed but ...." She shrugged.

Stephanie's brow furrowed. "Then that's curious too."

"Why?"

"Because ... two men ready to kill an ex-con and one very ordinary civil servant? There's no money in it. Who's got the money? There is something very *un*-ordinary going on." Stephanie held up her hands. "Now don't get upset. I know that Jeffrey Wallace was just shy of being a saint in your mind."

"Stephanie, what are you talking about?"

"My third discovery," she said. "Jeffrey Wallace was having an affair."

HOLLIS WALKED BACK TO WORK in a daze. Richard's speculation had been right.

She patted her purse with the contact information Stephanie had handed her from the police file. It indicated that Patrice Leoni—divorcée from San Francisco, mother of one adult daughter, retired social worker, and avid golfer—had been having an affair with Jeffrey Wallace for the past two years.

Stephanie was wrong about one thing: Hollis didn't think less of Jeffrey. In fact, after her meetings with Frances, she could well understand his attraction to someone who really cared about him. If Patrice was a good lady, Hollis was glad for him. She also understood that staying in his marriage—even reluctantly agreeing to make a trust to ensure Frances would be okay—was also Jeffrey's way. He kept his commitments, no matter what.

Hollis took out the paper with Leoni's number and closed the door to her office. Patrice Leoni's phone rang several times before bouncing to voicemail. Hollis hesitated before leaving a message.

"Miss Leoni, my name is Hollis Morgan, I'm a friend of Jeffrey Wallace's and I understand you—"

"Wait, wait," Patrice said, turning off her answering machine. "Ms. Morgan, are you still there?"

"Ms. Leoni? Yes, I'm still on the phone. I'm sorry to bother you, but I understand you were a … a friend of Jeffrey's and I was wondering if I could visit you. I have just a few questions."

"First, call me Patrice," she said. "And if you're calling me, you already know about my relationship with Jeffrey." Her voice sounded choked. "You could come over now if you'd like."

"That would be wonderful," Hollis said and then realized it

probably wasn't the right tone; she sounded too formal. "And please call me Hollis."

Hollis made a rush call to Gene and told him about her upcoming meeting.

"We're running out of time. Can you run a check on Patrice Leoni?" Hollis asked him. "Oh, and call the Angels together for Monday. See how many can attend, and I'll make space in my schedule."

Gene said, "I can't believe it. Not so much the having someone on the side ... I'm not a prude. But Jeffrey seemed so ... so not interested."

"Well, then we both were wrong."

CHAPTER 29

PATRICE LEONI LIVED IN A Victorian flat in the Dogpatch section of San Francisco, near its central waterfront district and nearby AT&T Park. It was an old neighborhood in the middle of gentrification. Artist's lofts and a bevy of new eateries sprouted monthly, prospered by growing word-of-mouth foot traffic and energized by popular appeal. In a few years the transition to another high-rent district in the City would likely be complete. Hollis just hoped it wouldn't lose its funky charm.

"Come in," Patrice said. She was a small-boned mixed heritage Asian woman who seemed unimpressive on first glance, until she smiled. Her expressive brown eyes and two deep dimples changed her from ordinary to extraordinarily attractive. She wore her jet-black shoulder-length hair in a page boy. It was hard to tell her age. She could be thirty; she could be fifty.

She led Hollis into an open-spaced living and dining room area, where she pointed Hollis to an overstuffed chair by the window. The room was decorated in a comfortable eclectic style. The furnishings weren't fancy, but they had been picked with deliberate care.

"Thank you for seeing me on such short notice," Hollis said. "I'm so sorry for your ... for your loss."

Patrice nodded. "From what I understood from Jeffrey, it's your loss, too. He talked about you, the whole book club actually—what do you call yourselves?"

"The Fallen Angels."

"Yes, the Fallen Angels, but he talked about you the most. He was very proud of you. He said that if he just had one success, he hoped it was you. He admired what you had done with your life." She looked off, past Hollis. "He was here when he drafted the recommendation letter to the court for your pardon."

Hollis felt a rush of heat go to her face. That letter was one of the main reasons she was an attorney. She said, "I messed up my life, and Jeffrey brought me back, so I owe him ... everything."

"I'm not sure he would want that responsibility. Knowing him, your debt has been paid." She gave Hollis a sad smile. "Let me guess why you are here. You want to know about our affair."

"No, your relationship with Jeffrey is your business. I want to know if there is anything you can tell me about who you think killed him."

Patrice looked away and fingered the fringe along the edge of a sofa pillow.

"Have you met Frances?"

Hollis frowned. "Yes. I'm the co-executor for Jeffrey's trust. I've had two or three conversations with Frances."

"I've never met her. I did see her once, from a distance. She was a guest speaker at a conference I attended. A friend pointed her out. She seemed ... self-possessed."

Hollis nodded.

Now that's an apt description.

"I loved Jeffrey and he loved me. Not enough to leave Frances, but enough to make me happy to settle for being his mistress."

Jeffrey?

As if reading Hollis' thoughts, she got up and stood by the brick fireplace that took up half of one wall. "Oh, I know he wasn't handsome or debonair. But he was witty, kind, funny … funny and …."

She burst into tears.

Hollis looked around and spotted a box of tissue on the dining room table. She brought the box over to Patrice, who smiled in embarrassment and gratitude.

"Jeffrey would hate this." She gently blew her nose. "He was not a sentimental man."

"No, he absolutely wasn't."

Patrice dabbed at her eyes and blew her nose. "I'm okay now. Would you like some tea?"

Hollis smiled. "I would love some tea."

They sat quietly for the first moments savoring the green tea and its jasmine fragrance. Then Patrice put her cup down and curled her legs under her.

"What do you want to know?"

Hollis ran her fingers through her hair. "I'm sure you know that Brian was arrested for Jeffrey's murder, but I'm not sure you know that the charges against him were dropped yesterday."

Patrice put her hand over her heart and shook her head. Hollis kept talking.

"The police arrested two men who they think murdered Todd. They also think there may be some link between Todd's killing and Jeffrey's murder."

"Todd is dead?"

Hollis closed her eyes. "I'm sorry. I thought you knew. Todd was killed a week ago. I was there. I mean we were having lunch when he had to use the restroom, and while I waited … he was … beaten to death."

She quickly related the details.

Patrice's eyes grew wide in disbelief. "I don't listen to the news; it can get to be too much. He was beaten by these two suspects? Why?"

"I don't know for sure it was these two men, although they'd been sitting in the restaurant and I ID'd them. And I don't know the connection to Todd or Jeffrey. It could be a prison vendetta being paid off. The police aren't sharing. In fact, that's why I wanted to speak with you. Can you tell me anything Jeffrey might have mentioned that could cast a light on why he was killed?"

It was clear from her distracted gaze that Patrice was still digesting the news about Todd. She got up, went to the kitchen, and brought back another pot of hot water for their tea. She sat back down, her face reflecting confusion and dismay.

"Jeffrey wasn't an unhappy man; he had made peace with his life. He was almost philosophical—except that he would never use that word. His marriage was unfortunate, although I have to tell you ... when Frances filed for divorce, he lost ten pounds, laughed more, and began to enjoy life." Patrice paused. "His relationship with Todd was ... was conflicted. Jeffrey felt so much guilt about his conviction. He told me he did everything he could behind the scenes to get that parole for Todd. But he didn't want him to know about what he'd done. I've never met Todd, but I know that when he was released it was the closest I've ever seen Jeffrey to tears."

Hollis sat back. This was a Jeffrey she never knew. She finished her cup of tea and poured herself another. She waved away Patrice's offer to serve and urged her to continue.

"Now, Brian was another relationship all together. I've known Jeffrey for many years. It's only been the last two that we ... we became intimate. He never mentioned his family at all before we became close. There were no pictures in his office and no photos—just that silly cat poster he had the nerve to encase in plastic." She smiled at the thought.

Hollis said, "I never knew he had a family either. He refused to talk about his personal life."

"Exactly," Patrice acknowledged. "So when I found out about his wife and son, I was a little surprised." She sipped her tea. "Jeffrey loved Brian, but he wasn't blind to his faults. That's how we first met. I was a social worker for the school district, and Brian had been acting out a bit in high school—nothing criminal, just teenage craziness stuff. But we like to nip these things in the bud before they spiral out of control."

Hollis nodded. "What was your perception about the father-son relationship? Did Brian love Jeffrey?"

"I think so. At least I'd like to think so. But he was so much like his father that their relationship had to meet a very high threshold, and I think Brian always thought he was a disappointment to his father. He wasn't, but there was nothing Jeffrey could do to convince him otherwise."

"Did Jeffrey approve of Brian's engagement?" Hollis asked. "Did he like the young woman?"

"What engagement? What are you talking about?"

Hollis rubbed her chin. "Brian told me that the reason for their big argument was that Jeffrey didn't want to give him the extra money he needed to get married to Gloria."

Patrice looked dumbfounded. "I assure you that Jeffrey didn't know Brian was getting married. I don't think he ever knew there was anyone serious in his life. Besides, can you imagine even asking Jeffrey for money to start a marriage? He would immediately point out that Brian clearly wasn't ready, and he definitely didn't believe in handouts."

Of course.

It was Hollis' turn to look dumbfounded. "You mean there's no woman in Brian's life?"

"Oh, Gloria was his girlfriend for a few months, but I think they broke up." Patrice looked past Hollis. "From what Jeffrey told me, she was a nice girl but more mature than Brian. I think she just moved on with her life. That doesn't mean he couldn't be seeing someone else that his father didn't know about."

Named Gloria.

"So what do you think they argued over?"

Patrice shrugged. "Jeffrey loved Brian, but he was always

pushing him to achieve. He would say that he could be the janitor, but be the best janitor." She sighed. "Brian preferred to take shortcuts. He didn't want to work as hard as his father, but he wanted the rewards and recognition."

Hollis nodded in understanding. "So you think Brian was after Jeffrey to give him money for some shortcut?"

"I can't say for sure." Patrice took a deep breath. "Brian had come to Jeffrey weeks ago, wanting to go into a startup business with a friend. Brian felt he could get his life focused if he worked for himself. Jeffrey drew a line in the sand; he said he would help Brian but not carry him. He told him he should come up with own resources to turn his life around."

Hollis noticed that Patrice's words were coming slower with each mention of Jeffrey's name. Her eyes were beginning to tear up again.

"I should be going," Hollis said. She picked up her purse. "Thank you for seeing me. Again, I ... I'm sorry for your loss."

Patrice gave Hollis a faint smile and wiped away a tear.

Hollis stopped on the front porch and turned back. "Patrice, did Brian know about you and his father?"

She looked puzzled. "Goodness, I hope not."

CHAPTER 30

HOLLIS FINISHED BRIEFING THE FALLEN Angels on her findings. They were all there except for Miller, who had to finish a project for work.

"Wow, who knew?" Rena murmured.

Gene said, "This is a lot to digest. Let's go over one bit of information at a time."

"Right." Richard nodded. "The un-tossed office .... I think those two guys just wanted Todd. None of us think these two guys were disgruntled parolees. But there is the chance they were doing a prison buddy a payback favor and Jeffrey was caught off guard."

"It doesn't hold up," Rena said. "First, the county building is secure. Jeffrey would have had to let the guys in—no way. Second, the police report says Jeffrey was shot up close. So, he likely knew his killer. Third, anyone who had Jeffrey for a parole officer and was headed back would have known that he played it by the book. There was a paper trail to justify his order. And they would know they'd be the first ones the police would look to. I think he was murdered because it was personal."

"I buy Rena's thinking," Gene said. "If the suspects from

Todd's killing weren't parolees, then why would Jeffrey let one or both into his office? He would meet them in an interview room. If they were hired, did your friend say who they might be working for?"

Hollis made a note to get back to Stephanie. "No, but I'll find out. I really don't think there were two guys in that office that night. It wasn't necessary; the killer had only to wait for Brian to leave." She paused. "Todd's case was different. It was a public place."

"Hollis, how did they know you and Todd would be meeting there? I mean did you tell anyone?" Richard asked.

"No, no, I didn't," Hollis said. "And I can't imagine that Todd would have mentioned it either." She wrote down: 'who knew about our meeting,' followed by several question marks.

They were all quiet for a moment.

Rena broke the silence. "So what was Jeffrey's mistress like?"

"Boy, did I pull that guess from the air," Richard said.

Hollis raised her eyebrows. "She's a real nice lady and seemed sincere. I believed what she told me, but I had to remember she was telling me her interpretation of events. She hadn't known Jeffrey that long—"

"But it sounds like she knew him well," Gene interjected.

"That's true, too," Hollis acknowledged. "Still, it would make all the difference in the world if Frances knew that she existed, or if Brian did, for that matter."

"Or Todd." Rena asked, "Could that be what Todd wanted to tell you that day?"

"No, I don't think so. Todd definitely wanted to talk about the trust," Hollis said.

"So, what you're telling us is that Mosley and company didn't have enough to make the charges against Brian stick when faced with more viable suspects?" Gene questioned.

Hollis said, "No, I didn't say that, but it's true. Would you want them to hold onto Brian without checking out two stronger candidates?"

"Of course not," Richard said. "But it was just luck you were observant enough to ID the dudes. Otherwise Brian would be facing some uncomfortable realities."

Gene played with his pen, making open boxes all over his pad of paper. "What do you want from us, Hollis?"

"I don't know. I'm stumped. We keep tap dancing around the motives. Why kill Jeffrey, why kill Todd?" She rubbed her forehead. "The Jeffrey we've been hearing about is not the Jeffrey we knew. The more I find out about him, the less I think I knew him."

"Nah, we all knew him the way he was." Richard spread his arms to include them all. "He was who we needed him to be."

Hollis nodded then stopped. "What did you just say?"

Richard gave her a curious look. "That he was who we needed him to be?"

"Right," Hollis said, more to herself than the Fallen Angels.

He was who I needed him to be.

THEY WERE BOTH OSTENSIBLY WATCHING television, but not really. They stared at the screen to avoid dealing with the emotion they couldn't or wouldn't express. Hollis sat on the floor, her back to the sofa, as John lay stretched out. She didn't know what to say. These moments of the unsaid were becoming uncomfortably more frequent.

He reached down and ruffled her hair.

"I've got to go to a training course in Chicago. Until I take it, I can't get my top security clearance, and I'm stuck reviewing case files in an unclassified area. It's only given every quarter, and the class started out full. But someone dropped out with the flu and a slot opened up. I think I'm going to take advantage and leave tomorrow evening."

Hollis froze. "How long?"

"A week. The seminar ends Thursday, the day of your hearing. I wanted to be there, but I may not get back in time."

She forced a smile and turned to face him. "I know, but

that's not so bad. You'd make me nervous anyway." She kissed him on the nose. "I'll pick you up from the airport and we can celebrate the evening you get back."

He gave her a hard look and turned to lie on his back. "You know about the elephant in this room, don't you?"

Hollis frowned. "What elephant? We're talking."

"No, we're not talking, we're having a conversation." He sat up. "I can't keep going on like this. I keep thinking—no, hoping—things will change, but they don't."

She crossed her arms. "Do we always have to keep talking about us? Can't we just enjoy the time we're together? Frankly, that's my biggest fear."

"What is?"

"It shouldn't be this hard, John," she said. "Maybe our relationship isn't ready to build a life on."

He shook his head. "It isn't hard. You just won't trust it."

"I trust you. It's me I don't trust. I've got a lot of baggage." She looked down at her hands.

He reached over and gripped her shoulders. "Everybody has baggage. Hell, I have baggage. Nobody is immune; it's called living your life."

Hollis got up and sat in the curve of his arm. She didn't want him to see her face, and her fear. He meant so much to her; she had done what she said she would never do again—let her guard down. She loved him with all that was in her, but what if they didn't make it? If she lost him now, would she lose herself again? Would her life spiral out of control again? She wrestled with the fear and the longing and lay very still next to him.

GETTING A MEETING WITH FRANCES proved harder than Hollis anticipated. It was clear Frances hadn't wanted to meet. All she wanted was for Hollis to file the trust, and her only concern was how much longer that would be. Once in contact, Hollis assured her the Thursday hearing date hadn't changed and there were to be no further delays. With that,

Frances grudgingly agreed to meet her the next morning at the Starbucks downtown.

That meeting scheduled, Hollis called Stephanie in an attempt to get a couple more answers.

"Does the report say anything about Brian or maybe Frances knowing about the affair?"

Stephanie responded, "Hold on. I knew you were going to come back at me with questions." Papers rustled. "No, it doesn't say one way or the other. For that reason, I bet they promised Ms. Leoni to keep things secret and not unnecessarily sully Jeffrey Wallace's reputation in exchange for her information."

"Makes sense," Hollis said. "Unless they needed her to testify, she could stay in the shadows. No need to cause unnecessary pain or embarrassment."

"That's what it looks like. Besides, it's no one's business. They eliminated her as a suspect in both murders."

"One last thing—does the report point out how the killers knew that Todd and I would be in that deli?"

Stephanie was silent as she scanned the documents. "No, I don't see a cross reference, but remember, I have Jeffrey Wallace's file, not Todd's. It wouldn't likely contain any information unless they found a link." She paused. "And before you ask, no, I can't get access to Todd's file. I don't think they're even finished with the report."

Hollis bowed her head in acceptance. It would have been helpful to know how Todd was targeted before she had her meeting with Frances, but she'd have to wing it.

FRANCES WAS DRESSED FOR BUSINESS in a charcoal-gray pinstriped pantsuit, an indigo-blue silk blouse, and black pumps with matching purse. Already looking at her watch, she was waiting impatiently when Hollis arrived at the downtown restaurant. She was on the phone and had spread out her paperwork across the top of the small table.

Phone in hand, she silently acknowledged Hollis and waved

her to the only other chair while she finished her call. Hollis motioned she was going to get something to drink, but while she was in line, she glanced back at Frances, who had put away all the papers and was now texting.

"I can't stay long, Hollis," Frances said. "I've got a real busy day."

"Got a horse running at Golden Gate Fields?" Hollis quipped and then immediately regretted it. She needed Frances' help.

"What does that mean?"

"Nothing, I'm sorry. I know you're accommodating me at the last minute, and I know you're really—"

Frances held up her hand. "Right, I'm busy so what do you want?"

"When is Todd's funeral?"

"There isn't going to be a funeral. Neither Brian nor I want the emotional upheaval. We will grieve in private."

I bet you will.

"Do the police think the guys I identified were the killers?"

"Er … yes. I want to thank you for your part in this whole awful … awful …."

"Mess?"

Frances glared at her. "I was going to say 'situation.' Todd … Todd had a way about him. He wasn't what he appeared to be."

"And what was that?"

Frances picked at a groomed fingernail. "He was sent to prison for a reason; once an ex-con always an ex-con."

Hollis felt her face flush. Frances looked at her in alarm.

"Oh, Hollis, I'm sorry, I didn't mean you. I told you how much Jeffrey thought of you, all of the Fallen Angels." Frances patted Hollis' hand. "I'm a silly woman; just ignore me."

I don't believe you for a minute. The swipe was deliberate.

"Todd was an unfortunate opportunist. He rubbed a lot of people the wrong way."

"Oh, don't worry. I think everything works itself out in the end." Hollis gave an airy wave of her hand. "Frances, I'm puzzled by a couple of things. I don't think it'll affect the filing of the trust, but I would feel a lot more confident if I had answers."

Frances leaned back in her seat. "What is it now? It's always something with you, Hollis. I spoke with a friend who was an executor for a trust, and he said it doesn't usually take nearly as long as ours is taking."

"Their trust probably didn't have murders occurring every few weeks."

Frances was silent.

"Frances, I've been getting a lot of hang-up calls lately, well, ever since I became co-executor. Have you had any problems?"

She frowned and bit her lip. "You don't think I'd do anything so childish, do you?"

"I take that as a no." Hollis went on, "I have just two more questions. Did Jeffrey say anything to you about adding Todd to the trust? And, do you know what Brian and Jeffrey argued about that day?" Hollis held up a hand to forestall her protests. "I know that last question is none of my business, but the Fallen Angels all cared about Jeffrey, and we're just looking for closure."

Frances smiled. "Don't worry, I'm not offended or put off. The answers to your questions are no and no."

"WELCOME BACK, MS. MORGAN, I'M thinking we should get you a field desk. You're here every week now, sometimes twice a week." Mosley held open the door for her to pass through. Leading the way to his office, he said, "So, tell me what was so urgent you had to see me today?"

"Detective, I've been thinking. How did those two guys know that Todd and I were going to be meeting there?"

"You should know that we let one of the men go. We checked him out thoroughly, but couldn't prove he was there in the alley. But from your lineup ID—number seven, a Jerry Ness— we found Todd Wallace's trace DNA evidence on clothing he'd tried to hide in a dumpster." Mosley gestured for her to sit but remained standing himself. "Now, he could have known you two were meeting at the deli because Todd Wallace was a regular. He went there almost every day."

"That's partially true. He went there to pick up his coffee from the cart in the morning. He told me so. But we were having a late lunch. Did Ness hang around for hours waiting to see if he was going to stop by?"

Mosley looked at her with a blank face. "Is that it? Is that your question?"

Hollis nodded. "Yes. So you're implying it's likely he'd been following Todd?"

Finally taking his seat, he rocked back and forth in his chair for a few seconds before responding. "That's the conclusion we came to."

"Who did Ness work for?"

"He says he was unemployed and looking for work. His high-paid lawyer says he's innocent and just in the wrong place at the wrong time."

"How could he afford to … oh, never mind."

"Yep, we figure he's got backing."

"Do you know who?"

"Evidently he's more afraid of what they'll do to him if he talks than he is of us."

"So right now you're unable to cross-check if he killed Jeffrey, too."

Mosley gave a slight wince. "Brian Wallace is still a prime suspect in my book, but the DA's office disagrees. They think Ness is a more likely candidate."

"How are you going to nail him?" Hollis asked.

Mosley gave her a sardonic look. "Just like they say, we're going to follow the money."

For once Hollis had a full day at the office. George had given her several new cases that needed to be researched including a recommendation for a legal approach. Whoever thought probate law was straightforward? It had more twists, turns, and upsets than she could ever imagine.

By four o'clock, she'd made major inroads into the stack of files in her inbox, and she was ready to brief George.

He sat and listened as she reviewed each matter. He asked a few questions and gave her specific advice on how to handle particular clients.

She'd saved the Wallace Trust case for last. It took several minutes to bring him up to speed with the happenings of the last few days.

George tilted back in his chair. "I know you're going to get prickly about what I'm about to say, but do you think you're in over your head? Could you use a little help? I can shift a few client meetings and we can focus on the trust together. The two of us will take a lot less time."

"You're right; I'm going to be prickly," Hollis said. "I can handle the Wallace Trust. I wasn't asking for your, or anybody's help. I've done the hardest parts. I only brought it up so that you would be aware of the doubts I still have about the assets."

He looked at her summary notes. "Don't worry. If the family members discover there were undisclosed assets or fraudulent distribution, we can file for a new hearing. Let it go."

Hollis bit her tongue. She had no intention of letting it go. Frances would go through the trust like a hot knife through butter. There would be no assets to retrieve later.

Still, George was right. She had to move on. The hearing was next week. She was out of time.

CHAPTER 31

———◆———

SITTING ON THE BALCONY DRINKING her morning tea, Hollis pondered for the umpteenth time what might have happened three months ago. Whatever it was, Frances was getting giddier by the day. She'd called Hollis twice the day before to make sure the trust hearing had not been cancelled.

She looked down at the phone viewer screen and saw the familiar number. It had been a mistake to give Frances her cell contact.

"Yes, Frances." Hollis only partially tried to hide the exasperation in her voice.

"I know you think I'm a pest, but I made plane reservations for Vegas the same afternoon as the hearing, and I told the buyers for my house they could move in early." Frances sounded breathless over the phone. "So, is it still on Thursday?"

"Yes, of course. Nothing has changed."

"Okay, that's good. And it's final, right? It can't change again? Will it take more days for it to be really final? Is there like a waiting period?"

"No, Frances. It's final on that day. Check with your insurance agent. You'll likely get your half of the insurance policy within a few days of the hearing." Hollis added, "Oh, and make sure they have your new Vegas address."

"Okay, okay, that's good." Frances paused. "Now, you told me that I don't have to split the insurance policy with the Public Library Foundation, right?"

Hollis sighed. "Frances, we've gone over this—"

"I know, I know, but this is the rest of my life we're talking about."

"No. The insurance policy identifies the beneficiaries. It's only the trust that specifies Jeffrey's community property share will go to the Public Library Foundation. And they only get whatever is left of the estate after you and Brian are dead." Hollis took a breath. "Jeffrey's insurance policy specified that you and Brian will split his policy fifty-fifty. It would have been shared with Todd had he lived."

"Such as it is," Frances said. "I told Jeffrey we needed more."

Hollis didn't bother to respond.

"Your legal fees are paid from the trust, true? I won't owe you anything, right?"

"That's right, Frances."

"Look, instead of putting the final papers in the mail. Can I come to your office Tuesday and pick up a copy? It would save you some time."

Really.

"That's two days before the hearing. The papers won't be stamped by the clerk recorder until after the papers are filed."

"No matter. I'll get the court copy in the mail. I just need to have what you filed."

Need to have it for what?

Frances consulted her calendar, and Hollis agreed she could come by the following Tuesday. At that their call ended; Frances had to rush off. She commented she was getting her nails done and having a Botox injection.

"I wouldn't want to stand in the way of progress," Hollis said under her breath.

"What?"

Hollis regrouped. "I said, we're finally making progress."

HOLLIS TOSSED THE SALAD ONE more time, and checked on the leg of lamb for the twentieth time. John, nursing a glass of Pinot Grigio, was waiting for her on the patio.

It was as if they both recognized that they had come to a crossroads.

All day she could feel his eyes following her. When she glanced at him, he would be peering at her with an expression she'd seen him use after he'd reached a decision. Even though he was only leaving for a few days, she knew she would miss him more than she thought possible. Still, there was a thickness in the air, and other than the common courtesies they had exchanged along with the light banter about his training, it had been underscored by silence.

He came and stood behind her, sliding his arms around her waist.

She smiled and half-turned. "It's not much longer to dinner."

"Good, it smells fantastic. Come outside and sit with me."

"I ... I ...."

Ignoring her hesitation, he led her by the hand and picked up a glass of wine he had already poured for her. They sat at the patio table.

"Yesterday, while I was packing to go to training, I tried to imagine all the reasons we should be together and all the reasons we shouldn't." He looked her in the eyes. "But when I got about midway through, I stopped, because it didn't matter. At the end of the day, at the end of the list, at the end of all the pros and cons ... no matter how it added up, or not ... I just want to spend my life with you."

Hollis gasped. Her eyes started to tear.

"John, I ... I—"

"And then I thought about what you said you wanted." He picked up her hand. "I am not Bill Lynley. I am not your ex-husband. I'm not going to take away your self-respect or leave you behind to clean up my mess. I'm not going to muddle your mind, so you can't judge right from wrong. I'm not going to put your life in danger and expect you to protect me."

She was unashamedly crying now. The years of pent-up disappointment and emotional fence-building required to keep her pain at bay had left her tired and spent. Her heart was exposed for the first time since her court sentence ten years ago, when Bill had walked away, leaving her to her fate and ending their marriage. Over the years she had sealed up her heart and was comfortable leaving it that way, until John.

John.

He held her and let her sob into his chest. Finally, she quieted. He handed her a cloth napkin for the tears.

Hollis' voice trembled. "I love you."

He nodded. "I know. I love you."

She leaned against him, beaming. "How much notice do you have to give to your landlord?"

He looked into her eyes and smiled. "It doesn't matter. I'll tell him tomorrow."

He held her face lightly and kissed her deeply.

SLOW TO ARRIVE AT HER office the next morning, Hollis tried to suppress the smile that kept creeping onto her face. She had woken up at three a.m. and looked over at John's sleeping figure, with his arm crossed over onto her pillow. From now on, he would be there for her. She would have someone by her side. She still couldn't believe her luck. Her smile wouldn't go away.

Later, her phone rang. She'd been distracting herself with work, finishing up a draft client letter. She hesitated a moment, bracing herself for Frances' voice, then saw who it was and picked up.

"Hollis, this is Vince," he said, swallowing. "I wanted you to know that I passed my test. I'm a high school graduate."

Her throat tightened. "Oh, Vince I am so proud of you." She gulped back a little sob of happiness. "You did it. You stuck with it, and you did it."

He cleared his throat. "No, *you* did it. You wouldn't let me get away with giving up."

"Well, you answered the questions. Now, when is the ceremony, and when do we celebrate?"

"I'm not going to the ceremony," he said. "You know, because of my mom and everything. She'll want to come, but she wouldn't do well—you know what I mean."

Hollis rubbed her eyes. "Yes, I know what you mean. Well, we can still do a dinner. Where would you like to eat?"

"You'll take me to dinner?" he said. "Say, you know that all-you-can-eat place in San Leandro?"

Hollis nodded. "Sure, but you can pick a nicer place, Vince. You can go to the all-you-can-eat place anytime."

"Maybe you can go there anytime, Hollis, but I can't," he said. "I've always wanted to go there. I've never been."

She mentally kicked herself for her insensitivity. "Then that's where we'll go. Are there any friends you want to invite?"

"You're my only real friend," he said. "Do you think Stephanie would come?"

Hollis grimaced at the thought of Stephanie's reaction to going to an all-you-can-eat restaurant—for Vince. She would have to do a little arm twisting.

"I'll ask her. I'm sure she will. But, what about young people your own age?"

He said, "No, not really." He took a long pause. "But who knows, maybe I'll make friends at Laney College."

Hollis caught her breath then squealed. "Vince Colton, you come upstairs right now!"

A wide smile spread across her face. In less than five minutes, Vince stood in front of her desk. She came around to give him an embrace.

"I don't care if you don't like them," she said. "You are getting a big hug."

She gave him a robust squeeze.

Vince said, "It's okay. I don't mind." He stiffened and accepted her hug.

"Are you going to apply to Laney?" Hollis asked. "Community colleges are a great way to get an advanced education. Have you spoken to a counselor? Do you need me to help you?"

Vince laughed. It was a wonderful, hearty sound.

She startled. She had never heard him laugh before.

He moved closer, keeping his arms to his side. "You've been great to me. I will never be able to thank you enough, but I think you'd want me to take it from here."

Hollis nodded. And for the first time in the short year she'd known him, she knew he was going to be okay.

That evening, the Fallen Angels came to a pause in their deliberations. They sat somberly in the same room that had witnessed so many of their discussions over the years.

Richard said, "I guess I always thought we would solve Jeffrey's murder and somehow pay him back." He passed his hand over his head. "Now, they may never find out who really did it."

"I thought we were getting close," Miller said, finishing a pale pink origami crane. "I always thought it was Todd." He paused. "That is, once I knew there was a Todd."

Gene shrugged. "I wanted to find the killer for Jeffrey, too. I thought if we worked together we could accomplish what the police couldn't."

Sitting next to him, Rena leaned over to pat him on the shoulder.

Hollis looked around at each of them in turn. "So, are we giving up?"

"What do you expect us to do?" Richard said. "The police are trying to link Jeffrey's murder to Todd's. You have to file the trust, and once that's done, what reason do we still have to poke around?"

Gene said in a quiet voice, "Hollis, I know you don't think the murders are linked—that Jeffrey's killer is still out there—but we've all neglected our jobs and violated some privacy law or another to come up with a lot of puzzle pieces that don't quite fit together. We gave it our best shot, and frankly, I'm just out of ideas."

She stood. "Then let's go through everything we know one more time."

They all groaned.

Ignoring them, Hollis walked around the table. "Why was Todd killed? Why is Frances so happy and so anxious? Why is Brian, who should be concerned, not scared? Why is the trust for a modest estate such a big deal? What happened three months ago that caused Frances to file for divorce?"

"You don't suppose Frances caught Jeffrey with Patrice Leoni, do you?" Rena asked.

Richard shook his head. "Oh no, Rena, don't encourage her. Besides, the police must have eliminated that angle weeks ago."

Rena said, "Maybe Frances kept quiet about knowing. She was proud and hurt. She would divorce him and go on with her life. After Jeffrey was murdered, there was nothing else for her to do. She may be a little greedy and insensitive, but I believe her. She wants the trust done with."

Hollis looked doubtful. "Nah, it's possible, but I don't see her keeping that kind of knowledge to herself."

Gene drummed his fingers on the table. "Rena may have a point. There may be something to the mistress angle."

She ignored them both. "It's about the trust. The trust is at the center of it all. We need to go back to square one."

"Don't you guys get it?" Gene looked at the others. "Hollis is not going to let us go home. They'll find our bodies here, rotting from mental overdrive." He took out a pad of paper. "Okay, one last time. Let's tackle each question separately."

He wrote at the top of one page: 'Why was Todd killed?'

"If we're brainstorming, suppose it was just a mugging?"

Miller said. "But I'm going to cancel my own idea. His death was personal."

Richard frowned and shook his head. "He knew something about Jeffrey's killing and he had to be silenced."

Rena rubbed her forehead. "But if we assume—like Hollis said—that it has to do with the trust, Todd didn't want anything to do with it. He was ready to walk away from the first editions. But Brian wanted the money from the sale of those books."

"Once Jeffrey was killed, only two people benefited from the trust," Gene said, "Frances and Brian."

"Excuse me," Richard said. "But remember, there was nothing in the trust to make it worth killing for."

"Wait," Miller said, "what if the first editions are more valuable than we thought? What if the first appraiser missed something?"

Rena picked up Gene's pad and tore off another sheet of paper. She made a circle of arrows. "If Todd was killed for the first editions, then either Frances or Brian could have wanted the cash that wasn't coming through the trust."

Hollis sat up. "I don't know. Those first editions were there from the beginning. It's an idea, but it doesn't feel ... I just don't think that's it. I wonder if Todd found out that Frances was hiding assets."

"Uh-oh," Richard said, gathering his jacket and cap. "We're going in another circle. Look, I've got to get home. We've got company coming over."

Miller glanced at his cellphone. "I need to get going, too."

Gene considered Hollis with concern. "Is there any way you could get another appraiser to look at those first editions on Monday?"

They all paused for her response.

"I guess." Hollis hesitated. "Brian has them. I can ask if I can show them to someone else. Say, Rena, while I'm checking with Brian, can you contact Nate and find out what, or if, there is word on the street about Todd?"

"Sure. What are you thinking?"

Hollis frowned. "I'm thinking Todd was silenced. I'm thinking they—whoever 'they' are—didn't want him to tell me something. It may have been about the first editions, but he said it was about the trust. But, to close the question, I'll follow up with an appraiser and eliminate the first editions from our consideration."

"Good," Richard said. "If you come up with anything, we can get together Tuesday night."

Rena put on her jacket. "That's cutting it awfully close to hearing time. Will that work?"

Hollis nodded. "We can always meet after the hearing if there is anything we can do to find Jeffrey's killer. Just because the trust is filed doesn't mean we have to give up."

They all left except Gene, who held back.

"You okay? I didn't want to scare you, but I'm glad you're still filing the trust next week. I was worried you might be in danger if you didn't file it on time. If you're being followed—"

"I'm fine." Hollis held up her hand in mild protest. "Gene, you know I don't scare that easy. I'm going to hang in there. I get the feeling I'm making at least one somebody very nervous. It's time I stopped looking for what makes sense and go for what makes crazy."

CHAPTER 32

———···———

BRIAN SOUNDED IRRITATED WHEN HOLLIS called to ask to see the first editions.

"I don't understand," he said. "They've already been valued by an approved expert. I have a certificate. Why do you need to see them again?"

Hollis hedged. "I'd like to have them in court with me on Thursday so that I can show the judge that at the time probate was filed, the asset was intact."

He grudgingly acquiesced. "Well then, I guess I don't have much choice. Come by whenever you want. I'm going to be home all day."

It was a gloomy first day of summer. Hollis parked in the driveway and picked up what looked like three days of newspapers scattered on the path to the front door. She waited for Brian to answer, and when he did, she gasped at his appearance. Unless he had multiples of his favorite outfit, these were the same clothes he had on days earlier when she visited.

Something was wrong, but she didn't have much time.

She could feel the adrenaline pumping into her chest, and she put her shaking hand in her pocket. Brian was too far into his own world and didn't appear to notice.

"Do you mind if I use your phone?" Hollis asked with only a slight tremor in her voice. "My battery is dead, and I need to check my messages. I have a tentative appointment after I leave here."

He pointed to a handset on the coffee table.

Hollis tapped in the numbers and gave Brian a tentative smile.

"I'll go get the books," Brian said, shuffling down the hallway.

Hollis quickly put the phone down, went into the dining room, and headed toward the cat poster, now jammed behind several boxes. Moving a container aside, she slipped her hand behind the plastic casing and felt for the gun resting on the bottom. Removing the Smith & Wesson, she returned to the living room and set the gun on the table in front of her.

Brian froze and set the books down. He appeared stricken, and his already pale face, bloodless.

"How did you know where to look? I'd hidden it here first, but ...." His voice was faint. "The police just gave me access to Dad's office furnishings two days ago."

Hollis didn't think this was a good time to say she'd finally understood Brian's guilty behavior. She knew he hated that poster. It was likely some symbol of a father–son dynamic she would never understand. Jeffrey had kept it on his wall for a reason. Mosley had noticed it too.

"You should have gotten rid of the gun," she said. "It was an accident, wasn't it? Do you want to tell me what happened?"

Brian looked at her, but he didn't see her. From his gaze, it was clear his thoughts had gone back in time to the confrontation that had changed his life. He stared at the gun.

"In the end, you're right, it was just an accident," he murmured.

"But how could it be an accident, when you brought a gun to your father's office?"

He looked at her. "Dad was more proud of his parolees than

he was of his own children. He spent all hours of the day and night making sure his 'caseload' was doing okay." Brian raised his fingers in air quotes. "He made sure you guys had extra help and attention, but me and Todd … we got the crumbs."

Hollis frowned. He hadn't answered her question. "Uh, Brian, what kind of problems did you need his attention for?"

He ignored her question again. "When I was a kid, I used to think that if I went to prison and got out, I could possibly have his attention all the time."

She moved closer. "So, what happened that night?"

"We were going to go out to dinner after he got off work, but he said something had come up and he'd have to reschedule." Brian's eyes glistened. "I wanted to tell him I was getting married. You know, a father and son talk, but he was too busy. He told me to hang in there."

Like the poster.

Hollis swallowed. "Do you really have a fiancée? Maybe he didn't believe—"

"Yeah … well, no … not now. It was over. But he didn't know that." He ran his hand over his head. "She didn't think I was much, either. That's why I wanted my own business. She'd have changed her mind. If I could have talked with him …."

"I'm sure if he had known you were going to tell—"

"So, I came by his office anyway." Brian paused. "I brought the gun. I don't know why …. I think I just wanted to scare him. To get him to see what he'd driven me to."

Hollis swallowed. "Did you fight?"

Brian nodded. "He told me I was acting like a child. I needed to grow up. He said all I wanted him to do was provide a shortcut. 'A reason not to work for something,' he said. He said it was a good thing I wasn't getting married. She was smarter than he'd given her credit for. He couldn't imagine why I thought I was ready to get married when I was so … so immature."

She winced.

Brian sat back in his chair. "That's when I shot him. He made me so angry. He looked at me as if seeing me for the first time. His hands clutched his stomach and the blood just started to pour out .... Then he fell to the floor." Brian's voice had dropped to a whisper. "I held him and told him I was sorry. But he was gone, just like that."

Hollis said nothing.

"I was scared and ran away. I took the gun with me. I'd bought it at a gun show. I didn't have a permit, so it couldn't be traced to me. I came straight home, hid it in my neighbor's yard, and then showered after I threw away the clothes I wore. I knew about gunshot residue, so I made sure it was gone. I guess I missed my shoes." Brian turned away.

"You left your dad there for the cleaning crew to find?" She couldn't stop the words from leaving her lips. "You were wrong. He didn't die right away. May be you could have saved him."

Brian finally turned to look at her and seemed to realize who she was. His smile was forlorn.

"Yeah. Aren't I a piece of work?" He paced back and forth. "I wanted the Fallen Angels to find something wrong with the trust. Dad was so proud of all of you. I thought you could figure it out. But you guys could never find anything. Frances didn't love Dad. My attorney told me she'd already started to divorce him. Then when I ... when I .... I guess she figured she didn't have to. I know she's hiding something. I'd rather give every dollar to the Public Library Foundation than let her have a dime."

"Look, Brian, let me help you with this. You don't have to worry about the trust. Even if the trust gets recorded on Thursday, it doesn't mean that we can't keep looking for more assets. You need to deal with the ... the other thing. Let me ...."

Tears formed in his eyes. "You know, I think it's best if you leave ... now."

She shivered. "Brian, you need help—someone to talk to. I'll come with you to turn yourself in. You don't have to drive there by yourself."

He gave a sad chuckle. "I have no intention of turning myself in."

He wasn't lying.

Hollis looked into his eyes. She wasn't afraid of Brian; he'd already shown his weakness.

"Let me call your lawyer. He's probably dealt with … things like this. He can advise you what to do next. There are all kinds of circumstances for … for manslaughter, maybe …."

"Thanks for trying to help, but please leave me alone."

Hollis started to protest, when he stood up, picked up the gun, and gestured her toward the front door.

She walked slowly to give herself time to think, but Brian reached the door first and held it open. She stepped out onto the porch and turned to face him, but he slammed the door behind her. She got out her phone and punched 911.

A shot rang out.

CHAPTER 33

—⁓—

Brian's suicide was only a blip in the paper the next day. Hollis had already texted the Fallen Angels to let them know. Richard and Miller responded with relief that Jeffrey's murder had been resolved. Gene was concerned that she was okay, and Rena invited her to her house for a drink. They all still wanted to get together on Wednesday before the hearing—for closure.

At home, Hollis turned on the public radio jazz station as loud as she dared and lay on her bed, staring at the ceiling and waiting for the numbness to subside.

"Goodbye, Jeffrey." The words came softly to her lips.

She was glad John was attending training in Chicago. She couldn't explain the frustration and sadness that clung to her over the realities of Jeffrey's and Brian's deaths. Hollis didn't want him to think it had anything to do with their moving in together, so she told him in an unemotional tone what had happened. From his soothing tone, she could tell he knew what she was going through.

On Sunday, she visited Rena, who was home alone with Christopher while Mark was visiting his family out of state.

"Here's to you and John. I am so happy for you both." Rena poured a glass of her favorite Malbec.

They raised their glasses and sipped.

Rena shook her head. "I don't know which is sadder—that Jeffrey was killed by his own son, or that his son killed himself because he felt so much guilt and despair."

Hollis mused, "First Jeffrey, then Todd, and now Brian. The only one left standing is Frances."

"Well, one thing's for certain: Frances didn't kill Jeffrey." Rena took a sip of wine. "And remember, she was at work when Todd was murdered."

"Yes, I know—how convenient. All along Brian believed she was hiding assets and he always hoped we'd find them ... in time." She paused. "Frances can't contain herself until the hearing on Thursday. I had to reassure her again this morning during her allocated five seconds of grief that her stepson's death would not slow things down."

Rena nodded with understanding. "But there's really nothing to keep the trust from filing on time, even I'm sick of her asking about it. Why does she think there'd be a problem?"

"Because I think she knows there's something out there that can stop it," Hollis said. "There's something she knows that she doesn't want me to find out. That's why she keeps checking in with me."

Hollis stared into her glass of wine. She knew she was in a race with Frances, but the stakes were elusive. A clock was ticking and Frances was heading for the goal line. Had she already said something that should have tipped Hollis off?

WHEN GEORGE FOUND HOLLIS IN the firm's library, she was surrounded by stacks of folders, newspaper clippings, and law books. She was tapping away at her laptop, plowing through the records and information the Fallen Angels had collected one last time.

"Still nothing?" he asked.

She scowled. "Frances is going to win this one, but I know she's hiding assets."

"Can't you get a continuance?" George glanced at a page from the top of the stack.

Hollis shook her head. "No, Brian already had one filed. After Frances protested, the court made it clear that they were not inclined to hold back distributing the estate for a second time, based on a hunch."

George stood. "Then, Counselor, you're now facing a lawyer's first reality check. You win some and you lose some—you just hope you win more than you lose."

"Yeah, yeah, I know." She ran her fingers through her hair. "But George, I'm *this* close to figuring it out." She put her thumb and forefinger a half inch apart.

"Well, let me get out of the way of your thinking process." George moved toward the door. "You may still want to ask for a continuance, based on suspected hidden assets. Maybe what you're looking for isn't in a law book."

She nodded absently and flipped open to another file. George gave her a sympathetic look and left.

WHEN TIFFANY CAME IN THIRTY minutes later, Hollis was still deep into her notes.

"Hollis, the appraiser is here to look at the Wallace's first editions. Shall I put him in the small conference room?"

She looked up. "Yes, that's fine. I'll be right there."

A note on the edge of a sticky caught her eye. She'd written it at the Fallen Angels meeting when Rena reported back on Frances' mob connections. Now, she marked it in yellow to remind her to look at it again when she got back from meeting with the appraiser. She picked up the Turneo first editions.

"Thank you so much for coming to my office," Hollis offered her hand to shake. "You saved me a lot of time."

She pushed the five books across the table for him to examine.

"Not a problem. My next appointment is in this building," he said. "The Franchise Tax Board offices are on the seventh floor. My quarterly tax payment is due. You know, sometimes I think I should just move my business to Nevada—no state taxes."

Hollis smiled and nodded in agreement, but then she frowned. "What did you say?"

"Some businesses have to pay quarterly tax payments—every three months. You know, so the Franchise Tax Board can get their money before the end of year."

She said softly, "Yes, I do know."

Hollis' mind raced over past conversations with Brian and Frances while the appraiser, wearing a special eye loupe, went through every page in the books. Finally he raised his head.

"I'm going to write my number down," he said. "I don't want to be influenced by anything you might say."

He scribbled a number on a piece of paper and put it off to the side.

"In my expert opinion, these books are in good condition for works almost ninety years old. Turneo was very popular in the twenties before alcoholism did him in at the age of thirty-seven. These books are the sum total of his work. He also wrote a few short—"

"I'm sorry, I don't mean to be rude," Hollis said, wanting to get back to her office, "but I have a time constraint I'm working under, and it would be helpful if you could …." She didn't want to be the one to finish the sentence.

He looked at her with understanding. "You want me to cut to the chase?"

She smiled and nodded.

"Well, while Turneo was popular in literary circles, he wasn't a Herman Melville or a Mark Twain. So, even though he wrote similar period pieces, his books aren't as valued." He pulled off his monocle. "To a collector they could be worth more than the market value. I can think of one Turneo collector off the top of my head who might be interested. What did the other appraisal come in at?"

"Ten to fifteen thousand, on the high end."

The appraiser nodded and reached across the table for his piece of paper. He slid it across to Hollis. It read, 'five to fifteen thousand.'

It wasn't about the first editions.

"The earlier estimates are valid." He packed away his monocle. "I think you have your answer, Ms. Morgan."

HOLLIS SAT IN HER OFFICE, deep in thought. She was waiting for Frances to arrive and collect her copy of the trust filing papers. While the final pieces of the story were falling into place, the picture formed was missing its core. The first editions were legitimately valued. Todd had not been cheated and Frances was far shy of the dollars needed for a casino.

Tiffany buzzed on the intercom.

Frances, seated in the conference room, appeared to be dressed for battle. She carried a black patent-leather tote and wore a black pantsuit with a red-striped blouse and matching red shoes. Her hair was pulled back into a low chignon.

"Hello, I'm in a hurry. Do you have my copy and something for me to sign?" Frances sat across the table facing the window, sunlight partially shining on her face.

Hollis pulled the papers out of her folder but let them rest on top.

"I know you did it, Frances. I don't know how you did it, but it's been about you the whole time," she said, shaking her head.

"I don't know what you're talking about." Frances' voice took on a hard edge. "Still getting those hang-ups? I know it would keep me on edge. Truth is, I have other things to do today. Let me sign and give me my copy. Then I'll be on my way. I'll see you in court tomorrow."

Hollis' jaw tightened and she snapped, "What happened, Frances? You were living an average life with Jeffrey. It might not have been exciting, but it was comfortable. He obviously let you continue your gambling addiction. Although I can imagine that for someone with Jeffrey's moral compass, it might have gnawed at him. What happened?"

Frances smirked. "Just give me my papers."

Hollis took a deep breath. "I know you're hiding assets. I know you must have jumped for joy when Brian confessed and killed himself."

Frances glared. "You have no idea." She gave a hollow laugh then looked quickly around the room. "Is this office bugged?"

Hollis wanted to kick herself. Bugging the room would have been a great idea.

"Once you sign this paper and I file it in court, you'll be adding on several other felony fraud charges to your already growing list of prison years," Hollis said. "You had Todd killed, didn't you? Did he discover your secret?" Hollis tapped the trust papers but didn't move to hand them over.

Frances half stood and grabbed across the table for the sheets. "Give me the form."

Her abrupt movement caused her purse to fall from her shoulder, emptying it in a rush across the table. Hollis leaned over, eyed the contents, and smiled. She pushed envelopes, coins, and a makeup bag toward Frances, who was frantically scooping items back into her tote.

Hollis pointedly handed over one of the runaway envelopes.

Frances reached for it, her face paling as she slipped the envelope back into her purse. She looked Hollis straight in the eye as she slung the bag over her shoulder. "Thanks, I've got it from here. There's nothing that can't be explained. Is this where I see the error of my ways and confess?"

"That's up to you, Frances." She slid over the papers.

Frances' voice was cold. "It's not going to happen, Ms. Morgan." Frances signed quickly, took her copy and returned the signed page. "You're going to lose."

Hollis smiled.

No, I don't think so.

HOLLIS RUSHED TO HER DESK and quickly drafted a new court

order. She convinced one of the firm's clerks to run it to the courthouse before the end of the day deadline.

Next she put in a call to Gene. He responded with his usual assurance.

"I'm lovin' this." She could feel his glee through the wire. "I may not get back to you until late, but I'll be at the Fallen Angels meeting tonight."

The rest of the day she spent getting ready for her morning court appearance.

She was a few minutes late for the Fallen Angels meeting and was surprised to see everyone there.

"We're all here, Hollis." Miller greeted her. "Even Richard."

"Very funny, crane man." Richard, looking nonchalant, glanced at his watch. "I won't be able to stay long, though."

Hollis smiled, wondering who got the short straw and had to twist Richard's arm.

Rena reminded her to dress for a photo op. "You want to appear confident and credible."

"It's only a hearing, not a trial," Hollis said.

"We'll take what we can get." Gene smiled.

For the next few minutes she quickly took them through the dress rehearsal for her first court appearance as an attorney.

CHAPTER 34

T HE COURTROOM WAS ALMOST EMPTY. There were a few small huddles of people, apparently waiting their turns. The Fallen Angels sat in the back of the courtroom, chatting among themselves. George had opted to sit in the viewer's section behind the railing and the attorney's table. Hollis appreciated that he didn't take the seat next to her. It might be interpreted as a sign of lack of confidence.

Frances Wallace sat across the aisle wearing dark glasses. Her lips formed a thin line of distaste.

All this Hollis took in. She was glad she'd finally convinced John not to come. He'd have to leave his seminar early to catch a flight, and he'd only make her more nervous. She promised to regale him with anecdotes over dinner that evening.

She'd had to beg him. "Please, John, just this once, let me get through this without any more spectators than I can handle. The Fallen Angels are going to be there, and that's bad enough."

"All the more reason someone who loves you unconditionally should be there, too." He held her by the shoulders and gazed lovingly into her eyes.

But in the end he gave in.

"I know you'd give me the same space," he said.

She pulled out the folder Gene had dropped off at the office early that morning and laid it on top of the others stacked in front of her.

The bailiff made the announcement for all to rise.

Judge Messina entered, wearing his black robe and an expensive looking sky-blue tie and matching shirt. He looked out over the courtroom and asked for the docket.

"Let's get started, I've got a long day," he said picking up a folder. He called out, "The estate of Jeffrey Wallace. Is the executor or administrator here?"

"I am, your honor. Hollis Morgan." She stepped forward in front of the table. "Unfortunately, the original executer took his life last week; however, I was authorized as co-executor before his death. I'm an … an attorney."

For a long moment the judge peered over his glasses at her, but said nothing. He picked up the file given him by the court clerk.

"I see Mr. Ravel is in the court," the judge said. "What are you doing here, George?"

George smiled and stood. "Just viewing, Your Honor. Ms. Morgan is one of our best lawyers. I'm interested in the outcome of the hearing."

Hollis breathed a sigh of relief that George didn't mention it was her first court appearance.

The judge peered at them both. "The outcome of a straightforward trust and will … what could be interesting about that? Well, we'd better get started. Ms. Morgan?"

Hollis cleared her throat and licked her lips. "Your honor, as it happens there is nothing straightforward about this trust. Mr. Wallace was murdered six weeks ago, and it was only five days ago that it was discovered that his son and executor, Brian Wallace, committed the killing."

Surprised, the judge took off his glasses as if to hear her better.

He looked down at the paperwork and asked, "Is that when you were declared the executor?"

Hollis shook her head. "No, Your Honor. A few weeks prior to his death, Brian Wallace asked me to sign on as co-executor and as such, to verify his concerns about his stepmother, Frances Wallace."

Behind her, Hollis heard the gasp from Frances. She could almost feel the plunge of the imaginary dagger in her back.

"Brian Wallace suspected that Frances Wallace, who'd filed for divorce shortly after the trust was drawn and funded, was up to something, but he didn't know what. He retained our firm to find out."

Judge Messina queried, "The trust has modest holdings. Did he think she was hiding assets?"

Hollis nodded. "Yes, but after spending much time searching, my associates and I could find nothing amiss except for a lot of little things that weren't quite right."

The judge looked past Hollis at Frances and then back. "Ms. Morgan, I must admit this is not the usual story I get in this court. But unfortunately I must urge you to wrap things up. I have here your petition asking for a continuance. Is that because you are looking for hidden assets?"

Frances stood. "A continuance? Please, Your Honor, there are no hidden assets. Ms. Morgan has irrationally pursued some vague notion that my late husband has—"

The judge hit the gavel. "Mrs. Wallace, this is my courtroom, and only I can speak unless I ask for someone else to speak. Since I did not ask you, sit down." He turned back to Hollis. "Ms. Morgan, I asked you the question."

"Yes, Your Honor, that was my intent. However, I don't think I'll need the continuance because since my filing yesterday I discovered the missing asset." Hollis came forward with a single piece of paper and handed it to the judge.

The courtroom was silent.

The judge quickly scanned the sheet.

"Ms. Morgan, would you like to ask Mrs. Wallace to take the stand?" He motioned toward Frances, "Or, would you prefer that continuance?"

Hollis took a quick glance at George, who gave her a slight nod of his head and then he got up and left the room.

"Yes, Your Honor, I call Frances Wallace to the stand."

Frances' heels clicked as she walked to the stand and took a seat. Even though her expression was deadpan, the muscles in her jaw flexed and tightened.

"We will swear you in, Mrs. Wallace," the judge said.

Frances stood and repeated the oath.

"Your turn, Ms. Morgan."

"Yes, Your Honor," Hollis replied confidently. "Mrs. Wallace, what is the recorded date of your trust that is under consideration in this court today?"

Frances' impatience was evident. "January twenty-sixth."

Hollis stood in front of her. "Did you purchase a California lottery ticket after that date?"

Frances turned pale, and the blood-red lipstick she was wearing shone like neon.

"Yes," she whispered.

"What is the date on the lottery ticket you purchased?" Hollis asked, staring at her.

Frances' eyes narrowed with hatred.

"You must answer, Mrs. Wallace," the judge said.

Frances licked her lips. "I purchased it on March sixteenth."

Hollis nodded. She'd had a hunch about when Frances had bought the ticket. "But that isn't quite true, is it? The purchaser was Jeffrey Wallace, who once a week bought a lottery ticket from the same location and turned it over to you. Isn't that true?"

"He purchased it for me," Frances retorted through clenched teeth.

Hollis ignored her. "Isn't it true that the ticket purchased on March sixteenth hit, Mrs. Wallace? It hit for twenty-eight million dollars, isn't that right? And didn't you file for divorce two days later?"

"Ms. Morgan, you may only ask one question at a time, giving the witness time to answer," the judge said.

Hollis nodded, reminding herself to breathe. "Ms. Wallace, didn't you file for divorce in Nevada two days after the lottery ticket you held hit the jackpot?"

Frances said nothing, but her eyes were darting back and forth as if reading the writing on the wall. Finally, she looked down at her hands.

"Yes, I filed for divorce." Her voice quavered.

Hollis went back to the table and picked up a sheet of paper. "California lottery rules specify that you have six months to claim your prize. Three months had already passed since the trust was created. You had to hold off claiming it until after your divorce was final and it became your separate property. So you only had three months to make sure it wasn't a joint asset. No one would be the wiser, including your husband. When he was killed, you must have thought you were on a lucky streak." Hollis paused, quickly glancing up at the judge, who was pointedly looking at her. She realized she hadn't asked a question. "Isn't that so?"

Frances rubbed her forehead. "I didn't kill Jeffrey."

Hollis walked back to the table. "No, you didn't kill Jeffrey Wallace. Brian Wallace did. But you did withhold the fact of the lottery winnings to everyone affected. Isn't that true, Mrs. Wallace?"

Frances' nose was turning an unattractive red.

"You must answer, Mrs. Wallace," said the judge.

"I only sent in the form. I hadn't collected the winnings. It wasn't verified, so I didn't know for sure." Frances gripped the edge of the witness box.

"This brings us to the murder of Todd Wallace." Hollis turned and caught the glance of a grim-looking George, who had returned to his seat. "You already had plans for the money.

You saw a new casino in Nevada as an investor opportunity with your name on it. But your new partners don't play around. They wanted absolute assurances that the trust would be recorded and you could come up with your share, or else. Is that correct?"

"I don't know what you're referring to. Maybe being an ex-con has twisted your view of honest people." Frances smirked.

"Or else ...." Ignoring the taunt, Hollis turned to face the judge and continued speaking. "Or else your stepson, Todd Wallace, would pay a high price. He'd found out about the lottery ticket and wanted a cut for his silence. But later he acquired a conscience. The day he died, he was going to tell me about the ticket. However, you and your friends couldn't afford to let that happen." Hollis looked up at the frowning judge and remembered his admonition. "So he had to be stopped. Isn't that right?"

From the way she stiffened, her eyes blinking rapidly, Hollis knew the answer.

Frances looked up at the judge, who glared back at her.

"Yes, yes, all right." Her shoulders slumped and she held her head in her hands. "It ... it just got out of hand. I told them I could handle Todd, but then when it was clear he was going to tell you ...." She started to sob.

Hollis stepped away from the stand and stood next to her own chair.

"Ms. Morgan, it is clear to the court that this is anything but a routine trust." Judge Messina put on his glasses. "There may be criminal charges involved. Mrs. Wallace will likely need to seek advisement from her own attorney. I will grant a continuance of thirty days. Bailiff?"

As if recovering from the testimony, the bailiff wiped his forehead and announced the next case.

Hollis turned and saw the smiling faces of the Fallen Angels as they waved and moved out into the lobby area. Mark was there too and he gave her shoulder a squeeze as George came around the banister to pat Hollis on the back. A police officer was waiting at the entry doors for Frances to make her way down the aisle. Hollis packed her papers and moved to the side as the next attorney approached the table.

She caught movement in the small balcony over the courtroom doors and looked straight into John's eyes. He grinned and gave her an acknowledging bow.

Epilogue

V INCE WAS AS UNCOMFORTABLE WITH attention as Hollis, so they both hated this gathering.

The Fallen Angels had reserved a table for a party of seven at Scott's Seafood in Jack London Square. The lunchtime crowd has dissipated and the mid-afternoon patrons were few. In the center of the table was a large fern with a balloon that read "Congratulations" and a second balloon painted with a diploma.

Hollis tried to remember the last time she'd owned a plant—a *living* plant. She'd transitioned to artificial plants when she went back to law school. It seemed more merciful.

"Hollis, why the look? Don't be mad. We had to do something." Rena smiled. "You were great. You must be on cloud nine. And you too, Vince. Your GED is a big deal. It took a lot of self-discipline."

Vince mumbled something under his breath. Hollis patted him on his shoulder.

She whispered to him, "Don't worry. I still owe you a buffet dinner."

"Hah, you all don't know her well, do you?" Stephanie

slid another fresh oyster into her mouth with a look of utter contentment. "She's afraid to be happy."

Hollis exchanged looks with John and gave a slight shrug.

"You guys know I don't—"

"Just once," Gene said. "Ms. Morgan, just once be gracious and accept our kudos and congratulations." He patted her on the back. "If it makes you feel better, just think that we're doing it for us, not you."

"What I want to know is how you knew about the lottery ticket?" Stephanie asked as she broke off a piece from the loaf of warm bread.

Hollis looked at Gene, who gave her an open grin.

"Frances came to my office to sign final forms. While she was trying to snatch the paper from me, her purse fell open. As she scrambled to put things back in her bag I noticed an envelope addressed to the California Lottery, attention Claims Division. And that's when it hit me. Or, at least it gave me the idea."

Vince paused from eating his hamburger. "But, Hollis, how did you know she'd hit the jackpot? How did you know the amount?"

"I didn't. But I knew Gene could find out from his newspaper. We knew someone had won the jackpot, and the lottery posts where the ticket was sold. Gene discovered a large win took place at a Bay Area market not far from Jeffrey's house. He was able to verify that she'd applied and was in the process of having her claim verified." Hollis patted Gene on the shoulder. "I could never figure out what the significance was of the three months. But then the pieces fell together. You only have six months to claim a lottery prize. But if she were going to claim this as her separate property, she needed six weeks to establish residency for a Nevada divorce. Francis hadn't planned on Jeffrey's death. After Jeffrey was murdered, the clock was ticking on having the trust filed. She didn't want the ticket proceeds in the trust because then she would have to deal with the Library Foundation and Brian as the executor and he could cause trouble. Her Nevada friends would not tolerate any delays."

Richard nodded in agreement. "She would cash the ticket as her separate property so it wouldn't pass on to Todd or Brian. Or perhaps she was worried they'd find out who actually bought the ticket and cause trouble." He raised his fork in the air. "Say, what happens to the lottery money now?"

Hollis' jaw tightened. "My initial research showed that there is nothing in the California lottery rules that prevents a convicted felon from playing or collecting lottery winnings."

"Then she's still going to get all that money," Miller grumbled.

A thoughtful quiet settled on the group.

Gene hit the table lightly with his fist. "I'm a firm believer in karma. Frances will get her just due and besides, as a felon, she's prohibited from participating in the ownership of a casino."

"Todd, now that's sad." Miller pulled out a small square of origami paper.

Hollis said in a quiet voice, "What's sad is that none of us knew what Jeffrey's life was really like. He was ... he was hurting. But, I guess the part that touches me the most ... I lost my hero." She paused and then continued, "I think Todd was going to blackmail Frances. He wasn't in the trust, but he'd found out about her winnings."

"How did he find out?" Miller asked.

Hollis sighed. "I don't know if we'll ever know for sure. Maybe he just stumbled on it the same way I did. But in the end he decided to be the man Jeffrey wanted him to be. He might have made the mistake of threatening Frances with telling me. Or maybe she was having him followed and he was seen meeting with me. I think one of her partners hired those two guys I identified to take care of him."

"So once you filed the papers for the hearing ...." Gene offered.

"So, once I filed the papers, everyone breathed a sigh of relief and my shadows backed off."

John squeezed her hand under the table.

"You know," Rena held her fork midair, "I just started reading a book by Jason Rivers. It's fictionalized non-fiction and it has a blackmail storyline something like we just came through. I guess life imitates art again."

"What's the title?" Gene asked. "If you guys want, I can get copies for all the Fallen Angels. We can make it our July selection. Vince, you're welcome to join us."

Vince shook his head. "Thanks, but maybe another time. I'm going to be busy going to college."

Hollis smiled at him, then at John, and then looked around the table at each member in turn.

"Well, here we go again."

R. FRANKLIN JAMES GREW UP in the San Francisco Bay Area and graduated from the University of California at Berkeley. In 2013, *The Fallen Angels Book Club*, the first book in the Hollis Morgan Mystery Series, was released. Her second book in the series, *Sticks & Stones*, was released in May 2014. James is married with two sons and resides in Northern California.

For more information, go to www.rfranklinjames.com.